Two to Love

Other Books by Lexi Blake

ROMANTIC SUSPENSE

Masters And Mercenaries

The Dom Who Loved Me
The Men With The Golden Cuffs
A Dom is Forever
On Her Master's Secret Service
Sanctum: A Masters and Mercenaries Novella
Love and Let Die
Unconditional: A Masters and Mercenaries Novella
Dungeon Royale
Dungeon Games: A Masters and Mercenaries Novella
A View to a Thrill
Cherished: A Masters and Mercenaries Novella
You Only Love Twice
Luscious: Masters and Mercenaries~Topped
Adored: A Masters and Mercenaries Novella
Master No
Just One Taste: Masters and Mercenaries~Topped 2
From Sanctum with Love
Devoted: A Masters and Mercenaries Novella
Dominance Never Dies
Submission is Not Enough
Master Bits and Mercenary Bites~The Secret Recipes of Topped
Perfectly Paired: Masters and Mercenaries~Topped 3
For His Eyes Only
Arranged: A Masters and Mercenaries Novella
Love Another Day
At Your Service: Masters and Mercenaries~Topped 4
Master Bits and Mercenary Bites~Girls Night
Nobody Does It Better
Close Cover
Protected, Coming July 31, 2018

Masters and Mercenaries: The Forgotten

Momento Mori, Coming August 28, 2018

Lawless

Ruthless
Satisfaction

Revenge

Courting Justice
Order of Protection, Coming June 5, 2018

Masters Of Ménage (by Shayla Black and Lexi Blake)
Their Virgin Captive
Their Virgin's Secret
Their Virgin Concubine
Their Virgin Princess
Their Virgin Hostage
Their Virgin Secretary
Their Virgin Mistress

The Perfect Gentlemen (by Shayla Black and Lexi Blake)
Scandal Never Sleeps
Seduction in Session
Big Easy Temptation
Smoke and Sin
At the Pleasure of the President, Coming Fall 2018

URBAN FANTASY
Thieves
Steal the Light
Steal the Day
Steal the Moon
Steal the Sun
Steal the Night
Ripper
Addict
Sleeper
Outcast, Coming 2018

LEXI BLAKE WRITING AS SOPHIE OAK
Small Town Siren
Siren in the City
Away From Me
Three to Ride
Siren Enslaved
Two to Love
Siren Beloved, Coming July 17, 2018
One to Keep, Coming August 7, 2018

Two to Love

Nights in Bliss, Colorado, Book 2

Lexi Blake

writing as

Sophie Oak

Two to Love
Nights in Bliss, Colorado Book 2

Published by DLZ Entertainment LLC

Edited by Chloe Vale
ISBN: 978-1-937608-85-9

Sign up for Lexi Blake's newsletter
and be entered to win a $25 gift certificate
to the bookseller of your choice.

Join us for news, fun, and exclusive content
including free short stories.

Go to www.LexiBlake.net to subscribe.

There's a new contest every month!

Dedication

To my mom, who gave me my first romance novel. You started me down this path and then made every mile all the easier for your support. I couldn’t do it without you.

2018 Dedication

It’s been years since I wrote this book, but the above dedication still holds and it’s bittersweet to read it. In the years between then and now I’ve watched your strength and dignity. As you taught me how to live a good life, you’re now teaching me how to leave that life with grace and love. I cherish every moment we have left. As it was then, it is now. This book is yours, Mom.

Chapter One

"She's a virgin?"

"That's what Stefan said," Nate Wright explained to his best friend, who had uttered the same question Nate had been asking himself. Though Stef was standing right beside them, he simply sighed and ignored Zane.

Nate watched the young woman through the two-way mirror. She lay back on the big bed, stretching her gloriously naked body. Only the constant darting of her eyes to the door gave an indication that she was anything but comfortable. Her right foot rubbed absently against the opposite leg, as though checking the softness of the skin. Nate would do the same thing in a few minutes, though it would be his hand running up her leg and finally making its way to its destination—her perfect, plump pussy. It was shaved and ripe looking.

If Stefan hadn't sworn she was a virgin, Nate would never have believed it. Of course, in a few minutes, she wouldn't have that problem.

"A twenty-five-year-old virgin?" Zane Hollister sounded as surprised as Nate felt. Nate looked over at his best friend. He was a giant of a man, and Nate worried that the young woman in question might be overwhelmed by his sheer size. He wasn't surprised to see Zane was practically salivating. Callie Sheppard was exactly their type. Nice breasts, ample hips, small waist, but she had some weight on her. Her face was sweet, but not model-like, with well-shaped lips that would look good wrapped around a cock. She wasn't a fragile thing who would break the instant they got a little rough with her. And they would definitely get a little rough.

Stefan Talbot threw Nate a look. It was his "dumbass is here why?" look. Stef wasn't Zane's biggest fan, but he was proving tolerant this evening. "Would you like the definition of virginity made plain to you, Hollister?"

Zane rolled his green eyes. "No, asshole. I just think she looks surprisingly comfy for a girl about to get her cherry popped by two strangers."

That aristocratic eyebrow of Stefan's arched up, and Nate knew the sarcasm was about to flow. "Well, unless the two of you have some superpowers I don't know about, or extremely small dicks, I think you should choose one to 'pop her cherry.'" He turned to Nate, and there was no mistaking the warning in his eyes. "I swear if he hurts her…"

Zane had the good grace to look surprised. He took a small step back and regarded Stefan seriously. "I wouldn't hurt any girl, much less one like Callie. She's seems very sweet and she's lovely. I'm sorry. I can't imagine she's gone this long and no man has claimed her."

That seemed to calm Stef. His stance relaxed, and the angry bull air about him deflated a notch. "I want you to be careful with her. I care about her. She's like a little sister to me."

Zane's eyes narrowed, a possessive look crossing his face. "Brothers don't normally see their sisters naked."

Stefan laughed. The sound conveyed his fondness for the girl in question. "If I had a big problem with nudity, I would rarely see Callie at all."

"What is that supposed to mean?" Nate was intensely curious about the girl he would spend the evening with.

"Callie's upbringing was a bit unusual, like many of us in Bliss. Her mother runs a nudist resort outside of town. Callie grew up there.

Oh, she lived in Bliss and wasn't allowed on the grounds as a teen, but she takes after her mother. She prefers her own skin. I know if I go to Callie's place, I'll probably find her in a hastily thrown-on robe. When she sees it's me, she happily throws it back off. It's just her way. There's nothing sexual about it. Callie is…innocent."

"But she doesn't want to be." Nate couldn't take his eyes off her.

Stefan waved away that thought with a twist of his hand. "I doubt an evening with you will truly take away her innocent air. That's why I picked you. I have some other friends, but I wanted you specifically, Nate. I know you'll be kind to her. I thought this whole plan was ridiculous, but she's determined to go through with it. If I hadn't set this up, she would have gone and found someone on her own."

The girl in question rolled over, offering Nate a look at her spectacular ass. Her cheeks were deliciously curved and flowed into a trim waist and graceful back. "That could be dangerous. Is there a particular reason why she wants a ménage? Usually only experienced women are interested in that."

Stefan's eyes hooded, and the floor suddenly had his attention. "You have to understand the way we grew up. Bliss is a small town. There were only the four of us the same age. In school, we were a very small class. It was me and Callie and the twins, Max and Rye Harper."

Nate had heard of Stefan's best friends. Stefan talked about Bliss, Colorado, endlessly whenever he was forced to return to Dallas for some family obligation. Sometimes Nate envied Stef's mountain home. He'd always wanted to go there and had never found the time. The others in their social circle couldn't understand why Stef would choose to forgo the best schools and a whirling social life, but Nate could see the appeal. It would have gotten him away from the constant pressure of being a "Wright." He could still hear his father yelling at him when Nate had told him he was joining the DEA. A "Wright," he'd been told, did not work in something so blue collar as law enforcement.

When he was running the DEA, he would show his father exactly what a "Wright" could do.

"We're still close," Stef was saying.

"She was in love with them," Zane commented.

Sometimes, not often, Zane had moments of emotional clarity. Nate knew they were usually followed by an enormous amount of beer drinking, but they were there all the same. He seemed to be having just such a moment as he looked at the dark-haired beauty through the two-way mirror. His hand lifted briefly as though he could touch her. He brought it down quickly and went back to brooding.

Stef nodded. "Yes, and they always viewed her as a little sister. It must have been hard to be the only girl in our group. By the time we were teens, the twins and I were experimenting with older girls from neighboring towns, and Callie was on her own in the sexual awakening department. We didn't make it easy on her. We scared off a lot of prospects. I didn't truly understand how that hurt her until recently. I want you to make her feel desirable."

"That won't be hard." Zane's pants were already tenting. He didn't do anything to hide his massive erection.

Stefan glanced down and then back up, shaking his head. "Like I said before, be careful with her. Callie's twenty-five today. She's sick of waiting. There's no one in Bliss even vaguely suitable, so she suggested we come here. No one knows her in Dallas. She can do what she likes in this club, and there won't be any gossip. Bliss is a lovely place, but it runs on gossip. I want to protect her. That's why I called you, Nate. I know you have certain kinks."

Nate felt a grin slide across his face. He did enjoy the occasional ménage, but no one in the world had more kinks than Stef Talbot. Pot, kettle, black as night. Nate himself simply preferred to enjoy a woman with his best friend. Stef's kinks were a bit more kinky. Stef's kinks involved all kinds of toys. He chose to let it go.

"Are you going to watch?" Stef had been known to.

"Hell, no." His childhood friend actually shuddered. "As I said, Callie is like a sister to me. While I will set up her little fantasy, I'm certainly not going to watch it. I'll be in the bar. I'm meeting some friends. I haven't seen them since the last time I was in Dallas. You're lucky I didn't ask them to handle this. They share, too."

Most men didn't have multiple sources to go to when setting up their friend's ménage fantasy. "Why us?"

"Because I trust you, and I've known you longer," Stef admitted.

"And deep down, I know that giant of an idiot you call a best friend won't hurt her, either."

Zane growled. At six foot five, Zane was a beast. Stef was pushing it. It was something he did from time to time, but Nate had no time to indulge Stef's need to get his ass kicked.

He'd talked about this long enough. He wanted to meet Callie. "We'll take care of her. Don't worry about it."

Stefan nodded and glanced out over the playroom of the exclusive bondage club they all belonged to. "I believe Mr. Lodge will send someone in to escort her back up to our suite when you're done. My friends are here. Thank you, Nate."

Stefan walked off to greet a dark-haired man and his blond companion, a slightly smaller male. The big cowboy held his hand out and greeted Stef. Nate turned back to Zane.

"I don't like him." Zane scowled as Stef walked away.

"I think the feeling is mutual." Nate had long ago accepted that his two best friends in the world were never going to like each other. Nate looked into the room they were about to enter. "The question is, do you like her?"

A slow smile split Zane's face. "Oh, yes. I like her quite a bit."

Satisfied, Nate opened the door.

* * * *

Callie Sheppard was startled by the sound of the door opening. She sat straight up in bed and wondered what the hell she was doing. It had seemed like a great idea at the time, but now a tremor of trepidation ran through her system. She was naked in a notorious BDSM club, waiting for two men to walk in and take her virginity.

It wasn't that she minded losing her virginity. She wasn't doing anything interesting with it in the first place. It needed to go, but now she worried this wasn't the way to do it. She wanted some affection and kindness. Would they give that to her? Oh, god, Stef had found her two guys for her birthday. She'd made him a loaf of zucchini bread and shared a bottle of cheap wine for his. What was she doing?

Could she run? She was naked. That didn't really bother her, but it could confound a lot of people.

"Hello." The deepest voice she'd ever heard pulled her from her panic.

She turned and hoped there wasn't a line of drool running out of her mouth as she caught sight of them. Best birthday present ever. Stef might be straight, but he knew how to pick gorgeous men.

She climbed as gracefully as she could off the big bed and faced them. They were perfect. The one who had spoken was tall. She doubted she would reach his shoulders when she stood against him. He was at least six and a half feet, and his body was corded with muscle. Every piece of him seemed chiseled out of granite. He was male model perfection, with a strong jaw and piercing green eyes. His hair was inky black and curled sweetly over his ears.

His partner wasn't quite as tall but still was no small man. He was a few inches shorter than the gorgeous monster, and his body held a lean strength. If the black-haired devil was a linebacker, this man was a swimmer. His eyes were a stark blue. His skin was sun kissed and smooth. Callie was fascinated with the idea of soft skin covering steel. His hair was cut in a military style. It was a rich brown. The intimate light of the room caught the gold and red streaks. He looked like a man who laughed often.

Everything inside her heated up at the sight of them, and she wasn't so scared anymore. Why the hell would she run from all that hotness? And they were handpicked by a man who would never, ever hurt her. She was safe with them.

"Hello." It seemed like a dumb thing to say to two glorious men when she was naked as the day she was born, but it was all she could think of.

"Hello, Callie." The other man's voice was deep, too, but there was an inherent friendliness to his Texas accent. It looked like Stef had found her a couple of cowboys. The blue-eyed man watched her. He gave her a small, calm smile, like he didn't want to scare her. "Are you nervous, sweetheart? We don't want you to be. Nothing happens here that you don't want. All you have to do is say the word and everything stops."

Their eyes were on her body. Callie had never thought much about her body before. It was a natural thing. She'd grown up in a household where nudity wasn't frowned on. She was comfortable in her skin, only now she wasn't. Now she was starting to feel hot and restless. They weren't avoiding her private parts the way the nudists politely did back in Bliss. These men stared boldly at her breasts, and her breasts seemed to be staring right back. Her nipples were hard nubs.

"Do I get a safe word?" The question came out on a breathy sigh. She'd always wanted to know what it felt like to truly submit. Stefan's subs always seemed satisfied.

The blue-eyed man's mouth turned down. "Your safe word is no. We don't have to play games. All you have to do is say no and we stop."

"But we can play games if you want to." That came from the big guy. His husky voice did all sorts of things to her libido. He walked boldly up to her and placed his hands on her hips. His touch lit up her skin. "Do you want to play, darlin'?"

Oh, yeah, she wanted to play. She was worried she didn't know how. His hands skimmed her hips and pulled her close. He was so big. He enveloped her. His mouth came down on hers. He was gentle but forceful. His tongue slipped past her lips and dominated her mouth. Callie had a moment of complete panic but forced herself to relax. She'd come here for this. She wanted to know what it felt like to be desired. She wouldn't get love out of this. She knew that. She wasn't as naïve as the boys back in Bliss seemed to think. But she might get the desired part, if the thick erection poking her in the belly was any indication.

His tongue coaxed now that she'd softened against him. He seemed more willing to take things slowly once she got involved. She let her tongue rub against his, enjoying the smooth glide. She could smell soap and man and something musky that heated her feminine parts to a froth. He pulled her into the cradle of his thighs. The denim was rough against her softness.

"Hey, don't hog the girl, Zane."

Callie felt a hand on her shoulder, and the big guy, Zane, broke off the best kiss of her life. It was one of the only kisses of her life, she admitted to herself. She was turned into a second hard body.

"My name is Nathan, sweetheart. But you can call me Nate." His Texas accent had gotten more pronounced as the room heated up. He cupped her hips and let his eyes trail the length of her body. "You are a beautiful woman, Callie Sheppard. We're going to take good care of you."

Callie sighed as he leaned in. His kiss was softer than Zane's but no less impactful. She felt it hum along her skin. She liked the idea of them taking care of her. She liked it a lot. Of course, they were only talking about taking care of her sexually, but she could dream. She let her hands caress the smooth skin of his shoulders and biceps. Her blood started to pound. This was nothing like the couple of times she'd fooled around before with sons of her mother's friends, or that disastrous time she'd tried to kiss Rye Harper. Those fleeting touches had been fumbling and awkward. This was a wave she had to ride and allow to sweep her away.

"Are we going too fast?" Nate whispered the question against her ear. There was no small amount of pleading in it. She could tell he wanted her answer to be a resounding *no* from the sound of his voice.

"I'm fine, Nate." Callie pressed herself against him, the cotton of his western shirt sensitizing her nipples. She kissed along his jawline. It felt so good to be close to another warm body, to be given leave to explore and play. She wanted them naked, skin to skin against her. She pulled apart the shirt under her hands. The pearl snaps popped, and his skin was hers to touch. She let her fingers run along the curves of his chest. He was all muscle, from his pecs to the six-pack that had her mouth watering.

"God, sweetheart, you feel perfect." Nate's head was back as he offered her his body.

"Yes, you do," Zane agreed, pressing against her back. His skin was warm against hers, so she knew he had gotten rid of his jeans and T-shirt. His hands slid from around her back and cupped her breasts. His thumbs stroked her nipples, and she could feel the press of hard flesh against the cheeks of her ass. Everything was beginning to whirl deliciously out of control, and Callie was going with it.

"You're sure you want this?" Nate seemed cautious, but his eyes were hot.

Callie nodded. She was sure. She wanted to experience something she'd fantasized about. There was a lot she hadn't confided in Stef. Her mother was sick. Callie would spend the next months giving her mother every bit of her energy and love. She would have to concentrate on keeping her mom's spirits up. She wanted one night where she didn't have to be strong, where she didn't have to face the future, where she could revel in the here and now simply because it felt good.

"Baby?" Nate's hand came up and brushed away a tear she hadn't known she'd shed. His eyes were a brilliant blue and narrowed in concern. "Are you afraid?"

The hands on her breasts were gone, wrapping around her shoulders and pulling her back into Zane's chest. There was a sweetness to his hold, as though he didn't want to let her go for a minute. That brought fresh tears to her eyes. No one had held her like that since she was a child. The gesture made her feel small and fragile and protected.

"There's nothing to be afraid of." Zane's voice rumbled along her scalp, his face pressed to the top of her head. "I promise I'll be gentle."

Callie shook her head. "I'm not scared. I'm just…emotional." Now wasn't the time or place to spill her guts. She wanted sweetness, not sympathy. She looked straight into Nate's eyes and asked for what she wanted. "I need to be out of myself for a while."

After a long moment, Nate smiled solemnly and leaned in to kiss her. His lips molded hers, and she felt Zane's mouth on her nape. She was wrapped up in them, and the sensations felt heavenly.

Nate stepped back and nodded at Zane. Callie glanced at Nate as he started to undress, then Zane swept her up into his arms and grinned down at her. It was a wild, feral thing, that smile of his. He was the bad boy of the two, no question about it. He cradled her to his chest and strode to the bed like she was nothing at all to carry. He tossed her lightly on the huge bed. Her eyes widened as she got her first real look at him.

"Oh, my god." His cock was enormous. It was gorgeous.

He stroked that monster cock of his, and a purely masculine look took over his magazine-cover-ready face. "Don't worry. I know how to use it."

Nate came to stand by his friend. His body was every bit as beautiful as Zane's. Nate's body was sleekly muscled, where Zane looked like a bodybuilder. Nate's mouth was turned up in a slight smile, and he rolled his eyes. "You know, you should never have shown her that thing first. Now she won't look at me."

"Yes, I will." She was breathless. Nate might not be quite as ridiculous as his friend, but he was amply sized as well. His cock stood at full attention, bobbing against his flat, muscled abs, almost reaching his navel. He wasn't quite as long as Zane, but he was just as thick. No one could accuse Nate of not being well-hung.

He winked at her. "I'm glad Zane hasn't ruined you for me, sweetheart." He crawled across the white comforter toward her. His big hand pressed her back into the mattress. "Lay back, and let Zane take care of you."

She closed her eyes and forced herself to relax. It was going to be okay. She knew it would hurt at first. Nate was distracting her as Zane moved her legs apart. His hands ran from her ankles to her hips, and she tensed, waiting for that big cock to start its assault. Nate's mouth trailed kisses from her neck down to her breasts.

Callie gasped as she felt Zane begin. It wasn't his cock seeking entry. His mouth covered her pussy. The feather-light touch had her shaking. It was an exquisite sensation and not one she had been expecting.

"You taste good, babe." Zane's deep grumble was a wave of pleasure rolling across her flesh. His fingers slid through her labia, parting her for the slow slide of his tongue. He licked and nibbled at her tender flesh. His tongue darted all around, lighting up her nerve endings. It wasn't enough. It felt so, so good, but it wasn't enough. She wanted more. She'd been nervous before, wondering if this was the right thing to do. But now, as his tongue worshipped her, she wondered why she'd waited. This was so sweet. Callie pushed her pussy toward Zane's face, begging for more. He growled and speared her with his tongue. His strong tongue went straight up her pussy and then he pulled out. He licked in forceful strokes from her clit all the way down. Callie was building toward something she'd never felt before. The minor pleasures she'd gained from her fingers were nothing like this.

Nate's lips pulled at her nipple. He rolled the one he wasn't suckling with his fingers. When Callie managed to get her head up off the bed, she watched the two men pleasuring her with their mouths and hands. It was a beautiful sight. Zane slipped a finger into her pussy.

"She's going to be incredibly tight." He moaned, coming up for air. Callie could see the evidence of her arousal on his chin and lips. His tongue came out to lap it up as he curled his finger deep inside her.

Nate came off her breast. "I think I need to try some of that honey of hers." He turned his body around and leaned over. While Zane added a second finger, Nate's tongue worked her clit. Zane added a third finger. He fucked her gently, curling his fingers deep inside. Callie's hands clawed at the comforter, and her hips moved restlessly under their ministrations.

"She's close." Zane was watching her carefully, his deep green eyes hooded with lust.

Zane was right. When Nate sucked her clit between his lips, she went off like a rocket. Every muscle she had tensed and released in a great wash of relief. It started in her pussy and rolled over her body like a wave. Callie cried out. Little tremors shook her as Nate continued to lave her clit gently now. Zane pulled his fingers out and moved up the bed.

"Up, babe." He pushed her up, sliding in behind her. "Don't worry about a thing. It won't hurt for long."

Callie opened her eyes, and Nate was on his knees, rolling a condom over his cock. Zane's hands smoothed down her hair. He whispered soothing words into her ear as Nate arranged her legs and started to penetrate her.

"Oh, Callie, baby, you feel so fucking good." Nate's face was contorted with the effort it took him to thrust slowly.

She tensed as his cock stretched her. It hurt. He was so big and she was small. He took his time, thrusting in slowly and retreating. He gained ground inch by inch. All the while, Zane told her how pretty she was, how he couldn't wait to be the man fucking her. She struggled to breathe as the pressure seemed to expand. Zane nibbled on her ear as Nate worked his way in carefully. She wanted to yell at him, to tell him to get it over with, but every time she thought she couldn't take another second of the maddening advance and retreat,

Zane would lick or gently bite her sensitive lobe, and she would shiver with the touch. Gradually, she relaxed, and Nate finally pressed forward. She felt something tear and then he was in. He was inside her body. It was wildly intimate. She felt so connected. The pain was a small thing in comparison to the pleasure they were giving her.

Nate held himself still. A fine sheen of sweat clung to his skin. It transferred to her where they touched, a sweet adhesive keeping them bound together. His body shook as he looked down at her. "Okay, now?"

She responded by wrapping her legs around his lean waist and pushing up to take him deeper. It still hurt a bit, but she wanted more. She wanted the deep connection she felt. His cock filled her, and she loved the way he started to shake when she clamped down on him. She pushed up against him, wanting to experiment with this feeling. It was delicious and decadent to be so filled with another human being. Behind her, Zane's cock pressed against her spine. Zane's hips were moving, twitching against her back.

"Fuck," Nate groaned and started thrusting. He leaned over and ate at her lips. He kissed her, never letting up on the slow slide of his cock. His tongue played with hers, fucking her mouth as he did the same to her pussy. He hissed and pushed himself up. Callie let her hands caress his waist. She wanted to touch every part of him. She let her head loll against Zane's neck. She was nestled in between them. What would it feel like to have them both?

"I'm not going to last." Nate's eyes were pleading. His face bunched up, and the muscles of his shoulders corded.

Zane seemed to know exactly what to do. His right hand slid in between their bodies and found her clit as Nate pressed in and withdrew. The pad of Zane's big thumb made circles around her clit. He started wide and got closer and closer as Nate tunneled in and pulled back out. Callie's head rolled against Zane's warm chest as the feeling built. Each thrust had Callie moaning.

"Please." She couldn't take it anymore. She had to know where this was going. She tried not to think because, even in her passion, that question scared the crap out of her. Even while she was fighting for her orgasm, she knew this was more than sex for her.

"Give it to her, Zane. I can't take it anymore."

When Zane pushed down on her throbbing clit, she cried out as she came.

The sound seemed to break something in Nate. His carefully measured strokes lost their rhythm, and his head fell forward. He ground his pelvis against hers, pressing Zane's hand between them, making her come all over again. She let her head fall back and felt Zane's mouth on her cheek, kissing her as he rubbed that nubbin of flesh that dominated her life in those moments. Nate pressed deep and then shouted as he came. He thrust one last time, holding himself against her before falling into her arms.

Callie let herself float for a moment. It felt so good to be between them, but Zane had a problem. "Zane?"

He laughed against her ear. "Already taken care of, babe. You were so hot I came like a fucking fifteen-year-old." He pressed against her back. She could feel he was already getting hard again. "But I'll be inside you soon enough."

Nate looked up, his eyes heavy. "One night isn't enough. Stay with us for the weekend."

A weekend? Not a good idea. She was crazy about them now. What would she feel like if she really got to know them? Could her heart handle it?

Callie decided she would rather have a broken heart than never to have risked it. She let her hands tangle in Nate's hair as she whispered her answer. One night was definitely not enough.

Chapter Two

Zane stared at Callie Sheppard several hours later. She looked slightly out of place in the big, elegant suite. Not that he felt comfortable here. It *was* comfortable. Like no one in their right mind wouldn't be comfortable here, but he was more used to motels.

Callie, though, would be much more at home in the woods. After all, that was where nymphs lived. The pretty ones, not the maniac kind. He'd known a couple of those, and some had been pretty but not the same way. There was something otherworldly about her. Ethereal. That was the word he was looking for. Callie was a fairy nymph. Right? He let his mind drift back to some old college classes and decided that she was definitely a nymph. A superhot, curvy, sweet-assin nymph.

"So, where are you from?" Callie asked.

Why had Nate left them alone? After they'd left the club portion of The Club—who named their club that?—they'd come up here and Nate had said he was grabbing some food for them and left them alone.

He swallowed nervously. He wasn't used to talking to women about anything serious. He searched his thoughts to come up with the last actual date he'd been on. *Was it a date if you paid for the beers and then screwed the chick in the back room of the bar?*

There hadn't been a lot of talking with that one.

"Fort Worth." It was simple enough. He could answer her questions. He'd just be really brief. "But I was born in Austin. My dad moved us to Fort Worth when I was eight, and then he was gone by the time I was ten. I think my mom always missed Austin, though."

Where the hell had that come from? She didn't care that his mom had been left alone. She had been a crappy mom, but at least he understood that much about her. But Callie was only making small talk. She couldn't really be interested in him.

"I bet you missed it, too. It must have been hard leaving home like that. I can't imagine living anywhere but Bliss." She leaned forward on the couch, the edges of her terry cloth robe gaping open. Her bags had arrived earlier, and she'd slipped into the comfy thing after her shower. He'd wanted to hop into the shower with her but held back. She was probably sore. He could be overwhelming.

God, he didn't want to hurt her.

"It was hard to leave. I didn't fit in real well up here." That was an understatement. "After my dad left, I didn't even feel like I fit in at home. My mom was on edge. I think she kind of wished she didn't have me."

"I'm sure that's not true."

"Nah, I was a hard kid to deal with." He didn't seem capable of stopping. "I got in trouble a lot. I wasn't very smart. She'd gotten pregnant real young and I screwed things up for her."

"That wasn't your fault." Her voice had dropped to a sympathetic tone. "You were a kid. You were her responsibility. And your father's. Was he not around after the divorce?"

"I actually don't remember much about my dad. Even when he lived with us, he worked most of the time. He spent a lot of time with his friends. He wasn't much of a family guy. After he left, Mom dated a lot. She partied. And then she started dating this guy who was an administrator at a private school. They got serious. He found out I was a pretty good offensive lineman. They had a great quarterback, but no one to defend him so he got me a scholarship."

"Is that where you met Nate?"

He nodded. "Nate was a pretty good quarterback. He was way

better after I started knocking down everyone who came after him. He was my roommate. We've been close ever since."

Callie scratched at the robe and readjusted it. She seemed uncomfortable. He couldn't help but think about what he'd been told about her. Had Stefan been telling them the truth about Callie?

"You can take that off if you want." He wouldn't mind her sitting around naked. It might be nice.

Her face bunched up sweetly. "Are you sure? I know the naked thing freaks some people out."

He was damn sure. The idea of being naked with her didn't bug him at all. As a matter of fact, it might be easier to talk if he could see her boobs. He pulled his T-shirt over his head. "If it makes you feel more comfortable, I can take off my clothes, too."

She shrugged out of the robe. "It's okay. I know I'm weird, but I like being like this. It feels natural. It's not like I don't wear clothes in public or anything. I'm actually quite prim."

He bet she would look like a cute librarian, if the khaki skirt and button-up blouse he'd seen her unpack earlier were any indication. It did nothing to lessen her appeal. Callie sat back, completely naked, and Zane realized Stefan had been right about his "almost" sister.

Damn but she was beautiful. She relaxed back against the mocha-colored sofa. She was sitting on top of her robe, her whole body on display, but there was oddly nothing particularly sexual about it. She was simply comfortable in her skin. There was a lovely air of innocence around her. It brought out his protective instincts. Zane knew that he'd beat the crap out of anyone who tried to break her of it.

"That was a fierce look. What were you thinking?" Her eyes were wide and curious.

He took a deep breath. He didn't want to scare her off. That was the last thing he wanted to do. She didn't need to meet his inner caveman yet. "Nothing, babe. I was just thinking I've told you an awful lot about me. Why don't you tell me something? Tell me something you've never told anyone else."

He wanted to know her. He couldn't put his finger on it, but she was important. Even if he wasn't sure he wanted her to be.

She gnawed on her bottom lip. "I don't think I have any secrets.

Not anything big. I'm pretty boring."

She was anything but boring, and suddenly he wanted her to know something about him. Something he hadn't even told Nate. "I'm starting a job in a couple of days, and I don't really want it."

"Why are you doing it, then?"

That was the million-dollar question. Why was he going into a job that scared the crap out of him? "I won't let Nate go alone."

He looked down, unable to stare into her eyes.

She nudged his head up. "That is the sweetest thing I ever heard."

He felt himself flush and quickly changed the subject. "Now, there has to be something you can tell me."

He let his hand sink into her hair.

"I've lived a pretty sheltered life," she said. "I grew up in a small town, but it's also the most tolerant place on earth. That bubble people talk about? We popped it a long time ago. You come to Bliss, people will accept you if you try even a little. But I was the only girl. That made things hard."

He wasn't sure why. If she'd been the only girl, things should have been super easy. She should have had every boy in her town panting after her. He would have been. He would have been her slave from the time he'd figured out what his dick was for. "I don't understand."

Her skin flushed the sweetest pink. "Uhm, the boys I hung out with, they thought of me as a sister."

"They weren't interested in you?" Did they not have eyes?

"Not in any way that wasn't friendly." She moved closer as a sly smile crossed her face. "So you can see I haven't had the same experiences most of my peers had. There are a lot of things that I haven't done that most twenty-five-year-olds take for granted."

His cock responded immediately to that sexy stare. He got the distinct feeling she wasn't talking about taking tequila shots. "What haven't you done, baby?"

She took a deep breath, her shoulders tensed, and she looked down. "Before today, I never had sex at all. Like in any way. I kissed a couple of boys, but that was the extent of my experience. I liked the way you kissed me down there. Oral, I mean. I am now a big fan of oral sex, but I've never given a guy a blow job. I think I would enjoy returning the favor, if you know what I mean."

Now it was his turn to force himself to breathe. It was hard to speak when all of the blood in his body had suddenly rushed to his cock. Like quickly. Head-spinningly fast. "You should definitely do that. Yeah."

Boy, that sounded smart. Dumbass. Why didn't he pull his cock out and shove it at her face? Damn, but he kind of wanted to do that.

Callie was licking those gorgeous lips and repositioning herself between his legs. Her dark hair curled around her soft shoulders. Her nipples were pointed. She had lovely breasts, soft and round and real. When her hands touched his stomach, it took everything he had not to come then and there. He took a deep breath and forced himself to calm down. Control. That was the key. It was the key to his pleasure, and definitely the key to hers.

"Not until I tell you to, sweetheart." He was aware his voice was deeper than before, his manner more formal. "This is my time with you, and I like to do things a certain way. I promise I won't hurt you, Callie. I won't force you to do anything you don't want to. I need you to trust me and give it a chance. Can you do that?"

"Yes."

He took a firm hold of his desire. "Good, then carefully get my cock out of my pants."

Her hands were trembling as she worked the fly of his jeans. He felt his cock jump and twitch, impatient to get out of its cage and into that soft, untutored mouth. No other cock had delved in between those plump lips or had that pert tongue on it. She'd never tasted another man. His balls drew up almost painfully. He sighed as she managed to pull his dick free from his boxers.

"What should I do now?"

So many things went through his brain. He picked the simplest command. "Suck the head, babe. Run your tongue all over it."

Her tongue came out tentatively. He hissed and fought the urge to force her head down and fuck her mouth. This time was for her. He wanted to let her explore.

"Lick it, babe. That's right." Her tongue was a butterfly running across his cock. She was killing him. Her tongue darted around the engorged head. She instinctively ran around the sensitive ridge. She licked her way up and down with a breathtaking precision, as though she was determined not to miss a thing.

"That is very good." Praise. He should praise her. "It feels perfect, babe. Now cup my balls and play with them while you suck the head into your mouth."

She was so obedient, never questioning him. It gave him an enormous sense of control, making him calm and content. He relaxed and let his hands find her hair. She was so fucking gorgeous.

"Holy shit."

Zane looked up to see Nate staring. He was holding a six-pack of beer and a large pizza. He let the beer drop and tossed the box aside. When Callie started to look up, Zane tightened his hold on her hair. "No, babe. You focus on me. If you don't like him watching, tell me now."

Her eyes were on him. "I don't mind, Zane."

Her tongue came out and swept up the arousal seeping out of his slit. Zane groaned. Callie set back to her task, tasting him, sucking him, driving him completely crazy.

Zane's eyes met Nate's. It wasn't the first time they had shared a woman, but Zane could see the difference. He definitely felt the difference. Callie was special. Nate's mouth hung open, but there was more than simple lust in his gaze. Zane's instinct was to tell Nate to get the fuck out. There was a part of him that wanted Callie all to himself. It was surprisingly easy to push the instinct down. Callie enjoyed this. She enjoyed being watched, being shared. She wanted this. And he wanted to please her.

"Pretty, isn't she?" Zane felt her smile against his hardness. Her tongue explored the base of his cock. If she ever got around to deep throating him, he'd come in a heartbeat.

"She's gorgeous." Nate stood to the side. He seemed more tentative than Zane could ever remember. Nate was confident. Nate was the one who plowed through problems. Now he stood watching, looking almost afraid to be on the outside. Zane didn't like it.

"You want to watch or join in?"

A smile lit his friend's face. His easy confidence was back just like that. "I'll watch. It's a stimulating scene, but I have to admit, if I were directing the action, I'd love to see how much of that monster of yours she can take."

That sounded like a fine idea.

"Come up here, babe." He pulled her up and into his lap. Her mouth was red and swollen. He couldn't resist cupping the back of her head and bringing her in for a long, slow kiss. He let his mouth slant over hers again and again, enjoying how she let him take control. She gave as good as she got, but she was so soft in his arms. His cock was throbbing, and he hoped he didn't go off the minute he got inside her. He reluctantly let go of her neck and fished a condom out of his pocket. With less finesse than usual, he managed to get it on. Foreplay. She probably needed more foreplay.

But she was already straddling his hips. He thought about correcting her, but he wanted it too badly. She was testing the limits of his control, and damn if he didn't mind. The fact that Nate was watching did nothing but make him harder.

"You take what you can," he whispered against her chest as she started to lower herself onto his waiting cock. He licked at a nipple, happy to have something to focus on other than the tight vise he was being forced into. Fuck, she felt good.

And she was so wet. He let his hand drift around to toy with her clit. The nub was soaked with her cream. Callie shook slightly as she worked her way down.

"Okay, babe?" He didn't want to hurt her. She was so small, so tight. His hands clutched her hips.

"I'm so full." Her voice was dreamy and her chocolate eyes slightly glazed. She managed to take him all the way to his balls.

She held herself there. If she didn't move soon, he was going to take over. He was going to flip her on to her back and pound into her. He would fuck her so long and so deep she wouldn't remember a time when he wasn't inside her. Of course, if he kept her like this, he could spread her cheeks and offer her ass to Nate. They could fuck her together.

"Oh, god." Callie pushed against his shoulders and lowered down again. She fucked up and down so sweetly he knew he was going to give her this. He let his hands drift to the curve of her ass, helping to direct her. His balls brushed that ass and they drew up, ready to go off any minute.

She leaned forward, grinding down on him. He could feel her clit coming into contact with his pelvis with every twist of her body. Her mouth opened, and she moaned as she came, thrashing her hips around, seeking every sensation to be had.

Then there was only one sensation Zane gave a damn about. Her pussy clamped down on him, and he shot off. He forced her down on him, holding her tight to his body as he emptied what felt like an endless supply.

Callie fell forward into his arms. He hugged her, not minding when he felt Nate's hand on her back. Callie was happy. She snuggled close. She didn't seem to mind that he was still tucked inside her body.

Zane looked at Nate over her shoulder and wondered if he sported the same look of slightly afraid wonder on his own face. They were all in trouble.

* * * *

Nate looked down at the girl sleeping in the big bed they had shared for the last two nights. He had never really thought about the whole marriage thing. He was twenty-five years old, and settling down seemed worlds away, but he wondered how his parents would handle meeting Callie. Probably as well as they took Zane. They had never thought Zane was a proper friend. He was forever doomed to care about people who didn't fit into his world.

Callie Sheppard wouldn't be comfortable in his father's high society any more than Zane was. Any more than Nate was in the end, or he would be starting a job in his father's company rather than what he was about to do.

The feelings he was starting to have for her scared the crap out of him. Simply looking at her sleeping made him feel like crawling back in with her and wrapping his body around hers. He wouldn't wake her. She needed the rest, but holding her made him feel good. Callie Sheppard was the funniest, sexiest, sweetest bundle of femininity he'd ever met. There was only one problem with it. Zane.

Nate shook his head and walked out of the bedroom. It had been the best weekend of his life, but it was hours away from ending. He hadn't thought about it for the whole weekend, but he had a job to do.

Zane stood in the sitting room of the suite, staring out over the Dallas cityscape. In the early morning light, he looked younger than usual. "I need to know something. Why are you doing this? I know why I'm going in, but you have money, man. You don't need a job. Why would you deliberately risk your life?"

How did he make Zane understand? All of his life he'd been on a path. He'd been bred to wealth. In his parents' world, a man's worth was marked by how much money he had and his potential to make more. His parents never saw him, merely the potential to carry on the family name and company.

"I need to make a difference." Nate wanted to prove he could be more than a rich kid, to his parents, to Zane. He was going to make a name for himself. "I need to find something that has nothing to do with my parents' wealth and conquer it. Does that make sense?"

"Honestly, it doesn't." Zane sighed as though the conversation made him weary. "But I know it means something to you."

Nate wasn't sure what to say. He definitely wasn't sure what he would do if Zane decided this wasn't the job for him. Zane had been his best friend for years. Zane had been the one constant in his life. His parents drifted in and out, paying attention to him only when they needed something, but Zane was always there when he needed him.

He'd never seen Zane so thoughtful, but it wasn't hard to figure out what had his best friend thinking.

Callie.

Callie could change everything if he let her.

Zane was quiet for a moment. "I don't want to leave her."

Damn it. That wasn't what Nate wanted to hear. He wanted Zane to smile and slap him on the back and tease him about sharing the woman Nate thought he might be able to love. Instead, Zane looked haunted.

They had shared women before but only as fun, wild nights. No one lived that way. He wasn't going to hop into bed with his friend and their shared lover on a nightly basis. "What are we going to do?"

Zane shrugged. His misery was evident in the slump of his shoulders. Nate felt a kinship. His own heart was heavier than he could ever remember it feeling.

"Leave," Zane said. "This was a weekend thing. I guess we could both date her, but damn it, I don't see how this works. Are we supposed to tell everyone we share a girlfriend?"

He said nothing but felt the involuntary tightening of his jaw. He didn't like it, but the thought of Zane escorting Callie around without him made him want to beat his friend's head in. The idea of sharing her hummed through his brain. He liked it. He also knew it wouldn't work. No one would accept it. Society didn't work that way. Callie would be called all sorts of names. And he'd seen firsthand how being on the outside of society hurt Zane. He wouldn't willingly put either of them there.

Besides, there was the unavoidable matter of their upcoming job to consider. It wasn't like they could simply walk away. There was too much at stake. They'd been training and working toward this for over a year. If either one of them walked away, the operation would have to be trashed and begun over again. All that work and time put in would be wasted.

Their careers would be over.

Zane sighed. "She deserves better than either of us can give her. For god's sake, Nate, do you remember what we're doing in a couple of days?"

Until this weekend, it had been all he'd thought about for months. This was the most important mission of their careers. It would make them powerhouses in the DEA.

In a few short weeks, they would be in deep cover. Their identities would be gone. Their lives would be put on hold. It wasn't fair to start something with Callie only to leave her. And they would have to leave her. One of the reasons they were perfect for the job was the fact that they lacked close ties to family or others. Their loyalty had to be to each other and the mission. Callie would be in danger if she was close to them. What was he thinking?

"I'll go wake her up." It wasn't a conversation Nate was looking forward to. Either they broke Callie's heart or she wouldn't care, and that might break his.

Zane's eyes flared, his jaw a stubborn line. "And tell her what? 'Hey, we had a good time but it's time to go?' No, we head out. It's better for her. She wasn't expecting anything. It was a wild weekend.

I'll write her a note. She's better off without us."

"I don't know, man," he said, hating the idea. "It seems cold."

Zane's eyes were stark as he stared at him. "If she cries, if she asks me to stay, I don't know that I'll be able to walk out, and you know what that means. I think if she asks me to, I'll wreck everything we've built to stay with her, so I'm going to write her a note and leave before I fuck everything up."

He turned and stalked away.

A vision of Callie reaching out and asking for something none of them could make work floated across his brain. Tears in her eyes. He would be the reason she cried.

Thirty minutes later, Nate felt something break inside as he closed the bedroom door. She lay asleep on her side, her arm reaching out. Her palm was up and open. For two nights she'd slept between them. She'd moved from one to the other, always cuddling. For two nights, he'd been warm and happy.

He knew he would miss her for the rest of his life.

"Are you ready?" Zane's eyes were rimmed with red. He looked toward the door as though he wanted to bust it down.

He grabbed his bag. "Yeah."

The sun was coming up as they drove off. He rolled down the window and stared back at the elegant building where he'd learned his capacity to care about a woman was far greater than he'd ever dreamed. Callie had gotten to him, but he couldn't drag her into the new life he was about to start.

Zane was right. She deserved better.

* * * *

Callie called out for them. She sat up in bed and stretched. Throwing back the covers, she walked through the suite looking for her men. She thought of them as hers now after two days in bed with them.

Nate and Zane.

It was heaven to snuggle down in between their big bodies. She had never felt as safe and cared for as she did when she slept between them. Her body was sore, but it was a good thing. She would snag whichever one she found first and have her way with him in the shower. They would take their time and soap each other's bodies. If she found them both, well, she would get extremely clean. After they got dirty.

She was well aware there was probably the dumbest smile on her face. Stef was going to make such fun of her.

And she would let him as long as she got to keep feeling like this.

She strode into the living room, the air cool on her skin. It seemed silly to bother with clothes. The drapes had been pulled open, sun shining in, but the place was filled with a heavy silence. In the days she'd spent with them, she'd gotten used to their habits. Zane usually had the television on ESPN if they weren't doing something, as though he couldn't stand the quiet. Nate was the reserved one. Nate could sit and be still for long periods of time, his mind lost in thought. Zane was the one who needed something to do.

Had they gone to grab breakfast? One of them usually stayed with her, but maybe they needed some guy time.

She was about to sink down onto the sofa when she saw a small envelope on the coffee table. She recognized it as the stationary from the desk, her name in clean, masculine writing on the front.

She stared at it for a moment, her heart sinking because that wasn't some "we'll be back soon" note. That envelope on the table could only mean good-bye.

With trembling hands, she opened it.

Thanks for the weekend. Have a good life.

No names. No phone numbers. They were gone and those eight words were all she had left. She should have known. For them, it had been nothing more than a good time. They hadn't said a word about the future. Of course they hadn't. It was just sex.

And she was in love with two men who didn't want her anymore.

She sank down to the sofa, tears blurring her eyes. It was over. This sweet respite from reality was done and she had to face the world. She let out her worry and all of her fears, holding back nothing. When the sobs subsided, she lay there, the sun on her skin, and for a moment she imagined they were still here with her, the moment trapped and time stopping so she never had to leave this place, this feeling.

After long minutes, she dried her tears, took a shower, and packed her things. Stef would be by to take her home, where she was needed so desperately.

She dressed, the clothes a reminder that she had work to do. She sat down to wait, the weekend playing out in her head like a movie she wanted to watch again and again. In the end, she couldn't blame Nate and Zane for not loving her. That hadn't been part of the deal. Who, besides someone with her lack of experience, fell in love in a weekend? They couldn't force themselves to feel something that wasn't there. They had been kind, and that was all she'd asked for.

They wouldn't know that she would dream about them forever.

When Stefan knocked, she put on a brave face and got on with her life.

Chapter Three

Six Years Later

Nate took a deep breath, the mountain air filling his lungs. The elevation was going to take some getting used to, but he couldn't argue with the fact that Bliss, Colorado, was a beautiful place. He looked out at the little town nestled in the Sangre de Cristo Mountains. Every way he turned, there was a stunning view. Stefan hadn't lied about that.

He slid out of his truck and straightened his tie. There was no more putting this off. It was his first day and he wasn't going to be late. No matter how much he didn't want this job, it was his and he would do it right. Like his name. Which was the only damn thing he had left now.

His boots crunched into the gravel that covered the parking lot of the Bliss County Sheriff's Office. It was a building just off Main Street. Inauspicious and small. This was his workplace now.

Shit, why was he so nervous? This was a huge step down, and he was practically shaking at the thought of meeting his staff.

What staff? According to former sheriff Rye Harper, he had an administrative assistant and one deputy.

Rye Harper. He had been Bliss's sheriff for years, but now he was quitting to train horses and spend time with his new wife. Callie had been in love with Rye Harper when she'd been young. But according to Stef, she wasn't the new wife. Damn, when was he going to forget that girl? Now that he was here, he couldn't stop the questions. Where was she? Had she come back to Bliss after that weekend they'd all shared? Would he be sitting in his office one day, look out the window and see her strolling by? What would he do?

It didn't matter. She probably wouldn't remember them anyway. Callie Sheppard was most likely married by now with a couple of kids. She would be thirty-one, and she would have gotten on with her life. She was probably still so pretty it would hurt to look at her.

If he did run into her, he would be respectful. God knew if he hadn't been good for her back then, he would be poisonous now. He didn't even know what to call Zane.

Toxic, maybe. He hoped the right word wasn't unsalvageable. The thought of Zane back at the cabin sent a weary sigh through him. This plan had better work. If Zane didn't start getting better, he wasn't sure what he would try. This was his last shot as far as Nate could see.

He stopped outside of the station house, the enormity of the last few years hitting him fresh and hard.

It was all gone. His money, their careers, possibly Zane's future. He had to make this work. There wasn't another choice. Guilt gnawed at his gut, and he wondered if the restless nights were finally catching up with him. He was so tired he wanted to sleep and pretend none of this was happening to them.

The door to the station house opened, and he was greeted by a tall man with reddish-brown hair and a friendly smile. "Sheriff Wright?"

That was his name now. He was the sheriff of a Podunk town, and he needed to be grateful for the job. "Yes. You Harper?"

Rye Harper held out his hand, and Nate shook it quickly. He couldn't help but assess the other man. This was the man Callie had loved. Tall, strong, with a laid-back cowboy vibe. He was sure Rye Harper had never had trouble attracting women. Still, what kind of idiot couldn't love that girl back?

"Welcome to Bliss, Sheriff Wright. We're really happy you were willing to take the job." Harper grinned broadly. "Me, especially. If

Stef hadn't convinced you to work out the rest of my term, those bastards were going to hold me to my contract. Can you imagine that? I didn't think the people here knew what a contract was. Anyway, I'm sure you'll like it here. It's pretty quiet. Come on inside, and I'll introduce you."

He wasn't so sure he'd like it anywhere. He might have passed the point in his life where he could have been happy. Still, he followed. It had been like this for months, ever since the day Zane's cover had been blown and their world had gone to hell. Since that day, he forced himself to shuffle through his days, a zombie moving more out of habit than any great desire.

Harper was talking as he walked through the door. "I'll be around if you need anything, but Callie can run this place with one hand tied behind her back, so I don't expect you'll have any trouble."

"What?" He heard the words come out of his mouth, but his attention was focused on one thing and one thing only. Her.

She wouldn't be strolling by. He wouldn't catch a glimpse of her some day. She was here. Right here.

He was stopped in his tracks, the world shifting and upending.

She was here.

"Nate?" Callie stood by the front desk. She was slightly older, but more beautiful than he remembered her. A prim skirt and a sweater hid her curves, but he knew they were there. He dreamed about them at night. No woman he'd slept with since could measure up. Just like that, he could feel her hips under his hands, tracing her skin while she moved over him. He could hear her laugh, see the way her skin seemed to glitter when the sunshine hit it in the right way. He could feel her arms around him.

The world seemed to narrow down to that one face. A bit of panic threatened to take over. She hadn't changed, but he had. He wasn't the same man who'd rolled in the sheets with her, who teased and played with her. He could feel his heart pounding in his chest.

"You two know each other?" Harper's sharp gaze moved from him to Callie and back again.

"Stef introduced us a long time ago," Callie said softly. She was wearing glasses. She hadn't worn them before.

He wanted to strip them off, along with that shapeless sweater.

"A very long time ago." Nate tried to recover. It would look bad to break down in front of his staff on his first day on the job. His mental breakdown could surely wait a week or two. He nodded briskly and put on a purely professional front. "Hello, Callie. It's good to see you again. I hope you're well."

Her face flushed. He could plainly see that it wasn't the greeting she expected. Her voice was strained when she replied. "I'm fine, Sheriff. Nice to see you."

Rye Harper slapped his hands together. "Well, then, I leave you in good hands, Sheriff." He was at the door in a shot, as though he couldn't wait to get the hell out. "You call me if you need anything, Callie. And be sure to explain to him about the nudists. There's a science fair the Farley twins are planning to enter. We'll likely have trouble there. Some idiot relative bought them a chemistry set. We'll be lucky if they don't blow up their barn. Oh, and we're coming up on Nell and Henry's annual mega protest. I think they're planning on chaining themselves to a tree or something."

The former sheriff looked damn happy he wouldn't be dealing with those problems. He grinned and was gone in a second.

And Nate was left alone with the only woman he'd ever loved.

He was going to kill Stefan Talbot.

"I didn't know your last name." She was quiet, but he heard every word. The station was empty other than the two of them. It was a far cry from the DEA office. And it was so far from the field.

So she was surprised, too. "Sorry. If I had known—"

Her eyes grew wide. "What? You would have warned me?"

The truth popped out of his mouth. He'd forgotten how to be polite. "I wouldn't have taken the job."

The blood left her face and the room went quiet. "Well, all right then. That's good to know."

He spoke quickly, taking a step toward her. Two seconds in and he was already fucking everything up. "Callie, it's not like that. I wouldn't want to hurt you again."

She shrugged. "You didn't hurt me in the first place, Sheriff. We had a fling a long time ago. That was all."

Damn, she wasn't any better at lying now than she was then. The hurt was written all over her face. He wanted to pull her into his arms and apologize. He kept his distance. "You're right. It was a long time ago and it shouldn't affect us today. I'm sorry to surprise you like this. Can we try to work together? I need this job. Harper said you can help me fit in around here."

"You need this job? I seem to remember you had a rather large trust fund. You told me you worked because it gave you purpose. I don't know that you're going to find that here," she said, her voice turning bland and unemotional.

"No more trust fund." He'd admit that much to her. He hadn't had any control over that. He hoped she never found out about the rest. "Bad investments. My father's company is gone. I'm going to work out the former sheriff's term, and we'll take it from there. I promise to treat you as professionally as the last sheriff."

She snorted, and a smile curved her lips. "That wouldn't be hard. The last sheriff used to pull my pigtails when we were babies. It's hard to keep it professional when you grew up together."

He hated Rye Harper. "Well, I'll be a good boss. Now what was he talking about? He said something about nudists and science experiments."

Maybe if he acted in a professional manner, she would go along. He had no idea how he was supposed to work with her. The idea of seeing her every day and having to hear about her husband or boyfriend...he wasn't sure he could do it.

Callie's hands went to the buttons of her sweater. She fingered them as though she really wanted out of the garment. He remembered that Callie felt more comfortable naked. She'd spent the entire weekend with them without a stitch of clothes on. Nate felt his cock swell at the thought.

Well, at least it still worked.

"Don't worry about it. He's trying to scare you. I already talked to Nancy Farley. She's keeping an eye on the boys. Nell and Henry are protesting logging practices by chaining themselves to a tree, but it's not one that's about to be cut down. This particular protest is meant to make us think about the trees. Also, I have an extra key in case I need to get them out quickly, though Henry is surprisingly good at escaping the things. As for the rest of it, well, it's nudists' retreat time. Sometimes they scare the tourists."

He stared at her for a moment, trying to figure out if she was joking with him. Nope. She seemed extremely serious. What the hell kind of town was this? "Well, if I catch them, they can spend some time in an orange jumpsuit. It's illegal to walk around like that. They need to keep to their place."

Callie stood up straighter. Her eyes lit up, and her hands were suddenly on her hips. "I think you'll find that a little tolerance will go a long way in Bliss, Sheriff Wright."

His tolerance was long gone. He hadn't been here fifteen minutes, but he could already tell the former sheriff had been very lax. "If I find someone breaking the law, I'm going to arrest them."

Callie's arms were crossed, and her lips pursed. "That should make for an interesting change then. Now, if you like, I'll show you around." She waved her hand. "That's around. There's your office. Your uniforms are hanging on the back door. Your deputy's name is Logan Green. He's on his lunch break. I'm going to lunch, too. I'll be back at two."

She was leaving? He just got here.

"Try to not arrest the whole town while I'm gone."

She walked out, and he was alone again.

* * * *

Callie tried not to cry, but as she shuffled down the street, the world swam in front of her. Shock. This was what shock felt like. Not the physical kind. The heartbreakingly emotional kind.

Why hadn't Stef warned her? Seeing Nathan Wright after all these years had just about floored her. When he'd walked in, her first impulse was to throw herself into his arms and plant a big kiss on those sensual lips of his. She'd been taken back to that weekend six years ago when he'd walked in and smiled at her and made her feel like she was a queen.

Then she caught sight of the coldness in his blue eyes. He hadn't smiled once. What the hell had happened to the man she'd met?

If he'd known she was there, he wouldn't have come. Knowing that made her feel smaller than she ever had. Her heart constricted. She wouldn't go back. She would call in and quit over the phone.

There was no way she could work with him. He could find an admin he liked more and she could…she could move on to whatever happened next.

She felt someone fall into step beside her. As though she'd conjured him, Stefan Talbot glided alongside, measuring his step to match hers. He'd probably been waiting outside the station house, watching for her. Callie turned away and tried walking faster.

"Callie…" Stefan's smooth voice practically begged her.

"Go away, Stef." She knew he played deep games from time to time. She never expected he would play them with her. Betrayal burned through her. It hurt, maybe even worse than Nate's total rejection. She had no illusions that Nate loved her.

"I can't. You should stop and talk to me, or I'll follow you around until you do." There was no threat, merely a simple promise. Stefan was used to getting his way. When he didn't, he tended to do whatever it took to force things to fall into place. Stefan liked a well-ordered house. "Let's go to Stella's. I'll buy you lunch and explain why I didn't tell you Nate and Zane were coming to town."

She stopped in the middle of the street. "Zane's here, too?"

"I suspect, though I haven't seen him. I doubt Nate would have left him behind."

"I don't want lunch. I want to go home for a while. If you follow me, you better tell me what you know." She gave Stefan her sternest look. Her best friend was a good foot taller than she was and every inch the elegant man. He had a face that made every woman who saw him sigh. Though she knew he was gorgeous, all she could see was the brother she should have had. Stefan Talbot was one year and two months older than she was. He had watched out for her almost all of her life. It would be good to know why he had stopped now.

"I didn't tell you because I thought you would quit." He had a habit of knowing what she was thinking.

"Why would I do that?"

"Because you were in love with Nate and Zane. Because you never got over those two."

And he knew her better than anyone in the world. Tears welled up again. When would she get that hard outer shell so many people got? When would she be able to contain her feelings? She turned and started back down the street toward the small cabin she'd lived in all of her life.

Stef was right beside her. His hand found her back. "I think he needs you. I don't know about Zane, Callie. I don't know him the way I know Nate. Zane's kind of a mystery to me, but I know Nate has been through a lot. He was involved in a deep cover operation for the DEA. From what I understand, it ended poorly. Zane was injured, and Nate blames himself. Couple that with the fact that Nate's family and finances imploded and he's not in a good place."

"Is Zane all right?" The thought of big, gorgeous Zane being hurt made her ache. Did he have some woman holding his hand? She hoped so. She hoped he was being taken care of. She wished she was the woman but wouldn't have him be alone for anything in the world.

"I think he's back on his feet physically." Stefan was silent for a moment. "The rest is a real question. Nate called me looking for a job. He wouldn't have done that if he wasn't desperate, and I think part of that desperation has to do with Zane. Like I said, I'm not close to Zane but I know how I would feel if I felt like I was losing my best friend. I would do anything to save her. Please, Callie. I think they need this place. And in order for him to start to fit in here, he's going to need you."

Callie began to slow despite the fact that she wanted so badly to stay irritated with him. Mostly she wanted to follow through on her first impulse and go hide in her cabin until she could run away.

"You should have told me. If you had said those things to me, I would have agreed and I would have been ready to see him." She might not agree with them, but he hadn't meant to hurt her. He slipped his hand into hers and pulled it to his chest.

"I made a mistake. I honestly worried you would leave. I know you've thought about it since your mom died."

She'd thought about it a lot. It wasn't that she wanted to leave Bliss. It was simply she wasn't sure there was anything more here for her.

He squeezed her hand. "I didn't want to give you any reason to go. Please don't be mad at me. I can't stand it when you're mad at me. You and Rye and Max are my whole world."

Poor little rich boy. She couldn't help but smile. Stef had given up a lot to keep his handpicked family together. "You're a jerk."

"I know." His smile was slightly sad. "So you'll stay?"

"For a while." It was all she could promise.

* * * *

The door to the small cabin came open, and Zane slammed down the book he had been reading. Was it really that late? He looked out the window, and sure enough, the sun was going down. He hadn't noticed the shadows elongating. Damn, he'd gotten lost. It was the story of his life lately.

"Zane?" Nate's voice rang through the cabin. It wasn't hard. There were only three rooms and a single bathroom.

Zane got up from the small desk that dominated the bedroom he'd chosen for himself and walked into the main room. It was tiny but served as both living room and kitchen. Naturally he hadn't done any of the stuff he'd promised he'd do. He'd been reading a lot since he got out of the hospital. It took his mind off…well, everything.

He rushed into the kitchen and opened the fridge. "Sorry. I'll have dinner ready in a minute."

Nate held up a bag. "You don't have to. I got burgers. The burger joint is supposed to be first class. I figured you'd forget."

Zane hated the feeling that rolled through his system. Useless. He was completely fucking useless. His legs worked again, but he was still half a fucking man. He couldn't even remember to cook dinner.

"Don't worry about it," Nate said as though reading his mind.

But he would. He pulled two beers out of the fridge. If Nate could put on that pansy-ass uniform and play at being a small-town sheriff, he could at least open the beer.

Nate was already plowing through his burger when Zane sat down. "Bad day?"

Nate shrugged. He was shut down, but Zane expected that. They hadn't talked, really talked, in months, not since long before he came out of the coma. He was okay with that. He didn't really want to talk, either. Talking wouldn't help anything. Talking wouldn't fix the things he'd broken. It wouldn't explain how they'd broken in the first place. That was what haunted him at night. The *why* was going to kill him because he was fairly certain there was no answer forthcoming.

Nate's eyes slid off to the side when he started to look Zane in the face. "It was fine. It's a shit-ass job. Nothing to it."

"Did you…" How did he ask it? Damn, but he wanted to know. "Did you hear anything about her?"

Nate let the burger fall out of his hands. He reached for the beer. "Her?"

He said it like he didn't know, but there was a hardness to his eyes that let Zane know he was lying with that question. It was a manipulation to see if he could get Zane to say her name.

"You know who I'm talking about," he replied, trying to keep his tone as bland as possible. "I know it was your first day, but I thought at least you might ask if she's still here. Don't you want to know?"

"Maybe I do and maybe I don't, but if I did I would find out myself. I wouldn't sit in this cabin and pretend like I don't exist. If you want to know if she's still here, go into town and find out for yourself." Nate stood and stalked off to his room, his dinner half-eaten and forgotten.

Zane didn't touch his. Damn it. It was still there. Even after all these years, Callie Sheppard was still between them. How was he supposed to tell Nate that he wouldn't go after her? The man should know. Fuck. Callie wouldn't want him now. All it took was one look in the mirror to know no woman would want him now. His face was ruined, and he wasn't sure he'd ever really had a heart to speak of.

He stood up and walked to the front door. He pushed through the screen door and moved out onto the small wooden porch. The previous owner had left behind a couple of crappy lawn chairs. He lowered himself into one, hoping it would hold his weight. He had a sudden vision of three Adirondack chairs, side by side by side. Three places for three people to watch the brilliant sunset. Three places for people to rest and be together at the end of a long day.

He took a swallow of beer.

Why wouldn't Nate put him out of his misery and tell him whether or not Callie was still in this mountain town? Was she married? Did she have a couple of kids? Did she think of him fondly or wish she'd never met him?

He settled into the chair, which showed no signs of faltering. The night air was cooling off. The beer was cold as it flowed down his throat. Everything was still here and yet in constant motion. It was odd. The world moved, but he could be still and nothing forced him to run. All the time he'd been in the hospital a ragged restlessness had ruled him. He hadn't wanted to be in bed and then he hadn't wanted to stand. Anything they brought him wasn't quite good enough. No food could fill his gut. No drug could quite make him sleep easy. He'd been on the knife's edge, cutting himself because he'd been too afraid to fall off.

Not here. Here things slowed down and the air was sweeter. He'd woken early this morning and a deer had been on the lawn. They'd stood there for the longest time, deer and man existing in the same place, considering each other. It had been a peaceful moment.

He could finally fucking think in this place.

But he worried if he left the mountain, he would have to face the fact that he wasn't the man he'd been.

What did he want? He sure as hell didn't want to be a burden to Nate for the rest of his life. Nate blamed himself for what happened, but he shouldn't. If Zane had been in the same situation, he would have made the same call and yet…

Nate wasn't the one who had to look in the mirror every day and see a monster staring back at him. Nate wasn't the one who knew how fucking mortal and helpless he could be. Nate wasn't the one who had broken.

Zane's eyes slid to the motorcycle that stood beside Nate's beat up truck. He could get on it and ride off. He could go anywhere and never have to be responsible again. There would be no expectations of him being the man he'd been before the end of the mission. No one would know him or care about him, and there was a certain amount of temptation to the idea.

But he owed Nate. He needed to make sure Nate was going to get his life back on track. He would make sure Nate was settled down here in Colorado.

Then he could disappear.

Chapter Four

Zane took a deep breath, banishing the thoughts that plagued him. He didn't have to think out here. He could let it all go. This place was so far from where he'd come from. El Paso had been dusty and hot, the sun scorching everything in its path. The very air had been dry. It was odd because he'd grown up in Texas, was used to hot summers, but something about El Paso had been different.

Or it had been the job. Maybe it had been the constant tension, the knowledge that any tiny mistake he made would put his life in the balance. And it had.

Colorado was different. Everything was green here. Alive. This place was so damn alive.

He watched as Nate's truck pulled away. They hadn't spoken this morning. Zane had waited until he was fairly certain Nate was leaving to walk out of his bedroom.

He stretched and pulled his sneakers on, warming up his long limbs in preparation for his morning run. He liked this time of day, just as the sun was coming up.

Where was Callie? He was almost certain she was here somewhere. Nate would have told him if she wasn't. He knew something about her. It was there in the way his shoulders tightened when Zane mentioned her name.

He started by the road, but quickly turned and jogged up the trail that led down by the river. The Rio Grande wound through the town. This particular spot was a deeper part of the river where he would often see people rafting and canoeing. Not that they saw him. He kept to the trees, preferring the fantasy that he was alone in the world.

His lungs burned as he climbed up and away from the river.

At some point he would be on National Forest land, but he didn't care. If the rangers wanted to run him off let them. And if some bear came along and decided to gnaw on him, then that was how it would be.

Nothing scared him anymore. He'd lived through the worst. He'd survived torture and pain. He'd lost more than he'd thought he had to lose.

Sometimes he thought he'd lost his soul.

He forced his legs to move, pushing past the pain. Hell, he welcomed the pain. The pain reminded him he could still feel something.

He reached the top of the hill and felt his muscles pushed to their max.

A field of green spread out in front of him. Perfect green. It was beautiful. Pristine and surrounded by forest, as though someone had carved out a meadow and hidden it.

A secret place.

He stood there, dragging air into his lungs and considering that piece of land. He'd run up a ragged spot where no grass would grow but there wasn't an inch of that ground that wasn't covered.

Why was it so perfect when other pieces of land got ruined? What protected it from insects and drought and blight? Why did it thrive?

Why? Fucking why?

The question welled inside him. It was always there, always sitting in his gut, eating away at him. Why? Why had he been the one who was tortured? Why hadn't he died?

He was still there, still in that chair where he'd learned how weak he was. He'd never fucking gotten out of it.

Zane took off, running like a madman down the hill and out into that perfect grass. The most insane urge to mess it up overwhelmed him. He wanted to pull it out, leave his tracks everywhere, maybe piss on it and see if he could get it to die.

A scream of rage burst from inside him, echoing through the space.

He stumbled, losing his balance and hitting that ground hard.

Every muscle pulsed with pain, and for a moment he couldn't breathe.

He stared up at the clearest, bluest sky he'd ever seen.

If this was his last moment, he would take it. He would lie here in this perfect place and let his body sink into the grass and ground beyond. He could become a part of it.

He closed his eyes, wishing he could forget everything and simply be.

"Are you okay?" A soft voice pulled him out of his agony.

He opened his eyes and stared up at the woman standing above him. She had ridiculously long brown hair and eyes to match. He placed her age at somewhere around thirty, though she could be younger. There was a startling air of innocence about her.

He was suddenly ridiculously aware that he wasn't wearing a shirt. He never saw anyone on his runs. Naturally the first time he lost his shit, he got caught.

"Do you understand English? It's an Earth plane language. Did you fall? I've heard there's a door to another plane somewhere around here, but my mother used to say they can be tricky to find," she said with a smile. "Might I be the first to say welcome?"

"Earth plane?" Had he hit his head?

She nodded and he realized she was carrying a basket. "Yes, that's what we call this particular plane of existence. Where are you from? You have the look of a mighty warrior. Are you from one of the faery realms? My mother claimed that's where I'm from. She's gone now, but she used to tell me all sorts of stories about the Seelie plane. If I had to guess I would say you're Unseelie, though. They have a bit darker look about them, though they shouldn't be judged for it."

"Lady, are you insane?"

Her smile widened. "Some people say so. Could you move just a tad to your left? You're about to ruin some very nice-looking curly dock."

Yep, he'd bashed his own head in and now he was in some crazy coma and she was a figment of his imagination. Still, he moved his foot. He rolled over as she knelt down and gently started to work what looked like a weed out of the ground. Her basket was full of green leaves and red berries.

"You think I'm some kind of fairy? I'm not sure how to take that."

She frowned at him. "Why it would be bad to be a fairy?"

He kind of got the idea that their relationship depended on how he answered that particular question. "It wouldn't be."

"Excellent," she replied. "And I didn't really think so. Though I wasn't joking about the door to other worlds. It's here somewhere. I know it. It's precisely why we have so much psychic energy. But I knew you weren't some lost Fae creature. They don't tend to wear Nikes. They like boots. Usually made of some kind of leather, and I disapprove of that as well."

His whole body hurt, but he was fascinated. Callie had told him this was a strange place with weird people. Of course, she hadn't put it like that. She'd used words like "magical" and "unique." This chick must be one of the unique ones.

"What should boots be made of?"

She kind of floated over to another patch of ground where she harvested her weeds. "Natural things."

"Leather's pretty natural." He wasn't sure why he kept talking, but it had been weeks since he'd had interaction with anyone but Nate, and lately their discussions consisted of whether to watch baseball or football.

And this chick kind of reminded him of Callie. She probably knew Callie.

God, he hadn't realized how lonely he was.

The woman's eyes had narrowed. "Yes, leather is natural. It naturally belongs to the cow. How would you feel if someone came along and brutally murdered you and then wore you as boots? You would be pretty upset, wouldn't you? And we wonder why we have such anxious livestock."

"You're Nell." He hadn't forgotten a word Callie had said to him that weekend so long ago. She'd told him about her hometown and her friends there, and she'd mentioned her friend Nell. Nell, the champion of all marginalized creatures great and small. "Nell Finn."

"It's Nell Flanders," she said with a smile. "I'm married to my soul mate. Henry. He's as gentle as they come and has such a deep connection to the earth. It's a beautiful thing to see. How do you know me?"

He managed to get to his feet. Everything still worked. Mostly. "I had a friend from a long time ago who lived here and told me a lot about the place."

He wasn't about to mention Callie's name. Nell would likely go right to her and tell her all about the crazy guy in the woods.

"Well, welcome to Bliss," she said. She gestured around the meadow. "I'm more than happy to share my grocery store with you."

"You run a grocery store?"

She twirled around, her skirt swirling. "The world is my grocer. I come up here in the mornings to gather ingredients. I like to get them when the morning dew is still fresh on the leaves."

"You eat weeds?"

The prim look was back on her face. "I eat the bounty of nature. I live in harmony with the land."

"It is beautiful here." He would give her that. "I come from a place that wasn't so pretty. I'm still trying to get used to it."

"Is that why I haven't seen you around town?" She found another mound of nature's bounty. "I assume you're the sheriff's partner."

He moved in, kneeling before she could and pulling the plant up for her. He held it out. "Yeah. I guess I need time to see if I can fit in here. I'm not so sure I do."

She gave him a beatific smile and accepted the hunk of weed. "Thank you. And why wouldn't you fit in? You have to know Bliss is a tolerant place. No one will think twice about your lifestyle. Love is love here. Though you might talk to your boyfriend. He's extremely cranky. I know an excellent shaman who could remove all his negative energy, and he would be so much happier."

The thought of Nate meeting with a shaman was pretty damn funny. But what? "Boyfriend?"

"Oh, are you married? That's lovely. I wish Marie and Teeny

would legalize their union. Not because I particularly believe they must have a piece of paper in order to love each other, but I would love a nice party. Max and Rachel and Rye's wedding was so lovely. Where did you get married? Henry and I were married right here in Bliss. Everything was recycled, of course, and we had the loveliest vegan cake."

"Whoa." Was that the rumor around town? "Wait. Nate and I aren't married. Like to anyone. Definitely not to each other." She started to give him the evil eye again. "Not that there's anything wrong with that. We don't swing that way. But again, totally cool with people who do."

"Then why are you worried you won't fit in?"

"Uhm, have you seen my face?"

"Of course. It's right there. You are an extremely attractive man. Not as handsome as my Henry, of course, but lovely all the same."

"I scare small children."

"Well, those must be very anxious children. Their parents should work on that. I've found children tend to be more accepting than their adult counterparts."

How to make her understand because it was suddenly important that someone did. Maybe if someone understood, he could feel better about the distance between him and Callie. He could feel good and settled that he was doing the right thing by staying away from her. "I'm not this meadow of yours. This place is perfect. It's so beautiful it almost hurts to look at it. Imagine there was one section of this place that was barren. That would be me. I'm that space and I bring everything around me down. I'm damaged."

She stared at him for a moment. "We're all damaged. We're all scarred. Sometimes you simply can't see the scars. Besides, perfection is boring. Perfect things tend to be the most fragile."

So no understanding there.

"I've got to get back," she said. "Henry gets worried if I'm gone too long. I hope to see you around town. You'll like it here if you give it a chance."

He nodded, knowing he likely wouldn't follow her advice. Despite her kindness, he'd come to know that sleepy little towns didn't welcome people like him.

She started to walk away, her basket swinging. She stopped at the tree line. "Do you know why this meadow is beautiful and fertile and green?"

He shook his head.

"Twenty-five years ago lightning struck here and started a terrible fire that almost took out the town. That happens a lot here in the mountains. The fire burned most of the land you see and for years it was dark. But not barren. You see, all the ash and waste that was left behind, the earth soaked it up and created something new and alive. This place is beautiful because it came through the crucible and survived. If you look closely you can see the signs that this land is scarred, too. It isn't perfect. It's strong and alive." She turned and disappeared into the woods.

Zane dropped back down, his muscles still weak.

This place had been barren? It was almost inconceivable, and yet somehow the land had slowly come back, stronger than before.

Was it possible for a soul to do the same?

Something moved in the distance. Something large.

Was that a moose?

Yep. That was one massive moose. It lumbered out into the meadow, staring at him before huffing and lowering its enormous head to the grass. He started to munch. It appeared Nell shared her grocery store with a lot of creatures.

He should probably run, but he found himself lying back. If the moose wanted to crush him, he would. Or they could share the space.

Zane stared up at the perfect sky and wondered if Callie was doing the same.

* * * *

"How much longer you planning on keeping me locked up, Johnny Law?"

Nate gave serious consideration to killing his one and only prisoner. Two weeks into his new life, and he was thinking about going out of it with a bang.

The station was quiet, with only Nate, his deputy, Logan, and the prisoner currently occupying the neatly kept rooms. Nate leaned on the reception desk and considered the man in the small cell. Bliss County Jail was a tiny operation with two simple cells. If he could catch a serious offender and shove him in there with Max Harper, he might be able to solve a major problem. If said prisoner shivved the mouthy horse trainer, then Nate wouldn't have to put up with the son of a bitch. Nate stared over at his deputy, Logan Green. The lanky, too-young-for-a-uniform boy had his nose in a comic book.

All in all, it was a long way from the Drug Enforcement Agency.

When Stefan had offered him the job of sheriff of Bliss, it seemed like the perfect place to start over. Of course, Stef hadn't mentioned that he'd have to deal with Max or crazy-ass Mel, who insisted daily that the aliens were coming. No one had bothered to warn him that he would be the law enforcement liaison to a nudist colony, or that once a year the new agers came in to soak up the vibrations or some shit that Bliss gave off.

It was a weird town, and he was rapidly getting fed up with it.

"Damn it, Max." Callie walked into the sheriff's office, pushing her glasses up her nose. Yeah, there was one thing he wasn't fed up with and that was looking at her. She was so adorable, Nate wanted to walk up to her and hug her. Of course, hugging would lead to rubbing, and he knew if he laid a hand on her, he'd end up humping her leg like a dog. She was such a sweet armful. Even dressed in a denim skirt and blousy shirt, she was sexy as hell. Why hadn't Stef bothered to mention that the woman of his dreams would be his secretary? Stef sure as hell hadn't forgotten that he had a past with Callie. Not that he seemed to care.

Two weeks in and he was starting to think he would go crazy if he didn't get his hands on her. Not that he was close to doing it. She barely spoke to him except to lecture him on all the things he was doing wrong. Then he would get sarcastic and broody and she would go back to not talking to him.

Callie completely ignored him. She blew past him, her hands on those curvy hips of hers, and plowed toward Max Harper. She never did anything without a great deal of energy. It was one of the hottest things about her. She was always moving, but Nate remembered a time when her energy had been spent and all she could do was sigh. He'd give anything to get her underneath him again.

But she was still off limits.

Harper's boots tapped against the floor. "Now, Callie, don't you yell at me. Talk to that tight-ass boss of yours. He's pulling people off the street for no reason. Can sheriffs get impeached? Because he should be impeached. Rye would never have done something like that."

Nate came off the desk, prepared to defend himself. He'd heard an awful lot about how the old sheriff handled things. Nate wondered if he would ever come out of the man's shadow. Everywhere he went, he was compared to Rye Harper.

He couldn't see her face, but he knew Callie was rolling her eyes. She had that sarcastic stance. He'd learned an awful lot about reading Callie's body language since he'd started the job. Mostly that was because he couldn't take his eyes off her.

"Rye didn't arrest anyone because he was as lazy as the day is long," Callie declared. "I could barely get him to write a ticket. Sheriff Wright is an actual, honest-to-goodness cop, and not some high school kid who didn't want to work at Stella's Diner."

Logan's head came out of the latest issue of *X-Men*. "Stella works too damn hard, if you ask me. This place is way calmer than the diner, what with all the tourists and having to deal with Nell and Henry's protests. And seriously, have you seen what happens when you get that guy's order wrong?"

Harper slapped at the bars of his cell. "I like my burger dead, man. Hal tries to cut corners by shoving a live cow in between two buns and calling it a burger. You want to arrest someone, Sheriff? Go arrest Stella's short-order cook."

Logan nodded as though happy to have confirmation of his life choices. "You see what I mean? Being a deputy is way less dangerous than working at Stella's. And I graduated three years ago. Stop calling me a high school kid. At least move me up to college. Speaking of college…I'm thinking about taking one of those online courses. Any way I could use the computer here?"

Nate narrowed his eyes, and Logan suddenly bolted out of his chair.

"I'll go catch some speeders. That's a good idea." Logan was smashing his hat on his head as he nearly ran out the door.

"Will you stop scaring the crap out of your deputy?" Callie frowned Nate's way as the door literally hit Logan's ass on his way out. The deputy yelped. "Do you have any idea how hard it was to get someone to agree to this job? This is a whole town full of antiestablishment hippies. They weren't lining up to put on a uniform."

Nate shrugged. Scaring the piss out of Logan was one of the highlights of his days here in Bliss. He attempted his most angelic look. "I have no idea what you're talking about."

Now he could actually see the eye roll. It was an expression she used a lot on him. "Sure you don't. I heard you recounting all of your so-called kills to him. Do you want to give that boy nightmares? And you…" She whirled back around to face the man in the cell. "What is your wife going to say?"

Max Harper grinned arrogantly. He wore jeans, a western shirt, and boots. The man was all cowboy, all the time. "She's going to say nothing because once I get my phone call, I'm calling Rye. He won't tell Rach anything. I have too much on him. We've got a nice, mutually assured destruction balance going on."

Nate sighed, a genuine sense of pleasure running through his system. This might be even better than giving Logan Green a bunch of baloney stories. This one was real. "Don't worry about that phone call, Harper. I took care of it for you. Your wife said she'd be here as soon as she…what were her words? Oh, yeah. She'll be here as soon as she sharpens a knife so she can cut your balls off."

It took everything he had not to burst into laughter at how green Max Harper got. The cowboy's hands fell to his sides, and he sat back on the cot. "You didn't."

"I did."

"You asshole. We had a friendly game going and you have to play hardball?" Harper looked like a little boy who had his toys taken away.

Was the man insane? "Friendly game? You call doing seventy-five miles an hour in a forty mile an hour zone a game? Then you didn't stop when I put on the lights and the siren."

"I was looking for a safe place to pull over." Harper shrugged.

"For ten miles?" He'd followed that son of a bitch all the way down the damn mountain.

There it was, that arrogant smirk that made Nate want to clobber him. "Those roads are damn dangerous. I was giving you a signal that I would pull over as soon as I could."

"You flipped me the bird, asshole."

Harper pointed his way. "See, now is that any way for a cop to talk? When my brother was the sheriff, he would never have used that sort of language."

"He cursed your name on a regular basis." A stern female voice was added to the mix.

Harper shifted back as though the bars wouldn't keep him safe from the terrifying newcomer. Rachel Harper was roughly five feet two and, if rumors were true, expecting a baby. Maxwell Harper was utterly terrified of his pretty, pregnant wife. She crossed to the middle of the room and stared a hole through him.

"Hi, baby." It was obvious Max was going for sympathy. All of the arrogance on his face had fled in favor of a sad-puppy look. "That man does not like me. He looks for any excuse to mess with me."

Rachel ignored him. She turned to Callie. "Does he need to make bail?"

"No," Callie said.

"Yes," Nate interjected.

Now it was Callie staring at him, and Nate understood Max for a moment. Nate might not have impregnated Callie, but she had a hold on him all the same. "You are not leaving him in jail until the judge gets back from his hunting trip."

"No, I need him to come home. I have a few words to say to you, husband number one," Rachel said.

"I can stay." Max nodded his head vigorously. "I don't want any special treatment."

Rachel stood in front of the cell. "Max Harper, you will get out of that cell and get your sweet ass into the car or there will be hell to pay."

A long, slow smile tugged at Harper's lips. He got up from the cot and stalked to the bars. "Hell to pay, huh? What kind of hell you going to put me through, Rach?"

Rachel cocked her head to the side as she stared at her husband.

"I think you know what I'm talking about, Max. I'm going to need at least twelve hours."

Max's face flushed. He suddenly seemed anxious. "I should get arrested more often." He turned to Nate. "I am very, very sorry for the shameful way I taunted you, Sheriff Wright." He snickered, his mouth curling up in a smirk. "Sorry, it's just the most clichéd name ever for a sheriff, but I utterly respect your authority."

The asshole didn't, but Callie was already getting the keys to the cell. He needed to hide the damn things. Every time he put someone in custody, his admin let them out.

The door to the station house slammed open, and Max's twin brother, Rye Harper, ran in, his boots sliding across the slick floor.

"Callie, I need to get Max out of here before…hey, baby." Rye plastered a smile on his face. "I was at the diner and found out Max had done it again. Damn it, Max, when are you going to grow up? Don't you know we got a baby on the way?"

"Yes, you're here to lecture Max." Rachel obviously wasn't buying it. "BS, Rye. You're here to bail him out and be his alibi, like you always are."

Max strode out of his cell and crowded his wife, one hand sliding across the nape of her neck, the other rubbing her belly. "Don't worry about it, bro. Me and Rach have a system worked out. If I screw up, then I have to be her sex slave for a while. It's a terrible punishment. It's going to get me on the straight and narrow one of these days."

Rye was immediately at her other side. "Well, I would like to point out that I was going to bail him out and then hide the evidence from you. That makes me every bit as guilty as him."

Rachel's laugh filled the station as she sent her husbands out to the car. The men ran to do her bidding, and she turned to Callie. "Sorry. Max is worried about the baby. You know how he gets when he's anxious. He tends to take it out on the world around him."

Callie hugged the pregnant woman, her affection obvious. "He's obnoxious all the time. It's part of his charm. Don't worry about it. I'll talk to that one about being more tolerant."

Nate stood a bit taller because he was pretty sure he was about to get lectured. Rachel left to follow her husbands. Husbands. Damn, as much as he hated Max Harper, Nate was also completely fascinated with the way the man lived his life. The Harper family consisted of the twins and their shared wife, Rachel. No one in town even blinked. Nate had caught some of the tourists shaking their heads when she smooched on both, but the citizens of Bliss took it all in stride. One of these days, he was going to sit down with Rye, who seemed far more reasonable than his brother, and talk about how it really worked.

But for now, he had to deal with Callie. He went on the offensive.

"You have to stop doing that." He made his tone firm. He wasn't Max Harper, afraid of one small woman. After everything he'd been through, he knew all about fear, and it didn't come in such a soft package. He'd been wary of dealing with her. He'd spent the last two weeks mooning over what he couldn't have, and now it was time to take the situation in hand. "You are my administrative assistant, Ms. Sheppard. If you want to be a deputy, you can take the test, and I'll put your name on the waiting list."

"If you don't like my work, Sheriff, you should feel free to fire me." She turned on her kitten heels and stomped back toward the front desk. She sat down on her chair and immediately began to straighten a bunch of stuff that was already neat and organized.

She had him there. He was never going to fire her. He couldn't even stand the possibility of her quitting. Hell, he didn't like the days she took off, and more often than not found some damn silly excuse to see her. Feeling utterly impotent, Nate stalked into his office and slammed the door shut. He slumped down into his comfy chair and pondered his situation. Zane was getting worse, not better. He hadn't been able to get him out of the cabin to come into town in the two weeks they had been living in Bliss. Zane still didn't know Callie was here. Nate hadn't told him for fear that Zane would take off on that bike of his, and Nate wouldn't see him again until he had to identify his body.

It had seemed like a good place to start over after everything that happened. He couldn't go back to the DEA, and there was no way Zane would go back even if they would let him. When he'd quit the DEA, Nate had been told that the director would hold his job, but he couldn't even consider it while Zane was recuperating. Zane's body had healed, but his mind was still in a dark place. He'd needed a place where Zane could get better, but the bastard didn't seem to want to recover. He wanted to brood. He wanted to rage. He wanted to beat the shit out of anything that came in his path. Nate kept hoping that would change, but now he wondered. Maybe they should have gone back to Dallas.

It would be easier if Callie wasn't here, but he needed her, damn it, and in more ways than one. Nate wasn't used to small-town politics, and he doubted anyone on the planet was used to Bliss politics.

He was fumbling, and he didn't know how to stop.

There was a brief knock on the door, and Callie popped her head in. If things were different, this would be the point where Nate would haul his hot secretary into his arms, shove her skirt up, and have his way with her. His eyes glazed over as he thought about freeing his cock and settling her in his lap. He'd lower that tight pussy onto him and fuck her hard. It would be a nice break. They got three a day. That might start to satisfy him.

"Are you still here or have you checked out?" Callie stared at him like he was from another planet.

Nate sat up carefully. His cock was painfully hard, but then it had been in that state for the last two weeks. "What's going on?"

"It's Mel. The aliens have landed, and he has proof." Callie wrinkled her nose. "You need to get out there and talk to him. I have the Detector 4000 out on the desk."

Every muscle in his body was suddenly weary. The Detector 4000 was one of the reasons he should have stayed in Dallas. It was a video game controller Stefan had "enhanced" with various bells and whistles to placate the town crazy—well, one of them, anyway. It made a lot of sounds and had lights that went off and told the user that no alien technology was in evidence.

It was complete bullshit.

Maybe it was time he took his job seriously. Nate stood up and placed the Stetson on his head. Yes, that was exactly what he needed to do. Why should he fit in? He was the sheriff. He was the authority figure for the town. Maybe the town needed to fit in with him. Yes, it was time to take this town in hand.

Callie watched him as he walked past her. "I don't like that look."

He waved her off. “Get used to it.”

Nate walked past the front desk, pointedly ignoring the Detector 4000. Mel would have to learn to deal with reality.

There was a new sheriff in town, and Bliss would have to face the music.

* * * *

Boy, he was about to screw up big time. Callie just knew it. She grabbed the Detector 4000 and raced after her boss, turning the sign on the door from *Come on in* to *Don’t commit any crimes. We’re fishing.*

He was already in the Bronco, starting the engine. Callie had quickly realized that Nate Wright was a man who took his time making a decision, but once he’d settled on his course, he was quick to follow it. She had to be fast or he’d be in trouble.

Before he had a chance to back out, she swung open the door and slammed into the passenger seat.

“Damn it, Callie, who is minding the store?” His lips thinned, and he looked pointedly at the station house. He was not amused by the sign she’d made when Rye had been sheriff. He’d been famous for his fishing afternoons.

She didn’t argue. It wouldn’t help to point out that no one would think a thing about the station not being manned. If there was trouble, they would call her on the radio or her cell. Nate hadn’t left his big-city mentality behind. She leaned across him and grabbed the radio. “Logan, this is Callie. I need you to get back to the station house.”

There was a slight pause. “Is he still there?”

She felt Nate stiffen beside her. Well, if he wanted his staff to like him, he should be less rude. Hell, she didn’t like him most of the time and she’d slept with him. Not that anyone knew that except Stefan. “No. It’s safe. He’s going out on a call, and I’m going to make sure he doesn’t cause trouble.”

She could hear Logan’s voice lighten. “Awesome. Then I’ll be right there.”

She would make sure to put a call into the station before they came back. More than once, she’d found Logan taking a nice nap on one of the cell cots. She didn't think Nate would find it amusing. She replaced the radio as Nate backed out.

"I swear I should fire you all. I've never been in such a shoddily run operation before." He kept his eyes on the road in front of him.

"Or you should feel free to head right back to the big city where everything is sunshine and roses." She kind of wished he would leave. It would be infinitely easier on her. Logan could be sheriff, and as long as absolutely nothing ever happened, everything would be all right. Of course, if anything went wrong, they were screwed. Still, she might be willing to take the risk. The tension was starting to wear on her.

"At least in Dallas we don't mollycoddle crazy people."

She was rapidly getting fed up with the sheriff's bad temper. He took it out on everyone, but since she was with him all the time, she got the brunt of it. "Well, if it helps at all, you won't have to worry about me for too much longer."

The Bronco stopped suddenly, the tires screeching against the pavement. She was glad she'd slipped on the safety belt, or she might have flown through the window. "What does that mean?"

She shouldn't have mentioned it. And why not? It wasn't like he hadn't made his displeasure of her services plain. She turned in her seat to look him in the eye. He was so gorgeous it hurt. She wondered what had happened to Zane. She'd asked the second day he'd worked there, but he'd refused to answer. She hadn't brought it up again, but she thought of Zane often. She wondered if Zane would be as disappointed to see her again as Nate had been.

"It means I'll be turning in my notice soon." She'd promised Stefan she would stay for a while. A month seemed long enough. She'd give him two weeks to find someone else. It was time to move on. She just wasn't sure where she was moving to.

"Why?" He asked the question softly, his eyes on her.

She softened slightly. "You know why. You're not happy with me. I'll find something new, and you can find an assistant you trust."

She wondered if he wouldn't give Laura Niles a call. Laura ran the cash register at the Stop 'n' Shop, but Callie had heard talk of her working for the FBI before she came to Bliss. Maybe Nate would ask to try out the tall blonde. She was willowy with light blue eyes.

Perhaps that was Nate's type. Hell, Laura was pretty much every man's type. There wasn't much of a call for plump brunettes, no matter how comfy they were in their own skin.

"I trust you."

She laughed but was well aware nothing about this mess was funny. "You can't stand me, Sheriff. I'm not an idiot. You don't want me around. I do get why Stef thought this was a good idea. I'll be honest, I don't understand why it isn't working. We're adults. We should be able to get along, but we don't. So I'll move on. I promise to make the transition as easy as possible."

He swallowed before he opened his mouth to talk. "I don't want a transition. I do want you around. I was just surprised to see you again." He turned his attention back to the road and started driving toward Mel's. "I'll settle down. I need a little time. That's all."

It was the first opening she'd had since he came to town. It bugged her, his obvious displeasure at seeing her again. It didn't make sense to her. It had been the best weekend of her life. She had no illusions that he felt the same way, but she had thought he'd enjoyed himself. "Why were you so angry to see me?"

"I wasn't angry."

He was going to be difficult. She wasn't surprised. She decided to push it. She was leaving anyway. If he got really pissed, maybe he would fire her, and she wouldn't have an excuse to hang around anymore. "You sure were. I don't understand. I didn't make a nuisance of myself. I didn't call you or anything."

Not that she could have. They hadn't left a number. Only a note. *Have a good life.* It hadn't been that great so far.

She watched as his hands tightened on the steering wheel. His eyes stared ahead, but she knew how uncomfortable this whole conversation was making him. If he'd been Zane, he would have turned to her by now and told her to stop asking him so many damn questions. But this was Nate, and he'd try to smooth things over. It was funny. She'd spent two days with them a long time ago, but she felt like she knew them so well.

It was an illusion.

His voice was soft now. "Callie, I wasn't mad. I was surprised, that's all. I don't want you to leave. Where are you going to work?

Logan is right about the diner."

She hadn't exactly figured that out yet, but she knew she had to make a change. Since her mom died the year before, she'd been in a bit of a fog. Five years of taking care of her had left Callie a bit dazed. She loved that her mother had managed to last so long before the cancer had come back and ravaged her body, but the long-term care had taken its toll. Her life had been on hold, but it was time to move forward. She owed it to her mom and herself. "Well, I was thinking about moving to Denver. I talked to Marie the other day. She knows how to sell property. I thought I'd put my cabin up for sale. There are plenty of people who would probably like to use it as a vacation property. I've got a nice view of the river."

Marie had been really upset at the thought of her moving. She and Teeny, her life partner, ran the general store and had known Callie all of her life. It hurt Callie's heart to think of leaving Bliss, but there was nothing for her here. She would never get married if she stayed. She would be surrounded by friends, but it wasn't enough. She wanted what Max and Rye had found with Rachel. She wanted a family.

The Bronco turned up the steep road that led to Mel's cabin. Nate was careful on the mountain passes, driving like a man who wasn't used to them. If only he was as careful with the people around him. "I don't think that's a good idea. You're a small-town girl. The big city would eat you up."

She smiled at the thought. "At least somebody would."

It had been so long since she had sex she couldn't remember what it felt like.

Nate stopped the car again. "Are you telling me you're leaving your home because you want to get laid?"

His voice held a hint of outrage, and Callie nearly laughed at the prim set of his mouth.

"Well, I've heard worse reasons." She didn't have to justify herself to Sheriff Wright, but she found it almost impossible not to explain. "There's no one for me here in Bliss. Unless I want to sleep with Logan, I'm pretty much on my own. And I really don't want to sleep with Logan, though he's tried." It had been sweet, but she'd had to turn him down.

"He did what?" Nate threw the car into park and was reaching for the radio.

She swatted his hand away. "What is your problem?"

"What's my problem? How about the fact that my deputy is hitting on my…secretary? It's wrong. It's setting us all up for a lawsuit." He reached for the radio again. Again she slapped his hand aside. He sat up and started the car moving again. "You're right. I shouldn't warn him that I fully intend to kick his ass. It might send him running."

She could see Mel's cabin in the distance. If she was leaving, she needed to use the time she had with Nate to try to get him to see reason. "You want some advice?"

"No."

"Well, you're getting it." She might as well go out with a bang. "Stop being such a jerk. You're getting a worse reputation than Max. If you don't watch it, these people will vote you out of office next year."

He snorted. "I'd like to see them try. Who are they going to elect? Logan? That boy can't get his head out of a comic book long enough to put his name on the ballot."

"Well, Nell said she might run." It was exactly what Bliss needed, a pacifist sheriff.

Nate threw his head back and laughed. It was the first genuine laugh she'd heard out of him since he'd walked into town. It lit his face and made her wonder what happened to the sweet, funny man who'd taken her virginity with such care.

"Losing an election to Nell would be like losing to a Disney princess. I swear, I expect small woodland creatures to follow that one around. And she wouldn't wear the uniform."

Callie smiled. The idea really was funny. "She wouldn't. Polyester isn't natural, and the shoes don't fit with the vegan lifestyle. But, seriously, Nate, if you don't watch it, they could run a rubber duck against you and that duck would win."

Nate turned up the long drive, the car tilting back as the four-wheel drive took over. "Good luck with the duck, then, baby." He stopped as though startled he'd used the term of endearment. "Sorry. I'll try to do the job to the best of my ability. But I don't think a lot of the people around here will appreciate it."

They were quiet the rest of the drive. She forced herself to turn away from the sheriff. He was too lovely, too remote. What had happened to him? Which man was the real Nate Wright? The playful, sweet lover she'd known years ago, or the hard, distant lawman she'd had in her life for the past two weeks.

She'd asked Stefan, and all she could get out of him was that Nate had worked with the federal government, his last job had gone sideways, and now he wanted a quieter job. You didn't get much quieter on the law enforcement front than Bliss. Of course, there were other things to consider.

"I got proof now." Mel jogged down from his one-bedroom cabin, his eyes darting around, trying not to miss a thing. He held a shotgun in his hand.

Nate's hand was immediately on the Colt in his hip holster as he got out of the Bronco and faced Mel. "You set that down now."

Mel stopped in his tracks. He was a tall, angular man. Deep into his fifties, Mel still had a strange innocence about him even as he held a shotgun. "Set what down?"

"The gun that you better not point this direction," Nate replied.

She glared his way. "You're going to get someone shot one of these days. And no, I'm not talking about Mel."

She walked up the trail and placed herself solidly between Mel and the sheriff.

"Goddamn it, Callie Sheppard, you get your ass back here. That man has a gun." Nate's bark cut through the peaceful afternoon with all the grace of a hacksaw. His face was red, and every muscle was at angry attention.

Callie sighed. Stef had been right to ask her to stay on. He'd simply been wrong about the timing. Nate hadn't integrated in two weeks, and she was beginning to doubt he would ever feel comfortable. "Everyone has a gun here, Nate. Except Nell and Henry."

"I told them they should, but they insist that the aliens are peaceful," Mel said, looking over her shoulder. "I promised to protect them when the invasion starts. I think I found a camp for the first wave. It's up here, Callie." He stared back at Nate and lowered his voice. "I don't trust that one. I think he might be one of them. Why did Rye have to quit?"

Because Rye wanted to be home doing what he loved. She didn't blame him, but sometimes she wished he hadn't quit, either. It left her in the unenviable position of protecting the town from the sheriff and vice versa. She turned back to Mel, who was fully dressed for war in his fatigues. It was always best to take Mel as seriously as possible. It settled his mind if he thought someone was working on the problem. "Why don't you show me this encampment?"

Nate was frowning fiercely as Callie turned and started to follow Mel. His long legs ate up the distance between them, and his hand was on her arm before she knew what was happening.

He spun her around on the small dirt trail. She had to put a hand on his chest to steady herself.

He growled at her, as fierce as any bear in the mountains. "You ever do that again and I swear I'll put you over my knee and spank you. And I won't care who's looking."

Callie could see it. She would be naked, the air cool on her cheeks. His cock would be rock hard and pressed against her belly. He would take his time because the anticipation was part of the tease. And then, his hand would make contact. She would squeal a little, and when he was done with the spanking part, he would turn her around and she would suck that big cock of his.

"What the hell are you thinking?" Nate asked the question in a hurried, hushed tone.

Callie grinned as they walked behind Mel. Nate's face was flushed as though he could tell what was going through her brain. When she glanced down, she realized at least one part of her fantasy had come true. The sheriff of Bliss sported an enormous erection in those khaki pants of his.

"Nothing. Nothing at all." She wasn't about to tell him what she'd been thinking.

Nate swore behind her but followed anyway.

Chapter Five

Nate trudged down the path following in Callie's wake. His temper was on edge. She was going to be the absolute death of him. He'd nearly had a heart attack when she put herself between him and that crazy with a shotgun. Did she think for a single second about what could happen? That gun could have gone off at any minute.

He had a sudden vision of Callie's chest blooming with blood just like…

Nate shut that shit down. He wasn't going to think about it. He also wasn't going to think about the way Callie's face had gone a little dreamy when he mentioned spanking that ass of hers. If, and it was a mighty big if, he ever got to date Callie Sheppard, he was going to treat her like a lady. He wasn't going down that dark path. It had already cost him years of his life and had almost killed Zane. He wasn't that man he'd become while working undercover.

Hell. He wasn't sure who he was anymore.

"It's right up here." Crazy Mel was pointing to a spot past a cluster of aspens. The locals called them quakies because of the way the slender trees shook in the wind. They were all over the property he'd bought. He'd gone home yesterday to find Zane sitting among them, staring at the sky overhead. Zane didn't talk much anymore. He seemed content to run around the woods, watch ESPN, and drink the occasional beer at the dive bar the next town over.

If he wasn't careful, Zane would end up providing the town with more legends. He would be the crazy woodsman.

Callie started to stumble over a rock. Nate grabbed her waist and balanced her. She shouldn't be running around the woods in leopard print heels. Her big brown eyes locked onto his, and he had to look away.

"Thanks." She pulled away and straightened her skirt. With a brisk nod of her head, she pushed through some bushes and followed Mel.

"It looks like a campsite."

Nate heard Callie's calm voice as he slapped the brush away and joined them in the circle of trees and shrubbery. He shoved aside all the emotional crap that was threatening to take over his brain and went into cop mode. Every instinct in his body was on high alert. It wasn't aliens, but Mel had found something.

"There's plenty of legitimate campsites in the area. There are national parks all over southern Colorado." Callie walked slowly around the small clearing.

The ground was hard, and it hadn't rained in days, so there was very little chance of good tracks. Still, Nate would guess there were at least three people who had spent the night in this space, maybe more. The grass was dented in body-like outlines in several places. They hadn't started a fire, but they left small clues that non-woodland creatures had visited.

The grass was disturbed, and the shrubs had broken branches. He quickly counted several cigarette stubs. It looked like this group rolled their own, and judging from the slight smell coming off one, it wasn't merely tobacco they were smoking.

"I'm getting nothing, Mel." Callie was pointing the Detector 4000 at the campsite. The device was humming, and a green light was blinking.

Mel scratched his head. "Really? You think it was some teens?"

She shrugged. "Guess so. Or people who didn't want to pay to camp in the regular places."

"Well, I shouldn't be surprised. I should have guessed. Aliens are real health conscious, if you know what I mean," Mel replied. "They don't smoke much."

Nate knelt down and used a pen to sort through the pile of butts. A few had red marks. Lipstick. He was doing a mental count when a smell hit him. His hands froze, and he turned to the left. That was where he saw it. On the ground before him, there were drops of black in the dirt, a pool of iridescent darkness. Motor oil.

He went cold at the sight.

"Mel, have you seen a bunch of motorcycles coming through recently?" He kept his voice even and calm when what he wanted to do was scream.

"Oh, sure, there was a bunch of them a couple days back." Mel gestured toward the road. "They came through wearing all that crap they wear. Why do they wear so much leather? I would think it would get hot."

They wore leather because it protected the skin better than anything else. They wore leather because it looked cool, and looking badass was necessary when running with the "one percenters." Nate knew that if a biker looked weak, he didn't last long with the Barbarians. He had the scars and the tats to prove it.

"You get a look at their vests, Mel?" Outlaw bikers wore three-piece patches on their vests. It identified the gang they were with. Nate would know. He'd worn the Barbarian MC patch for almost four years. God help him if they had caught up to him. And God help Zane.

"I didn't right notice, Sheriff. You see, I'm all about aliens, and these fellows were obviously human. They certainly smelled human, if you know what I mean. Those boys could use a bath." Mel looked around. "Well, I guess I can get back to working on the bunker then. I was worried I might not have enough time."

Nate stood, utterly frustrated. "Is there anything else you remember? How many of them were there? What kind of bikes were they riding? Did they have women with them?"

"Wow, that's a lot of questions, Sheriff." Mel seemed to consider the queries for a moment. "Now, as I remember it, there were a bunch of them, but not too many. They had a couple of women, but they were real tough looking. As for what they rode, well, they rode motorcycles. It was real loud, too. Hey, Callie, you think the loud motorcycles might have scared off the aliens?"

Callie opened her mouth to say something, but Nate had had enough.

"There are no aliens." He gritted out the words as he yanked the Detector 4000 out of Callie's hands. "This is a video game remote. They've been placating you for years, but I won't do it. There's too much serious shit going on to spend my afternoon traipsing through the woods to make you feel better."

Mel frowned. "Well, I ain't feeling better now." Mel leaned over and talked behind his hand. "I think they got to the sheriff, Callie."

"Something got to the sheriff." She was shooting daggers his way.

Nate wasn't taking it. He kicked at the dirt with his boot. What the hell was he doing? He was standing around with a kook when he should be…damn it. What was he going to do? Even if he could find the bikers who had spent the night here, he could write them a ticket, but that was about all. He wouldn't be able to arrest them. If the Barbarians had come to Bliss, they would be careful to hide. They would be careful not to do anything that would put them at a disadvantage until they were ready to strike.

"Sheriff?" Callie looked at him, her eyes worried. "Are you okay?"

Mel was shaking his head. "This is what they do. They probably probed him. He'll have trouble going to the bathroom for a couple of days."

"Damn it, there are no aliens." Nate took a firm stance. "And don't call the station again. The next time one of us gets called out here under false pretenses, I'm going to fine your ass. You understand? We can't spend all our time on your nonsense. You call in again, and I'll write you a big ticket."

Mel took a step back. Nate could see the fine tremble in his hands. "That's the next sign. The aliens will come after our currency. I knew it would happen."

Nate tossed the Detector to the ground and walked out of the clearing. He could hear Callie talking to Mel, soothing him with that soft voice of hers. She assured Mel everything was going to be okay and she would make sure of it.

He could use some soothing. Callie smoothed things over for everyone. He couldn't miss the way everyone in this crazy-ass town came to Callie Sheppard when they needed something. She spent most of her time building her friends up or talking them out of doing silly things. But did she have time for Nathan Wright? Hell, no. She would spend hours making sure that Mel felt secure, but could she spare a minute for her boss? Had she ever brought him cupcakes? She did it for Logan. Had she ever asked him out to lunch? Hell, no.

Nate was aware he was barreling through the woods with all the grace of a bear on a rampage. He hadn't exactly invited friendly gestures from his secretary, but that didn't matter now. He was fully in "woe is me" mode, and he didn't really want to come out of it. It felt good. He'd spent so much time worrying about Zane that feeling bad for himself was freeing.

"Hey!"

He stopped in the middle of the path, aware of the thrill that went through him. Callie was yelling at him. Her voice was filled with fire and begging for a fight. Damn if he didn't want to give her one. Nate whirled on her and was perfectly satisfied when she stopped in her tracks.

She stood stock still for a moment, holding that damn Detector in her hands again. He saw her take a deep breath before she got brave on him. "What the hell was that about, Nate? Do you really have to act like such a…a…jerk?"

He loved that hitch in her voice. She was so proper. "What's wrong, baby? You can't cuss? Say what you mean." He invaded her space. He knew he was on the edge, but he couldn't quite pull himself back. Those years he'd spent away from her weighed heavily on him. The very smell of motor oil had brought back too many bad memories, and he needed a way to burn them off.

He knew what he would pick if given a choice.

"I choose to keep my language free of rough words. And you were a jerk." She held her ground. He was counting on that.

He towered over her. "I was an asshole, baby. I was a motherfucker. I was a dick. I was all of those things. I was also right. Things are gonna change around here."

Her jaw set in a stubborn pout. "Oh, really? The great Nathan Wright is going to come in and teach all of us yokels how the world works?"

"Damn straight." Somebody needed to. As far as he could tell, no one in this town ever bothered to take their head out of their ass. They were all worried about their art or hurting someone's feelings. He'd heard an awful lot about karma since he started walking the streets of Bliss. And no one made him feel more like a dumbass than Callie Sheppard. She'd spent her time lecturing him on how Bliss worked. He wasn't supposed to give tickets to Henry and Nell for not having the proper permits when they stopped traffic on Fridays with their silly mime project. He wasn't allowed to arrest the nudists. He wasn't supposed to "display a threatening presence," and she'd told him to smile more. What the hell was that supposed to mean? She was trying to reduce his job to some sort of happy, glad-handing politician, and that wasn't going to happen. "I'm going to force this backward-ass town to realize that it isn't in a bubble. Bad shit happens, darlin', and you can't fight it with a poem or a goddamn piece of pottery. You sure aren't going to keep this place safe by holding hands and singing 'Kumbaya.'"

She raised her stubborn chin up. "Maybe we don't like the so-called outside world. Maybe we choose to behave in a fashion that all you realists look down on, but don't think for a second that these people can't handle themselves. And don't think they haven't faced hardships of their own."

"Yeah, a lot of hardship here. I can see that plainly. What's the worst thing that happened here lately? Stella run out of coffee?"

She pushed against his chest. "You're hopeless. Please take me back to the station. I'm going home."

She was so close he could smell her. He could smell the soap she'd used and the shampoo on her hair. Her small hand was on his chest, the heat of her body righteously close to his skin. Her upturned face was mere inches away, and suddenly Nate couldn't stand it. He growled as every instinct in his body led him. His hands clamped on her hips, dragging her to him. He saw the surprise on her face just before he descended, taking advantage of her slightly open mouth. He slammed his mouth down on hers, forcing his way inside. She struggled for the barest of moments before she flowered beneath him. Her arms wound their way up and around his neck.

She was short. He solved the problem by dragging her up against his body and supporting her with his hands on that curvy ass he'd dreamed of. He was rock hard in an instant and ground himself against her pussy, resentful of his pants and her skirt. She was a sweet weight in his arms. His heart pounded in his chest, his cock full of blood. He needed her. God, he needed her more than he could ever remember needing anything before.

He started walking, moving toward the large pine tree behind them. That would do.

"Oh, Nate." She moaned his name as he dragged his mouth from her lips across her cheek and jaw, settling into the soft valley of her neck. She didn't complain as he planted her back against the tree. Her skirt hitched up as her legs came around to circle his hips. Fuck, she felt good.

Anchored against the trunk of the tree by his body weight, Callie clung to him. She let her head fall back, giving him the flesh he sought. He pushed up the denim of her skirt. Every inch of skin he captured felt like a victory. He pumped his hips against her pussy, unable to wait until he freed his cock to play with her. He was going to brand her. When he was done, Callie Sheppard would know who she belonged to. His hands were on the buckle of his belt when he realized Callie was fighting him.

"Stop." She was pleading, tears running down her face. Her legs were on the ground again, and she pushed at his chest.

He stepped away from her like she was on fire. It took everything he had to stay on his feet. What had just happened? Had he dreamed she was responding?

"I'm sorry," she said through her tears. "I can't. I know I was…I know I led you on, Nate, but you don't even like me. I can't sleep with someone who doesn't even like me." The words came out in little hitches.

"Don't like you?" What the hell was she talking about? Not like her? She was all he thought about.

She was making a pointed attempt to get herself under control. She smoothed down her skirt and wiped her tears away with the back of her hand. Had he really been ready to toss up her skirt and fuck her right here in the middle of the woods? Yes. He had been this close to heaven, and it would have led him straight to hell. What had he planned to do after? Take her off to his shitty cabin and show her everything he had to offer, which was exactly nothing? Was he going to show her off to Zane like a prize he'd won?

It was all so fucked up.

"Yes, Sheriff, you've made it clear you don't particularly care for me." She slumped against the tree he'd tossed her against without any regard for her comfort. "You let me know on a daily basis how much you wish I wasn't around."

He shook his head at the thought. "I don't know why you think that. God, Callie, I've been crazy about you since the day I met you." There it was again. He didn't fucking think anymore.

Her eyes widened behind her glasses. "But you left me."

Take it back. Tell her you were joking. Tell her anything but the truth. "Zane loved you, too. We couldn't choose who got to keep you."

It had been much more complex than that, but he couldn't think. His brain was stuck on the way she felt, smelled, sounded. He wanted to do anything that might make her change her mind, even though he knew what a mistake it would be.

She was staring at him, her jaw wide. After a moment of complete silence, her mouth closed and she leaned over, picking up the Detector 4000 that had dropped from her hands sometime during their tussle. She started to march straight past him. Nate reached out and grabbed her by the elbow, unwilling to pretend none of this had happened. He'd fucked up, but maybe it was for the best. Maybe they could work something out. If he could see her quietly, it wouldn't hurt Zane. How much did he have to give up for his best friend?

"Did you hear what I said, Callie? I'm crazy about you." He started to pull her into his arms. If he could get his mouth on her again, he could convince her. She was so responsive.

He dropped her arm when she slammed the remote over his head.

"Damn it." He took a step back, but she was on the offensive now.

"You jerk! How dare you? You left a note. You left a stupid note. You say you were crazy about me, that Zane's in love with me, and all you could manage was a note and not one phone call in six years."

He backed up, arms over his head to ward off her blows. "Baby, there's more to it."

He'd had a job to do.

"Don't call me baby."

The blows didn't hurt at all, but he let her push him back. She didn't have it in her to really harm him, but she needed this. He'd pushed her over the last two weeks with his anger and complete indecision. He knew what he wanted. He simply didn't think he deserved it.

"I'm sorry, Callie." He was. He was sorry about all of it. He was sorry he'd left her, and he was sorry he'd just about assaulted her in the middle of the woods. And he was pretty damn sure it would happen again. Now that he'd touched her, he knew he wouldn't be able to leave her alone. Damn it. What was he going to do? He had nothing to offer her, and it would break Zane if he waltzed off with the girl. A voice whispered in the back of his head. *Max Harper didn't lose his brother when they fell for the same girl.* Why did he have to lose his best friend? Callie wanted them both once.

"You left me and I thought it was because…" She stopped and dropped the remote. She shook her head and turned on those little heels. Her hips swayed as she walked away from him, and Nate did what he'd wanted to do since she pushed at him. He let himself fall to the ground.

Holy shit, was he really thinking about it? Was he really thinking about sharing Callie Sheppard with his best friend on a permanent basis? How would it work? Who would marry her? Would either one of them marry her? Would Zane even think about going for it?

Then he just had one question running through his head as he heard tires screeching. How was he going to get back to the station? His honey had left him high and dry. The whole threesome thing might be a moot point since Callie didn't seem like she wanted to talk to him, much less join him in an alternative lifestyle.

"You look like you have a headache, Sheriff." Mel stood over him with a sympathetic nod. "That's what happens when they probe you. That and the other stuff."

This was his punishment. He was stuck relying on a man who thought the sky was falling. Nate got up as gracefully as he could manage with a raging hard-on. His erection hadn't gone away. In fact, it was only worse now that he was thinking about the possibilities. He reached into his pocket to pull out his…damn it. He'd left his cell in the car that was currently flying down the mountain. They were going to have a talk about her reckless driving.

After he managed to get her in bed. That's where he would do all his talking with Callie from now on. "Mel, do you think I could use your phone? Um, maybe I was a little hasty about the whole alien thing." He picked up the only slightly destroyed Detector 4000. "I'll get this fixed."

Mel slapped him on the back and smiled. "Don't worry about it, Sheriff. It was time to upgrade, anyway. Alien technology changes fast. We gotta keep up. Come on up to the house. I have a tonic that'll help get rid of the aftereffects of the probe and a helmet to wear that'll keep them from reading your thoughts."

Nate shook his head. He was definitely going to pay for that note he'd left her all those years ago.

* * * *

The door to her cabin slammed behind her, and Callie immediately dragged the sweater over her head. She tossed it to the side and unhooked the hated bra. Her skirt was next, and then she kicked her shoes to the side. She sighed, feeling slightly free for the first time that day. The feeling was immediately overwhelmed with anxiety as her fight with Nate replayed itself in her head in brilliant 3-D, with the volume too loud.

She ignored the guilty whisper in the back of her head that told her stealing a county vehicle and leaving the town sheriff behind was a bad thing. She'd parked the Bronco at the station and hadn't bothered to wake up Logan from his nap to go get Nate.

Jerk. Nate deserved a long walk back into town. She wasn't going to feel bad. He had made it plain. He didn't need help from a hick like her. He didn't need anything from her, except maybe some cheap sex.

She couldn't buy the whole "I'm crazy about you" thing. It wasn't possible. He was just a man saying what he thought she wanted to hear to get what he wanted. Wasn't he? She would have to be a fool to believe him.

She walked straight to the back porch and out into the warm afternoon. The sunlight and mountain breeze kissed her skin. It was quiet here. The cabin she'd shared with her mother was isolated from the rest of the valley. She walked down to the river. The Rio Grande ran through Bliss, splitting the town through the valley before it wound its way south and east. Callie sank onto the soft grass and stared at the water as it flowed.

If rumors were correct, the river flowed by the cabin Nate had bought, too. Not that he'd invited her there. Was Zane staying at the cabin? Was he staring at the same river she was? She smiled slightly. He probably wasn't naked.

She had to face facts. Nate was right. She was a hick. She'd been born in Bliss, and she'd lived her whole life here. This was the only place where she felt at home. What was she going to do in an apartment in Denver? Fade. That's what she'd do, and yet the thought of staying here when she could see the future so clearly seemed like a bad idea. She would end up being everyone's favorite aunt. Max and Rye's kids would run wild through town, and she'd wish her own were right there with them. Eventually Stef would get a clue and see what was right in front of him. He wouldn't be able to ignore Jennifer Waters forever.

She'd be the one on the outside, but then she always had been. Everyone in town loved her, but she wasn't an intimate member of any family. She could have a hot affair with the sheriff, but in the end, he would find something better and move on. As for Zane, well, he hadn't even shown his face around town. That was how much he didn't want to see her.

"Hey, anyone home?"

Callie turned and saw her friend Jen trudging down the small hill her cabin sat on. Jennifer was an artist who worked at the diner while she was trying to make a living off selling her work in the galleries. She was very good, and Callie had often thought she could be big if she went to New York. There was no denying what kept her in Bliss. She had come to convince Stefan Talbot to teach her and ended up falling in love with the man.

"I'm at the river," she called out.

"Well, hello, nature girl. I stopped by the station but Logan was the only one there. I decided not to wake him up." Jennifer was a cute brunette, her hair in a perpetual ponytail. She wore jeans and a T-shirt emblazoned with the logo from the diner she worked at. She plunked herself down beside Callie. It was only a minute before she'd shucked her clothes and lay back in the soft grass wearing only her undies. Jen might have been born in a conservative Southern town, but she fit right in here in Bliss. "I figured you would be here. Is the jerk giving you hell?"

She let her head find her knees, pulling her legs up as though the mere mention of Nate made her want to protect herself. "He's decided to bring us all into the real world."

Jen frowned. "The real world sucks. I grew up in it. I like it better here. What was Stef thinking? Why did he need to bring that guy in? Logan would have been fine. Or you. Why don't you put on some polyester and take over? Everyone goes to you anyway."

"Not going to happen." Though the thought made her smile. She wasn't much of an authority figure. Neither was Logan, for that matter. "And Stef was right. We do need someone who knows what they're doing. Though maybe not someone as hard-core as Nate Wright."

Hard. He'd been ridiculously hard when he shoved her up against that tree. Why had she pulled back? Oh yeah. A little thing called self-esteem. Did she really need that more than she needed an orgasm? And how long would she be able to hold out if he tried it again?

Jen came up on her elbows, her pretty face scrunched up in disgust. "Well, we'll vote him out of office if he keeps it up. Did you know he warned me not to jaywalk? I was crossing Main Street to go from the diner to the Trading Post, and he stopped me. He told me next time I would get a ticket. I'm supposed to walk all the way to the gallery and then wait for the stoplight to turn red. Seriously? Doesn't he have anything better to do?"

Yes, he did, and that was why Nathan Wright wouldn't be here two years from now. He would get some time under his belt and move on. His family money might be gone, but she doubted his connections were. Nate would move on, and she would be alone again. She didn't think she could handle it. Everywhere she looked, the road led out of Bliss.

She sat back up. If she was really leaving Bliss, maybe she should go out with a bang. Nathan Wright wasn't the only one who could scratch an itch.

"I don't like that look." Jen stared at her. "I see that look a lot in the mirror, and it always gets me in trouble."

Trouble sounded like fun. Maybe it was time for everyone's favorite aunt, who never cursed or threw a fit, to cause a little scandal of her own. She'd spent thirty-one years easing the lives of the people around her, smoothing the way for temperamental Max, listening to Rye's love problems, being the girl on Stefan's arm at family events because he didn't "do" long-term relationships. And that was just the boys she grew up with. She was the one Stella called when her fry cook decided French fries and burgers didn't soothe the inner artist in his soul. She was the one who listened to Mel's latest alien theories. She was the one who sat through the Repertory Theater's dress rehearsals and gave notes and went to every artist in Bliss's gallery show. And who listened to her? What would they listen to, even if they were willing?

She was Callie Sheppard, doormat of Bliss.

"Seriously, sweetie, whatever you're thinking, don't." Jen got up, picking up her clothes as Callie rose to her feet. She followed behind her as Callie turned toward the cabin. "The naked thing is really a great way of thumbing your nose at society. You should stick to that."

She glanced back. "I'm not thumbing my nose at society. I like the way it feels. And whatever I'm about to do tonight isn't about society. It's about me. It's about..." It was time to be a little vulgar. "It's about getting laid. Callie Sheppard is on the prowl. What do you know about that bar on the far side of the mountain?"

Jen turned a bit green. "Are you talking about Hell on Wheels? The biker bar? Tell me you're talking about another bar. You want to know what I know about that bar? I know you shouldn't go there because we'll never come out alive. I say *we* because I can't let you go alone."

It would be nice to have company, but she didn't want Jen to feel obligated. "Don't be silly. How bad could it be?"

She walked into her cabin and hoped she could find some slutty clothes because she intended to find out.

Chapter Six

The sun was starting to go down over the tops of the mountains when the door to the cabin came open. Zane turned from the back window, surprised at the sight of Nate coming home from work early.

"I'm fine." Nate slurred every syllable as he stumbled through the door.

Zane felt his eyes widen. There was a tall, angular man trying to help Nate. The man looked to be in his fifties and had a strange hat on his head. It was a trucker hat with tin foil coming out the edges. Now that he looked at it, Nate's Stetson had foil peeking out of it as well.

"What the hell is going on?" Zane asked.

The tall man took a step back. Zane was used to it. He knew what he looked like.

The older man squinted and then slapped Nate on the back. "It's okay. He seems human."

Nate smiled beatifically. Damn, he was drunk and still in his uniform. What was going on? "He's not human. That's Zane, Mel. Don't worry about the frown. He's a brooder. It's his thing. I wish he got paid for it. If he got paid for brooding, we would be millionaires and that would solve so many problems. Zane, we need to put that on your résumé. Brooding."

Mel nodded, as though that made sense somehow. He looked

back and forth between him and Nate, seeming to form some sort of opinion. "Well, now I've always found it best that couples acknowledge their differences. He's seems nice enough, Sheriff."

"What?" Zane was having trouble following the conversation.

Nate stumbled to the green 1970s refugee couch. It had come with the cabin and opened into one of the most uncomfortable beds Zane had ever tried to nap on. Nate didn't seem to have the same muscular issues with the couch that Zane had. He pulled his hat off his head and settled it over his face. He didn't bother to get rid of the foil liner, just let it lay there, covering his mug like a burrito wrapper.

Zane looked to the thin guy. "What is wrong with him? Has he been drinking on the job?"

It wasn't like Nate. Nate was freaking Captain America. Nate was upstanding and by the book.

Nate looked up from his place on the couch. His fingers fumbled when he tried to lift his hat, and both the Stetson and its tinfoil inner lining rolled away. "Hell, no. I do not drink on the job. I am completely off duty. That's what happens when a hot honey steals your squad car. I'm gonna spank her for that. Stef is right about the discipline thing. Girl needs some discipline. But I ain't been drinking. I've been doing community service. I gotta start fitting into the community. Callie told me to."

Zane felt his gut clench. Callie? Was Callie the hot honey who needed discipline? And why was Nate talking about it?

Mel was pulling on the quilt that lay on top of the couch. He placed it over Nate, who settled back down with a loopy grin on his face. Mel picked up the hat and made sure the foil was secure. "Don't you worry about the sheriff now. We got it all fixed up. He needs to wear his hat when he's out, and it'll be fine. You see, he got probed."

Nate seemed to think that was hilarious and started laughing, his knees drawing up. "I've been probed. Hell, I almost got to probe her. Got so fucking close. It would have felt really good to probe her."

"I gave him my special tonic. He'll feel better tomorrow. I drove by the station and got his keys and his phone, but he shouldn't be driving yet. Because of the cure. Takes a while. You'll see, he'll be all better in the morning." Mel was nodding.

He didn't think so. He was pretty sure Nate would be in a shit-ass mood tomorrow, probably sooner. Nate had never been able to hold his liquor, but he never stayed drunk for long. He always sobered up fast. And what did he mean by probing her? Was he talking about Callie? "What's in this tonic? Whiskey?"

Mel nodded. "So you've had it before? I make it myself. It keeps the aliens at bay. They can't metabolize it, so they stay away."

"Got to get rid of the aliens so I can concentrate on Callie. Can't let her quit. She's a good secretary." Nate sighed like a man who knew what he wanted. "She's still so pretty, Zane. Her breasts feel so good. And she can kiss. Damn, for a girl so innocent, she tastes like sin. I'm gonna marry her."

Zane felt the pounding in his head start. He looked down at his best friend in the world. Every time he'd asked about Callie Sheppard, Nate had shrugged him off, telling him that if he wanted to know he should go see for himself. Bastard. Now he understood the game Nate had been playing. He'd had her all to himself for two weeks. No wonder he spent so much time at the station. Callie was there.

"God, you have no idea how sweet she is."

No, he didn't, and he never fucking would because Nate had taken her without giving him a chance. Not that he had one. His hand went to his face, where the scar ran from the base of his skull all the way down to his jaw. He could still feel the knife splitting his skin. He'd thought nothing could hurt as much as that knife.

He'd been wrong.

Betrayal bit through him. They'd made the decision about Callie together a long time ago. Now Nate was going to change his mind and Zane hadn't even had a chance. He couldn't stay here. His hands were on the keys before he really knew what he was doing.

"Hey, where ya going?" Nate was trying to get up but got caught in the quilt. "We need to talk. You might say it's crazy, but I been thinking about something."

Yeah, Zane bet he'd been thinking about something. He'd been thinking about Callie and how he could steal her. He had zero interest in Nate's thoughts. He turned to Mel, who still looked ridiculous with tin foil covering his head. "You should call his deputy and tell him the sheriff is indisposed."

"Zane, where ya going?" Nate struggled to get up.

"I need a beer." He was out the door in a heartbeat and headed for Hell on Wheels. *A* beer? He would probably drink a dozen, and it wouldn't help.

An hour later, he knew he'd been right. He was only into his second beer, and it didn't even begin to obliterate the image of Nate and Callie. Who was he kidding? And could he really blame Nate?

Fuck, yeah, his inner asshole said. Inner Asshole usually warred with Reasonable Guy. This time Reasonable Guy was perfectly silent. Reasonable Guy agreed with him. Turned out Reasonable Guy had a thing for Callie Sheppard, too.

And what the hell had he meant about the brooding? Inner Asshole was spewing some serious venom. Who the hell did Nate think he was? They had agreed that she was off limits long ago. They had agreed that she deserved better. Maybe Nate had simply decided *he* was better.

Maybe Nate had decided he was sick of putting up with Zane's shit and was ready to move on.

He slumped forward, his elbows on the somewhat dirty bar. He called for beer number three. The low light of the dive bar revealed the other patrons. Leather and denim seemed to be the dress code, though some of the women wore bikini tops under their vests. Zane made a quick roll call of the MCs in attendance. The Animals, the Wasters, and the Colorado Horde were there in decent numbers. Zane could tell from the three-piece patches they wore on their leather vests. There were a couple he didn't recognize, but he wasn't worried. If someone figured out who he was, they would kill him quick.

Now the Barbarians, that was another story.

In the background, Zane heard the small door to the prefab building swing open but turned back to his beer. The big bartender swung a fresh mug of whatever was cheapest in front of him.

The man shook his head, his eyes narrowing. "Damn it, there's trouble."

Zane looked up, following the line of the bartender's sight. Two newcomers stood in the doorway, two women who looked to be a bit lost. Zane struggled to see them through the smoke. There was one with dark hair and a banging body, and a thinner, taller one with lighter hair piled in a bun on her head. He liked the short one. She had long, thick hair and round breasts. Yeah, he could do that one. Maybe he would try since it wasn't going to happen with Callie. It wasn't like he was married or anything. If she didn't mind ugly sons of bitches, he'd give the girl a ride.

Or he'd fix her car. That had to explain it. The two women were so out of place, they had to have had car trouble. The hot one was dressed in a yellow sundress. It exposed an expanse of creamy, ivory skin and made her look like a little piece of the sun, walking through the clouds. The other girl had given it a better shot. She had on a denim mini and a tank top, but still looked out of place due to the innocent air surrounding her. There wasn't a place for innocence in here.

Zane sighed. Everyone was staring at the out of place women. If he was half as heartless as he pretended to be, he would leave right now. Inner Asshole wanted to do exactly that. He wasn't responsible for a couple of chicks who likely wouldn't give him the time of day under normal circumstances. But Reasonable Guy finally woke up, and Zane knew he was going to protect those ladies. They were going to get in trouble. Already he could sense the sharks beginning to circle. A couple of the men by the pool tables were watching them, obviously planning their moves. They weren't the kind to take a polite no for an answer.

That old familiar tightening in his gut began. The adrenaline started to flow freely. Yeah, maybe a good fight was what he needed. He could pretend it was Nate he was punching the shit out of.

"This is the worst idea, ever," the woman in the denim mini was saying as they sort of floated through the cloudy bar. Maybe one of them had a lick of sense.

"Oh, I think it's charming, once you get past the smell," the other one said. She approached the bar, and Zane got a good look at her face.

He turned as quickly as he could, praying she didn't see him. Fuck. What was Callie doing here? The adrenaline was still flooding his system, but he turned from fight to full-on flight mode. Both Inner Asshole and Reasonable Guy were in full agreement. It was time to run and as fast as he could.

He started to push back the stool but stopped. If he ran, she would be alone in here with those sharks. She was about to be in serious trouble. Damn it. He couldn't do it.

He pulled his cell out. This was Nate's job. She was Nate's girl.

Get to Hell on Wheels. Callie and a friend have decided to have a girls' night out.

He threw in a text to Stefan Talbot just in case. As pissed as he was, he wasn't about to let Callie get hurt because she didn't belong to him. He would watch over her until the others got here.

Then he would run.

"I would like a…I don't drink very much. Maybe a Cosmo. Those always look good on TV." Callie's voice was bright and optimistic.

"I got beer and tequila. I can get you a whiskey, but that's about it." The bartender did not seem amused.

"We'll take the tequila." Callie's friend nodded and wiped off her barstool before sitting down.

Zane watched her through the sooty mirror behind the bar. Damn, she was gorgeous. Should he wait for Nate or Stef? Or man up and do what needed to be done? He wanted to toss Callie over his shoulder and haul her out of this bar.

"You are being surprisingly negative, Jen." Callie pushed a pair of glasses up her nose. "Why can't you see it as an adventure? We're like Thelma and Louise."

"Thelma and Louise died, Cal."

Callie shook her head. "Nope. I choose to believe they made it across the Grand Canyon in their convertible. Why do people keep trying to get me to see the dark side of life?"

The bartender set two shot glasses in front of them and poured out the gold liquid. He set down a shaker of salt and two lime wedges. Zane had a sudden vision of himself doing body shots off Callie. He would suck salt off her nipples, shoot tequila from her navel, and who needed a lime when her pussy tasted so good? Damn it, his jeans were getting awfully tight.

The girls bit down on the lime, completing their first round. Callie's friend Jen seemed more acquainted with the procedure. "Is that what Sheriff Dickhead did today?"

Now Zane was listening closely. He leaned in so he could hear over the loud jukebox playing classic rock.

Callie motioned for another. She turned to her friend. "Sheriff Wright made a heavy pass at me, which I politely turned down. That's all."

Zane wanted to fist pump, but it might call attention to him. So Nate wasn't in so good with their former lover. Nice. Maybe he still had a chance.

Then he caught sight of himself in the mirror and remembered the real reason he hadn't gone after her. Scars. He was made of them now.

"You turned down that hunk of man? What are you thinking? I know he's a jerk, but he's a completely hot jerk. Seriously, you drag me out here tonight because you want to get laid, but you turned down the perfectly safe hot guy? What is wrong with you?"

They were already on their third shot. What were they thinking? Who was going to drive them home? And he thought Callie had been smart to turn down Nate since he was a backstabbing, half-woman stealing dickhead. Goddamn it, half of Callie was his.

"Wow, that works fast." She rejected a fourth shot with a wave of her hand. "I turned down the sheriff because I have some self-respect. The sheriff has made his opinion of me plain. He doesn't like me or my town, so I will not sleep with him whether I want to or not. However, the episode pointed out the fact that I have been lax in dealing with certain bodily needs."

"You're horny."

Jen seemed good at stating things plainly. Zane could appreciate that. And Callie wasn't the only one who was horny. God, if he wasn't afraid she would run the minute she got a look at the left side of his face, he would shove her up against the wall and take care of them both.

"I am seeking a bit of physical affection, that's all."

Jen sighed. "Then let me call Stef. He knows people, people who would be nice to you."

Callie's hands came down on the bar, slapping angrily. "No. I am not so pathetic that I need Stef to find someone willing to sleep with me again. Not again. I know I'm not the world's most beautiful woman, but I'm not hideous, either." She turned to him. "How about you? You looking for a date?"

Zane wondered if the floor would magically open up and swallow him whole.

"Wow." Jen was staring at him in the mirror. Her face was a wide-open book. "That is amazing."

He put his head down and started getting off the barstool. There was no way he would stand around and take their pity. He could watch over them from afar.

"Well, that figures." Callie's hands were on his arm.

He turned because there was nothing to do now. She'd recognized him. He looked at her, drinking in her face for the first time in years. Whatever she was thinking, it wasn't that she felt sorry for him.

Her pretty face was frowning at him. "I go out to find someone who might want me, and I run into you. That's perfect." She turned back to the bartender. "I changed my mind. Hit me again."

At least now he could do something. "You give her another drop of liquor, and I swear I'll tear you up when you least expect it. You understand me?"

The bartender took a step back. Zane was satisfied with the way the man turned a little white. He pulled the tequila bottle back. "Sorry, sweetheart. Bar's closed for you. I don't think I want to see what that ugly son of a bitch could do."

"That is not a nice thing to say!" Callie pushed her empty shot glass toward the bartender. "I am not tipping you anything above the normal twenty percent. You're rude to your customers. What kind of service professional are you?" She turned back to him, crossing her arms over her chest. "Please feel free to flee. I promise I won't chase after you." She gave him an imperious wave of her hand.

He felt his face set stubbornly. He would not let her know how much she affected him. "I was here first, Callie."

"Well, of course you were. Tell me something, Zane, how long have you been in town?" There was suspicion in her voice, and her eyes were brown lasers cutting through him.

"Couple weeks."

"That's what I thought. You've been here a couple of weeks and you didn't bother to call."

Jen was at her side, but her eyes were on him. She looked utterly fascinated. It made him uncomfortable. "You know this guy? Wow, Cal, he is stunning. Hi, I'm Jen and I would really like to paint you."

He ignored her. He was too busy paying attention to Callie. "I didn't think you would welcome a call from me. I figured you were married and stuff."

Her smile held not a hint of humor. "Well, I showed you, didn't I? Not married. Not dating. Still alone. I haven't even…"

For the second time that day he felt the world shift. Was she saying what he thought she was saying? She hadn't had sex since him and Nate? How was that possible? Her face was a flaming red. "Babe, I couldn't call you."

Was she looking at him? Could she not see his freaking face?

"You're like a fallen angel. It's really beautiful." Jen's nose was a bright red. Girl couldn't handle her tequila.

"You couldn't call me? Well, as I see the cell phone in your pocket, I can only assume you couldn't call me because you didn't want to." There were tears shimmering in Callie's eyes, and his heart was going to shatter if she cried.

"Babe, look at me." He turned his face straight to her, so she couldn't miss a single inch of the scars that ran down the left side of his face. Besides the long one, there were two others. One on the side of his jaw, deep and puckered, and one across his forehead. He'd damn near lost his eye. Only Nate had managed to save him. She couldn't even see the scars on his body.

She snorted. "Yes, you're horrible. All of your hotness is gone. Don't give me some lame story about how a few tiny marks are supposed to make me not want you. They're scars, Zane. Get over it. You're gorgeous, and you know it. Just be honest. You slept with me as a favor to Stef, and that was it. It's fine, but don't lie to me."

"You slept with him?" Jen's mouth was wide open as she looked between them.

"At least Nate was honest enough to tell me he didn't want to see me," Callie replied.

"You slept with the sheriff, too?" Jen asked.

He was going to beat the sheriff to death for putting that look on Callie's face. He felt his face bunch up and was sure he sounded like a pleading boy. God, if he still had a chance with her, he wanted to take it. If she could see past how awful he looked, he'd do anything for her. She'd haunted his dreams every night for the past six years. The fact that she was here and still thought about him, too, well, it floored him. "I wanted to see you. I wanted to see you so bad. But you can't possibly want me like this. You have no idea what I'm like now. And these aren't the only scars I have. They're everywhere."

Callie shrugged. She was on her feet. They were encased in dainty sandals with ladybugs on them. "Like I said, Zane, at least Nate was honest with me."

She stalked off toward the dance floor, and Zane was left staring after her. Her ass swayed as she approached the jukebox.

"Seriously, you have to let me paint you. You are amazing."

He squinted at the brunette. "What are you talking about?"

He needed a minute to catch his breath. If he went after Callie, he would be on his knees in a second, begging her to give him just one night. Just one. He needed to get this situation under control because she hadn't reacted the way he'd expected.

"I'm talking about the dichotomy of your face. It's amazing. The things you must have been through. It's really beautiful. I've never seen anything like it."

"Are you insane?"

She shook her head vigorously. "Oh, no, I'm an artist."

She slid into the seat Callie had recently vacated. Zane had a sense of her leaning in, but his eyes were firmly on Callie. So far no one had crowded her, but two assholes in leather vests and blue jeans had eyes planted on the delicious treat.

Jen was still talking. "You're the perfect model. So beautiful."

He had no idea how to respond to the drunken artist. But maybe she could help him out. "Why hasn't Callie gotten married?"

Callie's body was swaying slightly to the sounds of Metallica. The two guys eyeing her were talking to each other and then looking back at him. He growled a little and bared his teeth.

"See, wow, that's hot. You're very alpha male. I can capture that on a canvas. Ummm, I guess Cal isn't married because she never found anyone. It's hard in a small town. And then there's the fact that she's always busy. And her mom only died last year."

Zane turned suddenly. "Her mom died?"

Jen nodded. "She had cancer for a really long time. Callie took care of her. Callie takes care of everyone."

Yes, he remembered that. She was concerned with the comfort and well-being of those around her. Even during their crazy weekend, when she should have been content to let them treat her like a princess, she had taken care of them. She had rubbed his scalp when he got a headache and cuddled against Nate after he'd gotten off the phone with his dad. She hadn't asked questions, simply been there. He bet everyone took advantage of her nature.

"So, you slept with my friend and then dumped her?"

Maybe Jen wasn't as wasted as he thought. "I didn't dump her. I had a job to do."

Jen's lips pursed. "Must have been a great job to leave someone like Callie."

It hadn't been. It had been hell. He'd give anything to go back to that moment in the hotel when they'd made their decision. He would call his boss and quit and slide back into bed with Callie. If Nate wanted to go, he would have let him. But Zane would have gotten under those covers. Unfortunately, he knew all too well he couldn't go back. "You think Callie and the sheriff have something going on?"

"Well, I certainly do now, given the fact that they have some sort of super-freaky past where she slept with both of you. Did she do you at the same time?"

"None of your business." They hadn't. He and Nate had decided she was too green to take her together. There hadn't been time to prepare her. He'd dreamed about it, though. Apparently Nate didn't have the same thoughts. He was planning a sweet vanilla life with the girl of their dreams. Screw that. She hadn't run away. She'd been pissed off that he hadn't come for her. Well, he could fix that. He wasn't giving her up. He jumped off his barstool. "And you can tell that town that she's taken."

"She is?"

He nodded. She would be once he was done.

* * * *

Callie tried to focus on the jukebox menu, but all she could see was Zane's beautiful face. He had a few scars. Anyone could see that, but she wasn't stupid. He was still a gorgeous giant of a man. His hair was longer than she remembered. It was pitch black and curled at the ends. His face was so masculine it was as though someone had carved it. His jawline was perfectly square, and he had a sharp blade for a nose. His eyes were a deep green, and intelligence still sparked out of them.

That was a lie. There wasn't a lick of intelligence in him if he thought she was falling for that whole "I'm not good for you" crap. Like she hadn't heard that before. Next he would want to be her friend because he didn't like her that way.

Story of her life.

She was not going to cry. Nope. No crying allowed in the tough biker bar. If she thought it would be hard living in the same town with Nate, how bad would it be with Zane here, too? It would happen all over again, watching two men she cared about search for what they wanted when what they wanted wasn't her.

Tears made the jukebox menu a watery mess. What had she expected? They'd had a couple of nights together years ago. It meant the world to her, but they had probably had so many women, she was lucky they remembered her face. She couldn't be mad at them. It was the way the world worked. Women like her didn't get guys like Nate and Zane.

"Hey, pretty lady, you with that rough rider back there?"

Callie looked up into a very rugged face. There were two of them, bikers both, or so their leather vests proclaimed. They appeared to belong to some form of horde that claimed Colorado as their home. The men had no right to call Zane rough. They were far rougher than Zane.

"No, I'm not. Please excuse me." She wasn't with him, and now she wondered what the hell she was doing. Was she trying to punish Nate? Jen had been right. This was stupid. She pulled out her cell and dialed Stef's number. He picked up immediately.

"Callie?" Stef sounded harried, and she could hear movement, like he was in a car.

"Is that her?"

Was Nate with him? Why would Nate be with him?

"Yes, it's me. I'm sorry to bother you, but Jen and I need a ride. We're at the bar on the other side of the mountain and we've had a bit to drink. I don't feel safe with either of us getting behind the wheel." She was feeling a little woozy.

"Give me that phone." She heard the sounds of a tussle, and then Nate's voice was the dominant one. "You stay right where you are, Callie Sheppard. Do you understand me? What the hell were you thinking?"

Callie moved the phone away from her ear. He could yell really loud. "Sheriff, please stop. The signal is fine. I can hear you. I need Stef to come get me."

"I'm coming to get you," he shot back. "How dare you walk into that bar? What were you thinking? Do you have any idea the kind of men who run around that bar?"

"Zane, apparently."

"Yeah, who do you think called me, baby? Now you go to the bar and sit your pretty ass down, and don't you move. Don't you leave Zane's side. I will be there in ten minutes, and then we're going to have a talk. I have an awful lot to say to you."

That didn't sound promising. "Maybe I don't have anything to say to you, Sheriff."

"Good, then you can listen. Do not disobey me. I have a headache and a half because you left me with Mel. I took that damn tonic of his because I'm the idiot who's trying to fit into this weird town to please you."

When had he started doing that? She sighed sympathetically. "Yeah, you really shouldn't drink anything Mel gives you. He tends to put rotgut whiskey in all his tonics."

"And that's illegal." Righteous Nate was back with a vengeance.

It was time for some more advice. "Nate, how do you expect to be sheriff in this town if all you care about is what is or isn't illegal?"

He sputtered. "Just stay where you are. What got in your head to go to someplace called Hell on Wheels, I have no idea…"

In the background she heard a third voice. It seemed like Nate thought he needed to bring the cavalry. "Uh, Sheriff, I don't think I'm allowed to go to that bar."

She heard Nate huff at Logan Green. "What the hell is that supposed to mean? Are you a deputy, son, or not?"

"Oh, no." He was bringing along Logan? That was a bad idea. Marie was going to have his hide. "You can't bring Logan here."

"My moms will get really upset," Logan explained.

Then there was a whole lot more cursing, but the phone fell out of her hand when she was twirled around bodily. She gasped as the biker from before was squeezing her wrist. He was short but stout as a bull, and from the way his fingers tightened around her wrist, he was as strong as one, too.

"If he don't claim you, then we will, right, Bone?"

The gentleman named Bone nodded his assent. He was slightly taller than his compatriot but didn't have his thick build. "Damn straight, Len. This one is real pretty. Nice tits."

Maybe Jen had been right. She should have gone down to the gas station and tried hitting on tourists. Callie attempted to pull her wrist out of Len's grasp. "Please excuse me. I really need to go."

She would go wait outside for Stef. If the sheriff walked in here, all hell would break loose and someone would get hurt, possibly him.

"You heard the lady."

Callie looked up, and Zane was a hulking presence behind the two men. Bone and Len were big, nasty-looking men, but Zane made them look like boys in comparison. He had gotten rid of his jacket, and his big biceps were on full display. She could plainly see he'd added some ink to his body. His jaw was set, and his eyes were cold. She had a sudden desire to put her arms around him and soothe that look off his face.

After he'd taken care of the men who were attempting to assault her, of course.

"Take your hands off her right this second, or I'll break them," Zane growled.

Jen was suddenly behind her. She slipped her arms around Callie's waist, anchoring her.

"I won't let them take you," Jen promised.

Len simply dragged Jen along, too. "Get your own fuck for the night, asshole. This one is ours."

Jen held on, and Callie was being tugged in two directions, then she was on her ass on top of Jen, looking up from the floor. Zane had Len dangling in the air, one big hand wrapped around his opponent's throat.

"I warned you."

Bone took the opportunity to attack, but Zane simply used his free hand to punch him squarely in the face. There was a satisfying crunch, and Bone slumped to the floor.

"I'll deal with your friend later. Now, I think you owe my lady an apology." The words came from between Zane's gritted teeth, each one an order. Callie wished she could be enough of a pacifist to be alarmed by Zane's propensity for violence. In this particular case, her female parts differed with her political beliefs. They were completely aroused watching that giant of a man defending her honor. And his possessive use of the word "my" was another thing she would argue with if she could stop drooling over the way his jeans molded to every muscle in his legs.

"I'm sorry, lady," Len spat out.

He didn't sound sorry. He sounded pissed. The room was filled with smoke and loud music, and potential violence throbbed through the air. Callie looked around. No one was dancing or drinking anymore. Every eye in the place was on Zane and the man he dangled in the air. Her mouth went dry. No one in the place looked like they were about to step up and help Zane out. They were looking at him like a group of hungry lions. Even Zane seemed to feel the tension filling the room. He set Len down and reached for something at his waist. When his hand only met his belt, she could see his eyes tighten. According to Nate, Zane had been a cop, an agent with the DEA. He was looking for his gun out of habit, but it wasn't there anymore.

His eyes never stopped moving as he spoke. He looked around the room as though assessing the threats. "Babe, I recognize some of these people. When Nate gets here, I want you to run to him. He'll protect you. For now, damn it, just run."

Jen was on her feet helping her up when Callie screamed. Another big biker came from behind Zane, brandishing a pool cue. There was a loud crack as it came down across Zane's back with brutal force.

"The Barbarians say hello, pig!"

Zane hit his knees.

"Callie, no!" Jen screamed as she pulled away.

She moved from the relative safety with Jen with one thought and one thought only in her head. *Don't let them hit him again.*

She threw herself across Zane's back. There was the terrible sound of a man shouting and the pool cue hit, but on the floor next to her.

"Get out of the way, you stupid bitch!" Len screamed.

She slumped across Zane, feeling his muscles moving as he threw her off with a roar that filled the room.

Zane was yelling, but she wasn't sure at whom. She forced herself to sit up before she got crushed under boots and heels. She was surrounded, and Zane's hands finally pulled her up and into the cradle of his chest. His palm covered her head, forcing her down against him. She struggled to see.

"She doesn't have anything to do with this," Zane said.

Len was grinning now, showing off a plethora of teeth in severe need of dental attention. She wound her arms around Zane's waist. He was the only thing that seemed real now.

"I think the girl has a lot to do with this, pig. You see, there's a bounty out on your head, Hollister." Len pulled out a wicked-looking knife and held it up for inspection. When Callie tried to move her head to see, Zane pulled her back. He encircled her as Len continued to talk. "Ellis might be in jail, but he's still got power. He wants you bad. He's willing to pay."

That name seemed to trigger something in Zane. "Let the girl go and you can do what you want with me."

"No." Callie struggled against him. He held her fast. "No."

She wasn't about to let that happen. She wasn't going to stand by while they hurt him.

"See, I think that you'll fight like hell if the girl isn't involved." Len sounded like the leader of this group.

Callie could hear the thundering of Zane's heart. It matched her own. Complete terror swamped her as she realized there was no way out. Something terrible was about to happen. She felt Zane huff. She tilted her chin up and could see the blank look on his face. He looked like he couldn't care less, but she could feel him. She could feel his heart racing, the fine tremble in his hands as he clutched her like he was afraid she would die if he let her go.

His voice was a chilly grumble. "I don't guess you would believe me if I told you I haven't seen her in years and she doesn't mean anything to me?"

Callie shook her head against his chest, and he gave her a little tap. He wasn't good at the lying part. Even she had to acknowledge the man felt something for her.

"Nope. Not for a minute. Get her." Len's order boomed through the room, and Callie felt Zane's arms go so tight around her she was sure she would pass out from lack of oxygen. There was a press of bodies around them. And they needed to spend some serious time on hygiene.

"You can let her go or I can shoot her here."

Zane leaned over and pressed his mouth against her ear. "I'm so sorry, babe. Nate will come. I know he will. You stay alive long enough for him to save you. He'll take care of you."

He kissed her forehead, and she was pulled away from him.

She hadn't seen him in years and should have hated him for leaving her, but Callie wept as they were separated. She cried and fought the men who held her. Vaguely she could see some big brute had his hands on Jen, but her vision was swamped with the sight of Zane being forced to his knees. His face remained gorgeous and cold, the line of his scar seemed redder and more intense.

Len stood over him, regarding him with utter disdain. "Ellis is offering a lot of money for you, boy. Ten thousand dollars and all I gotta do is cut the Barbarian tat off your chest and hand it to him like a scalp. Fitting, huh? You got that tat to prove you were a Barbarian for life. When I'm done, that's all that's gonna be left of you." Len made a short, sharp movement with his knife and four men surrounded Zane. "Get him on the table. If he struggles, slit her throat."

Zane offered no resistance as they lifted him, straining despite the fact that there were four of them. "The sheriff of this town is in love with her, too. You kill her, and he won't ever stop hunting you down. You remember Nate Rush? He goes by Sheriff Wright now."

Len's face fell momentarily. "Fuck. Rush is here, too?"

"He's the sheriff!" Jen struggled in a big, tattooed guy's arms. Of course, that could describe most of the people here. Callie felt tears start down her cheeks as they shoved Zane onto the green felt of the pool table.

"I ain't afraid of no hick sheriff. I don't believe Rush would sink that low. That man is addicted to adrenaline. Crazy motherfucker, that one. No way he's wasting away in some sleepy mountain town. Try again, Hollister." Len's dark eyes gleamed in the smoky light as he pulled Zane's head up by the hair. "Don't you know ain't no one gonna stick by you? You look in the mirror, you freak? Even if that pretty thing could look past your ugly mug, what do you think she's gonna do once she finds out the things you've done? She know how many men you killed? She know how much meth you moved?"

Callie saw the light die in Zane's eyes and realized her belief in nonviolence had reached its end. If she ever had the chance, she would kill that biker, and she wouldn't hesitate. Len raised the knife over his head. There was a loud bang, and Callie waited for Zane's head to slump forward, her heart breaking, but it was Len who screamed and dropped the knife.

"I would step away from him if I were you." Nate's voice rang out.

He held a pistol in his hand. He stood in front of the bar with Logan behind him and Stefan to his side. But there was no question who was in charge of this little operation. Nathan Wright stood tall and lean, and Callie felt safe even as some jerk held her.

Len no longer had the knife but refused to back down. Suddenly there were a whole bunch of pistols in people's hands. Callie felt the press of cold metal against her skull.

"You okay, Callie?" Nate didn't look at her. His eyes were kept on Len.

"I'm fine. I probably won't become a regular at this establishment." The words came out on a shaky sigh.

"Oh, we're going to talk about your choices. You might never see the light of day again, baby." His mouth was a flat line.

Stefan stood beside him, his hands around a shotgun, his eyes moving between Jennifer and herself. His jaw was tight, and she knew she and Jen were in for a stern talking-to. Callie was damn glad she was merely Stef's almost-sister and not one of his subs.

"We seem to be at an impasse, Sheriff." Len cradled his hand against his chest. Unfortunately, he had several people watching his back. "Here's the deal. I'm gonna take Hollister and the girl, and we're gonna leave. I'll even give you the tall brunette. I promise to leave the girl alive somewhere down the road."

"No fucking deal."

Len sighed. "Sheriff, I don't think you understand. You're outnumbered and outgunned. You got a civilian and a deputy who looks like he should be somewhere having his mama change his diapers."

Nate never wavered. "Be that as it may, I'm not an idiot. I recognize you. You run with the Horde. You won't let her live. Give me the girl, and you can take Hollister."

"Nate!" She couldn't believe he would even offer the deal.

"You go, Callie!" Zane had his head turned. He barked the order at her. At least there was some fire in his eyes. At least he looked ready to fight again.

She couldn't leave him here. "I'm not going anywhere without you."

"Callie!" Jen was yelling now, and Stefan looked ready to shoot.

Nate held the pistol plainly aimed at Len's head. "You got one shot at this. You run now and I'll probably be so concerned about getting my woman and my friend back that I'll let you go. If you walk out of here with Zane, I'll hunt you down. You even think about walking out of here with her and you'll wish you'd never been born. You think I can't do that?"

"Fuck," Len cursed. He looked between the sheriff and Zane and finally shook his head. "Scatter!"

All hell broke loose. Callie was shoved to the floor, and it wasn't a second before a huge body covered her. Zane. She went limp under him, grateful to be so close to him. She heard banging and yelling as the bar emptied. There was the loud roar of bikes being revved and then blessed quiet.

She felt Zane sigh heavily, and then she could breathe again.

Chapter Seven

Nate heard the last chopper fade off and finally allowed himself to relax long enough to get really mad. "What the fuck did the two of you think you were doing?"

He wasn't the only one. Stefan was yelling, too, his normally pristine manner shoved to the side in favor of one pissed-off alpha male. It was good to know he wouldn't be alone in handing out the ass kickings this evening.

"Jennifer, I asked you a question, and I expect an answer," Stef barked.

Nate recognized the brunette from Stella's Diner where she was a waitress. The slender woman's hands were trembling, but she stood up to Stef.

"We were getting a drink, that's all," Jen replied.

"Really, is that all?" Stef didn't sound like he believed her. Nate wasn't sure he did, either.

Nate was ready to get his two cents in. He saw Logan slump into one of the chairs and breathe deeply. He seemed prepared to stay out of this particular fight. Smart boy. While Stef yelled at Jennifer from afar, Nate had no intention of letting Callie Sheppard off so easily. "You wanted to get a drink, did you, baby?"

With some help from Zane, Callie stood. She primly smoothed

the skirt of her yellow sundress. "Sheriff Wright, I am grateful for your swift action." She nodded at him, like that was going to placate him. "I know I, for one, will definitely vote for you over the rubber ducky the townspeople intend to run against you."

He could still feel the blood pumping through his system, charged with adrenaline. His head pounded from the hangover that was just now taking over his system. He was still shaking a bit and had been since he'd read the text Zane had sent. Thank god he was a light sleeper and his cell chirped at every new message. It was starting to hit him what might have happened. Zane could have died. Callie would have been tossed on the pool table and taken by any fucking biker who could get it up.

Jennifer was shouting something at Stef about not belonging to him, but Nate was watching Callie.

Zane stepped in front of her. "Now, Nate, you need to think before you say something you can't take back."

The sight of Callie peeking from behind Zane's wide form sparked something primitive in Nate. "Don't you dare hide behind him."

"I'm not hiding behind him," Callie protested. "He's really big. He takes up all the space."

And now that he thought of it, he had a bone to pick with Zane, as well. "And where the hell is your gun? Did you let them take your weapon? What the fuck is wrong with you?"

Zane frowned, his dark brows forming a *V* above his eyes. Callie had managed to get out from behind him, but he simply slid a bulky arm around her chest and hauled her back against him. Again, Nate's inner caveman was clawing at his insides.

Zane hadn't spent two weeks pushing her away. Zane hadn't made an ass of himself. Naturally Callie clung to him.

"I wasn't carrying," Zane admitted.

"What? Since when do you run around unarmed?"

"Nate, Zane has been through something traumatic. He needs some time to process," Callie began. Her palms ran soothingly across Zane's forearms.

"Zane almost died and you with him." And what about him? Nate had been through hell, too. First he'd drank god knows what trying to get in good with a clinically insane person to please her. Then he'd been forced to watch as the two people he loved most in the world were threatened. Oh, god, he loved them. He loved Callie, and he loved Zane. Not in a weird way, but his life would be incomplete without the big bastard. It suddenly struck him that he'd lived most of his adult life with Zane.

Callie's big brown eyes were round beneath her glasses, and she reached out to him as though trying to bring him into their circle. "Nate, it's all right now."

It wasn't. It was so past all right, he wasn't sure he could handle it. "That is the most naïve thing I have heard you say."

"Hey, don't be so tough on her," Zane interjected.

He turned on his partner. "Fine, how about I be tough on you? How about I point out that you're in a fucking biker bar? What were you thinking?"

Zane's jaw went mulishly tight. "That I wanted a beer."

"This isn't the only bar in the county."

Zane's eyes studied the top of Callie's head, and Nate knew what he wouldn't say. This was the only bar where people wouldn't stare at his scars and then look at him with sympathy. Or look away. Here, those scars were somewhat expected. The only place Zane felt comfortable was the one place he should never go back to.

"I will go where I like and do what I like." Jen's voice rang out in the empty bar.

The look on Stef's face could only be called a sneer. "And that is why I will not train you. This attitude may suit your selfish needs but it's precisely why you'll never fit into my world."

The waitress went a pasty white. "Stefan, I didn't mean…" She stopped and went still.

Callie turned to her friend, moving between the girl and Stef. "It was my fault. I asked her to come with me. I was feeling a bit reckless. I came here to find someone to spend the night with, and she was worried about me."

"What?" Nate practically screamed the question. She'd done what?

Callie shrugged. "Like I said, it might not have been the best idea. I immediately ran into Zane, who cut me off at the bar and proceeded to snarl at any man who looked at me. I will admit, there were not a lot of decent prospects here. So, you can't blame Jen. She was only trying to help."

"What Jennifer should have done was call me to let me know you were making a huge mistake." Stef's face was set. Nate knew that look. Callie should stop talking. Nate had known Stef for a long time, and Stef wasn't listening to anything but his own rage now. "She should have trusted me to handle the situation. She knows nothing of trust, and therefore there can be nothing between us. Now, Jennifer, you have two options, you can go and get in the car, or I can carry you there."

Tears running down her face, Jennifer walked out the door. Stef turned to Callie. "As for you…"

"No, Talbot. She's not yours to discipline." Zane's words came out in a low, predatory growl.

Stef looked like he wanted to argue. Nate stepped between them. Zane was right on this one. "Stefan, I appreciate the backup, but this is between the three of us. It would be best if you left. Take Logan with you. Zane and I will handle Callie."

"Is that the way it's going to be?" Stef glared at them, every muscle in his body bunched and coiled.

Nate wondered if they were about to have it out. It would be worth it. Callie was worth it. "Yeah, that's the way it's going to be."

A small smile broke over Stefan's face and he sighed in obvious relief. "Excellent. Then perhaps it was worth it after all. Callie, good luck, dear. Call me if you need anything." Just like that, Stefan was back to being the smooth artist. Nate had always envied his friend's ability to change like quicksilver. Stef walked to the door. "Come along, Logan. I'll take you home. I'm sure someone has told your mothers that you went into a biker bar with guns blazing by now."

"Damn it," Logan groused. "Do you have any idea the lecture I'm about to get? Have you ever had a big, overprotective lesbian lecture you?"

Stef laughed. "No. But thank you for the warning. I'll be sure to drive away as quickly as possible so Marie can't catch me. Good night."

It was blissfully quiet. Nate looked at Zane, who seemed ill at ease, and Callie, who couldn't possibly be as calm as she looked. "Callie, get in the car. Since you stole mine earlier, I'll drive yours back. Zane can take his bike."

She opened her mouth.

"No arguments." Nate barked at her, unwilling to argue. "And Callie, passenger seat. If you decide to take off, I will show up at your house, break down your door, put you over my knee, and I won't listen to protests, darlin'."

Her jaw dropped open. "Nathan Wright, how dare you?"

He wasn't about to back down. "I dare."

"Do what he says or as soon as he's done blistering your backside, I'll do the same." Zane let her go.

Her head swung back and forth between the two as though sizing up their true intentions. "You are both cavemen, aren't you?"

Finally, she understood them. She turned and flounced off, yellow skirt floating around her knees. He looked at Zane, and they followed after her. The night air was cool on his sweaty skin, and Nate was glad for it. He was on edge, and he knew it. After Callie slammed the car door shut, he turned to Zane.

"You want to tell me what happened in there?" His eyes shifted around. He saw Zane doing the same. Looking for danger. Once a cop…

"Apparently, Ellis isn't done with me. He put a bounty out on me."

Simple words coming out of his friend's mouth, but they shook Nate to his core. Brett Ellis was the president of the Barbarians. He was also the man who'd tortured Zane and nearly killed him. When would they be done with this? They had put the man in prison, but his arms had a long reach. "And now she's on their radar."

Zane nodded, his face a careful blank. "I'll head out in the morning."

Ah, the expected response from self-sacrificing Zane. No way that was going to happen. "No, you won't. She'll still be on their radar. I don't suppose you had the good sense to act like she didn't mean anything."

He shrugged. "I tried, but I'd already beaten up a guy over her, and then I pretty much pleaded with them to let her go, so no, there's no way they believe I don't care."

Damn it. He let his eyes close briefly as he considered the problem. Well, he'd wanted a reason to throw the three of them together. Now he had one. He intended to make the best of it. "We have to stay close to her. They won't let her be. If they're after you, the best way to come at you is through her. I didn't help the cause tonight. They know I care about her, too. We can't let her out of our sight. You'll have to suck it up and show your ass around this town."

That suited Nate just fine. Zane needed to come to the same conclusions he had. It was foolish to not try to figure out a way to make this thing work between the three of them. This was the perfect place to start. No one would care in Bliss. They could take their time and ease into the situation while Nate made plans for them. He would take it slow, move them toward what he wanted.

He was a patient man. Well, he could try to be a patient man.

Zane frowned, but Nate could see the softness in his eyes as he looked over at Callie sitting primly in the car. "I don't think she's going to like having us on her ass twenty-four seven."

Nate bit back a groan at the thought of her ass. Fuck, he was going to die if he didn't sleep with her and soon. "She'll live with it. You're her bodyguard. I can watch her at the station house, but what happens when I go on a call?"

A grim look of determination crossed Zane's face. "I'll be there. I'll watch her."

At least they had a plan, and it was good to see Zane emotional about something. He walked to the two-door piece of crap Callie drove. He wondered briefly how he was going to fit and where they stored the hamsters that obviously powered it. As soon as they had some cash, her ride was getting an upgrade. "I'll see you at home. You follow, and don't let us out of your sight. And Zane, you don't get caught without your ordnance again."

He slammed the door and held his hand out for the keys. Callie dropped them in and stared forward, not looking at him for even a moment. "You be as pissed as you like, darlin', so long as you mind me."

Callie faced the road. "You can't expect me to obey you outside of work, Sheriff."

His hands tightened on the steering wheel. He hated the distance she was putting between them and had no intention of allowing it to go on a moment longer. He'd seen the way she'd clung to Zane. She had done the same thing to him earlier in the day, only to push him back because she was afraid. He knew he'd had a large hand in giving her that insecurity, but there was no room for fear anymore. "Nate. Don't you call me sheriff again. Not at work and not at home. My name is Nate."

She set her pretty lips in a stubborn pout. "I don't think that's a good idea."

"Don't think at all, darlin'. Look where your last idea landed you." He turned and stared at the road ahead.

It got really dark in the mountains. He concentrated on the twin beams of light that illuminated the road in front of him. It struck him suddenly that it took two lights to really see the way through and keep things safe. Turn one off and you could be blindsided. Something tightened in his heart. It would take two of them to keep Callie safe, two of them to really love her. He had to find a way to convince them.

"You should turn here, Nate." Callie's head followed the road he should have turned down, the one that ran to her house. "You missed it."

"No, I didn't. You're coming home with us, and you'll stay there."

Now she was looking at him. He felt that thrill he got when Callie was flustered and angry with him. He shouldn't like to needle her, but she was so cute when she was pissed. And passionate.

"I certainly am not. I am going home, and then you can ride back with Zane."

"Not happening. First, you were right. Zane takes up all the space. I can't fit on the back of his bike. I'd have to ride on the handlebars like an eight-year-old. That's illegal, so then I would have to write myself a ticket. If I have a ticket, how am I supposed to go on being Sheriff? I owe it to this town to be a role model. If I step down and the rubber duck takes over, chaos will ensue. So you have to come home with me in order to fight chaos."

He turned toward the road that led to the valley his and Zane's cabin was in, thinking about how nice it would be to have her there.

"That is the silliest thing I ever heard." But there was a slight curling of her lips. It satisfied him.

* * * *

She knew she should protest. She should force him to take her home. This was definitely a case of "what would Nell do." Callie's hands twisted in her lap as Nate efficiently handled her car. The top of his head nearly brushed the ceiling, and despite the fact that he had the seat all the way back, his knees were up. She doubted Zane would be able to fit at all. Zane. He was here and, at the very least, he didn't want her to be horribly murdered by bikers. That was something, right?

She could still feel the press of him against her skin, his weight holding her down. She'd been able to sense his panic when he realized they were surrounded. A lump formed in her throat. They had been surrounded. Those men…they had been intent on killing him. The sudden image of Zane's big body still and silent brought a sob to her throat.

"Baby?" Nate's voice was softer than she'd heard it in six years. He sounded like he had back then. "Oh, baby."

He pulled the car in front of the cabin he'd bought. Callie knew it as Marnie's old place. The elderly woman had moved into an assisted living home in Alamosa. Callie loved her cabin. She'd played there with Marnie's grandkids when they came up for the summer.

He could have died…

She heard the driver's side door slam. She couldn't hold it back anymore. She put her head in her hands and sobbed. It all crashed in on her. The weeks of being near Nate, her loneliness, how scared she'd been tonight. It crashed over her like a wave that had been building for years, and she trembled with the force of it. Her car door opened, and Nate unhooked her seat belt. Before she could protest, he pulled her into his arms. One hand went around her back, and the other hooked under her knees. He cradled her against his chest. Callie gave in to the irresistible pull of another human being comforting her.

"What's wrong?" Zane's voice was a soft accusation.

"She's coming down," Nate stated quietly.

Zane nodded. He rushed to the cabin door, unlocking it and clearing the way.

"I wasn't high," she protested through her wretched tears. It came out on a hiccup.

"Of course you weren't, darlin'." Nate swept her through the small living room and sank down on the couch. He gently directed her head to the crook of his neck. "You had an adrenaline rush because you were in a dangerous situation. It helps keep you alert and aware during the crisis, but it has some aftereffects. Now you're crashing down. I feel it myself."

"Me, too, babe." Zane was kneeling close to her. His hand stroked into her hair.

She rubbed her face against Nate's neck. She should stop and put some distance between them, but it felt too sweet to be held. It had been so long since she had arms around her, skin pressed to hers, the scent of another filling her senses. She felt Zane moving next to Nate. She shivered slightly as his head nestled into her shoulder. She was fitted to Nate, and Zane was connected to her, the three of them linked together like pieces of a puzzle.

"Callie, baby, we're in a dangerous position."

She wasn't sure if Nate was talking about the stuff with the bikers, or the fact that every nerve in her body was so aware of the two men touching her they were singing a chorus. Her tears were drying up, subsiding into little tremors. Those tremors were rapidly having more to do with the slide of Zane's hand along her thigh and the way Nate's breath heated her cheek than her earlier fear.

Zane's voice was a low, husky growl. "You're going to have to stay with us for a while, babe. It seems like our past is catching up and you're caught in it. That biker gang won't go away. They'll be looking to mess with you because they know that would hurt me."

"Us. Hurting you would hurt us," Nate corrected. He brushed the hair back from her face. His blue eyes were serious as he forced her to look up.

God, she must look a mess. She didn't cry prettily. When she started, she went all out. She got red in the face, and her nose lit up like Rudolph. She tried to pull away. His hand tightened on her hair, firmly but gently keeping her where he wanted. It should have bothered her. Instead it made her soften against him.

"Callie, these men are dangerous. You have to trust that we'll do what it takes to protect you," Nate said.

Zane's head rubbed restlessly against hers. "We won't let anything happen to you."

He groaned as his hand found the naked skin under the skirt of her dress.

"We'll take such good care of you." Nate's mouth hovered over hers. So close and then he was brushing his lips against hers, the kiss so sweet it pierced through her.

Oh, boy. She was rapidly approaching the point where she wouldn't be able to make a good decision. The tequila was still running through her system. It was time to slow things down. She understood the need to stay here, but she wasn't about to sleep with them. Except when she opened her mouth to protest, Nate's tongue slid in.

Push him away.

Her arms weren't listening. One wound around Nate's neck while the other wandered off to encourage Zane.

Zane slid off the couch, kneeling at her feet. Nate's tongue was gliding against hers with a silky grind. Callie felt Zane pull off her shoes. He held her feet in his big hands, surrounding them with his heat. They were both so hot. The heat that came off those large bodies could keep her warm all winter.

Nate's palms cupped her face, holding her still for his dominating tongue. He was done with gentle caresses, it seemed. His mouth slanted over hers again and again, challenging her to keep up with him. Callie let him lead, her tongue playing against his, a feminine response to his male dominance.

She sighed as Zane gently bit at the arch of her foot. She'd never thought of a foot as being erotic, but the sensation was overwhelming. Her legs started to move restlessly. Zane held her, putting a stop to that.

"No, Callie. You relax. You're not in charge of this. We are." Zane's deep voice had a direct line to her pussy. It pulsed with need. She stilled, and Zane kissed his way up her leg, licking and biting and awakening every inch of her skin.

Nate's hands pushed down the straps of her dress. He kissed her hard on the lips one last time before twisting her body around. His hands on her waist, he spun her forward so her back was to his chest and used his knees to spread her legs wide. She could feel the hard line of his rigid cock against the seam of her ass. She wiggled against it.

"No teasing," Nate barked as he pulled down the bodice of her dress, baring her breasts. "Damn it, Callie, where's your bra?"

His hands cupped her, his fingers immediately playing with her hard nipples.

"I don't like them. I wear them at work but nowhere else." She hated them, actually. She knew her breasts were too big to go without, but they were still somewhat perky, and she saw no need to give in just yet.

She looked down, and Zane was grinning up at her, the look on his face so sweetly lascivious she thought she might faint. Whatever he was planning in that brain of his was going to feel good. She was sure of that.

He tossed her skirt up, and his head disappeared. "Damn. No panties, either."

Nate pinched her nipples, rolling them between his thumb and forefinger. She felt her breasts swell under his plucking fingers. Her head rolled back. She gave up the fight. Not that she'd given it much of a go. She wanted them, even if they broke her heart.

"I'm fine with the panties." Nate's breath was warm on her neck. "But I don't want anyone watching these breasts. They're soft and round, and every man with eyes will want to watch them bounce."

Zane came out from under her skirt. "Let 'em. I don't mind them looking, but I'll kick the ass of anyone who tries to touch." He shoved her skirt up, exposing her to the air. "This, on the other hand, is a different matter. God, I missed this."

He knelt back down and shoved his nose right into her pussy. The sensation was so startlingly intimate, she nearly jumped up. Nate's hands tightened, keeping her close.

"Calm down, darlin'. Let Zane taste you. He's been wanting to taste you again for years."

"She smells so good." Zane's words vibrated against her flesh.

"Is she wet?"

The men were talking around her like she was a sweet plaything, existing only for their pleasure. She sighed and gave herself over to the fantasy. It was so nice to let go. Every day of her life, it seemed, was about being in control and taking care of someone else. This was heaven. She needed it so badly.

Zane's fingers slid through the flesh of her pussy. Callie felt a fresh coat of arousal covering her.

"She's past wet, bro. She is soaking." He pushed a big finger deep into her pussy, grunting as he rotated it. Callie quivered. "She's also tight as a drum. That's what happens when you wait, babe. You get tight as a virgin all over again."

Nate's tongue traced the shell of her ear. "What do you mean wait?" He gasped a little. She could feel his breath on her ear. "You haven't had anyone but us, have you, baby?"

She wanted to lie and tell them she'd had a hundred men since them. It would make her feel far less vulnerable than the truth. But they would see through her. Besides, there hadn't been anyone. "No one but you."

She'd never wanted anyone the way she wanted them. What she had felt for the Harper twins had been a girlish crush, an attempt to hold on to what she knew. Nate and Zane were different. Her heart had been engaged the moment she laid eyes on them, and she doubted it would ever change.

"Now, Zane, since this woman of ours has been kind enough to wait until our dumb asses came back to her, maybe we should reward her."

Zane's finger eased out. He brought it straight to his mouth and sucked the cream off it. "I was thinking the same thing. A woman like Callie deserves a reward."

He winked at her, his hair falling over his eyes as he knelt back down and out of view.

She gasped when his tongue slid through her juices. Liquid pleasure coursed through her. She sagged against Nate. The hard muscles of his chest became the only thing that seemed concrete. Zane's soft, strong tongue lapping at her felt too heavenly to be real.

"That's right, darlin'. Give over. Just relax, and let us have you."

Nate's hips moved against her ass in a slow grind. "We're going to take such good care of you." His Texas accent was amped up. Every word dripped honey.

She wanted to believe him. She wanted to believe that this time they would stay. It didn't matter. She would at least have this night. Zane ate her pussy, seeming to savor every inch. He sucked the flesh into his mouth and then fucked his tongue deeply into her channel. Over and over, he sucked and then speared her with his tongue. It wasn't enough. It felt so good, but it wasn't even close to being enough.

"Please." She wasn't too proud to beg. She never had been. She wanted to wrap her fingers in Zane's thick hair and force him to fuck her hard with his tongue, but Nate's arms bound her.

"Please what, darlin'?"

"Please make me come." It had been so long.

"She wants to come, Zane."

Zane's head came up. She wanted to cry at the loss. "Fine, I'll give you the first one, but then you don't come until I'm inside you, understood, babe?"

She managed to nod. That sounded fine to her. Zane's eyes stared at her breasts as he parted her with his fingers and worked his way up. Even his fingers made her feel full. He pumped slowly into her.

"Nate, I think I need to taste one of those luscious tits of hers." Zane licked his lips. She could see the evidence of her arousal coating them.

Nate's hands cupped her breasts, offering them to Zane. Without missing a beat, Zane leaned over and sucked a nipple into his mouth. His tongue whirled around the nub as his fingers continued their steady rhythm. She bucked against Nate.

His left arm tightened around her waist, and his teeth nipped her ear. "You stay still."

She shivered at the erotic pleasure-pain that bite caused. As though he knew what his partner had done, Zane bit down on her nipple as his thumb found her clit. The combination of sharp pain and grinding pleasure made her scream as the orgasm washed over her. As she came down, Zane continued to thumb her clitoris. Little aftershocks caused her to shiver. Zane tongued the nipple he'd bitten softly, caressing it, as though in apology.

She dragged in long gasps of air and let her hand find the silk of Zane's hair while she rested against Nate.

* * * *

Zane took one last soft drag off that sweet nipple before deciding his dick had been in agony long enough. If Nate was in the same shape he was in, Callie was in for a rough ride.

"Hands and knees." He stood and quickly shrugged out of his shirt. He didn't take any time to think about the scars on his body. A part of him knew that Callie wouldn't care. She hadn't cared about his scarred face, but that didn't matter. He was far too eager to get inside her. It was all he could think about since the moment he realized she would have to stay with them. If she was living here, he would be on her four times a day if she let him. God, he felt like a beast in full rut. He shoved his jeans off. His cock was already poking out of his boxers.

Callie's eyes were slightly sleepy. "What?"

He decided not to argue. It was better to show her what he wanted. He picked her up. "Nate, pull out the couch. It should be the perfect height."

Nate's eyes heated. They were definitely on the same page. Nate quickly flipped the back of the old couch down. It made a flat surface. It was uncomfortable as a bed, but it looked like the perfect way to get Callie in between them.

While Nate stripped, Zane pulled the dress over Callie's head and tossed it aside. She wouldn't need it tonight or, possibly, tomorrow. He drank in the sight of her perfect hourglass figure. Her nipples were still tight from his attention. Her breasts full and heavy. Her pussy gleaming with moisture. Her eyes languorous. She was the perfect picture of a well-loved woman.

He pulled her close, every inch of her pressed against him. His cock pushed at her belly. He forced her chin up so she had to look at him. "Babe, I want you on your hands and knees on the couch. Face Nate and spread your knees wide for me."

Her sweet face was a little dreamy as she nodded up at him. He couldn't help but smile as he plucked her glasses off her nose and laid them aside.

"Hey, what if I need to see something?" She wasn't vigorously protesting. Her hands ran along the sides of his chest. The soft caress made him want so much more.

"I think you'll be able to see what's coming your way, babe." Zane slapped her ass gently. Nate was in place, his face flush with arousal. He stroked his cock as he waited on the other side of the now flat couch. "Do what I asked."

She climbed onto the couch, giving him a spectacular view of her ass. Her ass was made to squeeze and take a pounding. Callie was petite in height, but she was lush and curvy. She wasn't delicate anywhere but her sweet soul. She'd been made for sex—pussy sex, oral sex, anal sex. He'd get in there soon enough. For tonight, her pussy would do, but he intended to play. She was perfect for him. Them. She was perfect for them.

Zane strode across the room and grabbed his bag. He didn't have the toys he needed. He would buy those specifically for her, but he had a couple of things that would help. He grabbed a bottle of lube and a stack of condoms.

Nate approached her. He stroked her hair gently before wrapping his fist in it and guiding her head to his engorged dick. "Lick me, darlin'."

Callie's tongue came out obediently and fluttered across Nate's cock. His partner's head fell forward.

"Oh, yes, just like that."

Her head bobbed up and down as she sucked. Nate's cock disappeared and reappeared as he fucked his way into her mouth inch by inch. Zane felt his balls draw up at the sight. He was harder than he could ever remember. He stroked his cock for a moment as he watched them then rolled on a condom. He got on his knees behind her sweet ass. She wiggled it back as though anticipating his entry. He had something to do before he got to that.

He lubed up his right hand. He dribbled a line of the slick stuff along the valley of her cheeks. She had the most adorable dimples in the small of her back. Zane caressed them briefly before parting the globes. Callie stiffened.

Zane gave her a sharp smack. "Don't you stop what you're doing. You suck that cock, babe." He sensed her hesitation. "I'm just playing. Nothing but my finger tonight."

Nate took control, growling at her to be still. He softened the command with long strokes of his hand on her hair, and she went back to work.

Zane found the gorgeous, tight rosette of her ass. It was perfect and would fit him tighter than any glove. He worked the lube in, his dick throbbing. He massaged the puckered hole, dipping in to the first knuckle of his middle finger. A small plug. He'd have to work her up slowly. He gently pushed in to the second knuckle. Callie moaned around Nate's cock, and her asshole quivered around his finger. He thrust gently in, back and forth, stretching her. After a moment, she pushed back against him. She ground her ass against his hand.

"Fuck, if you want to go together, you better be fast." Nate was struggling. His face was contorted in a familiar look of agony. Nate pumped into her mouth. "She feels so good. Our woman knows how to suck a cock."

Zane pulled his finger out, her little rosette clenching all the way. Now it seemed like a damn good thing the place was so small. He moved to the sink and washed up, all the while watching her as she sucked Nate hard.

His partner was right about one thing. He needed to get inside her and quickly. It had been a good thing he'd given her that first orgasm because he wasn't sure he would last long. He moved back into place and gripped her hips.

He lined his cock up to her pussy and plunged in. She was so tight he had to wiggle and fight his way in. Her pussy was slick, facilitating his penetration. She moaned and ground back against him. Nate was holding her head, fucking her mouth freely now. Zane knew he had one thought and one thought alone. He wanted to come. Zane wanted that, too, but he was the one responsible for Callie now, and he'd have to hold off. Her tight pussy pulsed around him. His eyesight dimmed, and his brain felt fried. God, he was never going to last.

"Finish off and help me, man." He managed to get the words out as he tunneled further in. Almost there. He was almost all the way in. Callie's ass tilted up, and he slid home, his heavy balls touching her skin, getting coated in the cream that was pouring off her. He held her hips, forcing her to be still. He wanted a moment to savor the feeling of being buried inside her. He wanted to take her without the stupid, idiotic rubber between them. He would fill her up, and he wouldn't let her wash it off for a while. They could sleep that way, stuck together, juices mingling.

Fuck, he was going to blow.

"Oh, yeah." Nate moaned and ruthlessly pounded into her mouth. His hips swung forward, head fell back, and Zane could hear Callie hurrying to drink down the semen. Zane's hips started moving of their own volition, little thrusts back and forth. An appetizer.

Nate came out of Callie's mouth with an audible pop. Free from her duties, Callie shoved herself back at Zane. His dick was impaled fully, and there was no stopping now.

"Finger her clit, please." Zane was begging because his balls had drawn up. He couldn't go until she did. How did she do this to him? He could fuck for hours, but she had him coming like a schoolboy.

Nate moved quickly. Zane could see his partner was already getting hard again. He moved to the side and slid his hand under to find her clit. Zane was pretty sure Nate was accurate because her pussy clamped down like a fucking vise, and she moaned. He felt her come all around his cock, and his leash was off. He hammered into her with no thought to her comfort, only the blinding need to mark her. She was his, and he didn't mind that she would be sore in the morning. That was what it meant to be his woman. In exchange, he would follow her around like an awfully big lapdog. He was fine with that. Any dude who wanted to call him pussy whipped hadn't fucked Callie. And never fucking would.

Zane gritted his teeth against the roar that came as his cock exploded. Semen streamed out of him, pulsing over and over. He ground into her until he didn't have anything left and then pushed one more time, staving off the moment when he had to leave her.

He slumped forward, his body covering hers, pushing her into the fabric of the couch. When he looked down he could see the smile on her face.

"You okay, babe?" He'd ridden her hard.

"More, please." Her breathy request made his cock jump again.

Zane could feel Nate on the couch with them. He should roar and shove the other man away, maybe beat the shit out of him. Why didn't he feel that?

Because Nate loved Callie, too. Because Nate would protect her with his life.

He kissed her and reluctantly pulled out. "I bet I can arrange that, babe."

Despite the earlier events, he felt lighthearted. He forced himself off the couch. Nate already had a condom in his hand and was rolling it on his dick as Zane was pulling his off. Nate turned Callie over and had her spread eagle and penetrated in a heartbeat.

"Oh, baby, you feel so good." Nate thrust in and out. Callie wound her legs around his waist.

Zane watched them. Again, no hot need to grab a knife and kill the man fucking his woman. Instead, Zane knelt by Callie's head and kissed her. She was the one. He had known that for six years. He'd been through the fire, the crucible as Nell had called it. Was Callie the one who could make him whole again? Could make him alive again?

She was sweet and funny. She made him laugh, and somehow, when she was around, he was sure he would be okay. How did petite Callie make his big, dangerous ass feel safe? His tongue tangled with hers, and he knew he wouldn't question it. He loved Callie Sheppard. He needed Nathan Wright.

God, could they make it work?

It didn't matter. Not tonight or for the foreseeable future. They were stuck together. Nate was groaning on top of Callie, and she was coming again. Zane saw her face flush, heard the sweet purr that came out of her throat. Zane let his face get buried in that mountain of hair on her head. He loved the scent. This would happen again and again while they were protecting her. Maybe, after a while, it would be something none of them could live without.

Suddenly that didn't seem like such a bad thing.

Chapter Eight

Nate could smell it. Though he wasn't sure what "it" was. That scent was bad news though. He knew that much. It filled the air with a sickening acrid scent that clung to everything. It was a little like a barbecue, but there was a coppery tone to it. The smell was making him sick, and he didn't need it. He needed to be steady. The heat from the August sun had baked the Texas border town to a crisp, and now that it was dark, the ground still held the sizzle. Sweat was dripping off his forehead, getting into his eyes and burning.

Nate held the Glock tightly in his hands and glanced at the men around him. He was their leader in this case, and that meant he had to lead by example and not give in to panic.

Stay calm. Remember your training.

It was so fucking hard. He'd been Nate Rush, outlaw biker, for years. Becoming DEA Special Agent Nathan Wright again was difficult. Nate Rush wanted to walk in, guns blazing, and damn the torpedoes. Nate Wright knew what would happen if he did. Rushing in without a good plan would get Zane killed in the crossfire. He needed to give the MET time to get into position around the warehouse. He'd already risked a lot to get to El Paso and organize the mobile enforcement team. He wasn't going to screw it up now. The guards who surrounded the warehouse were dead or hog-tied in the back of the MET unit's van. There were only the core members of the Barbarians to deal with, but they wouldn't go down easy. He had to think of this in terms of his job—get in, arrest the bad guys, collect the evidence, get out alive.

But that professional thought didn't do anything to calm the churning in his gut. Zane was in there and had been for hours. When Nate had left, Zane had been tied to a chair while the gang took turns using him as a punching bag. Why wasn't Zane screaming? At least he'd been spitting bile and vitriol when Nate had managed to slip away hours before. He felt like he hadn't breathed in hours and hours, not since that moment when he realized Zane's cover was blown.

The leader of the MET made a chopping motion with his hand. It was the go signal. Nate kicked the door in and entered hell. He heard gunfire and finally realized what that smell had been.

Zane.

"Sweetie, you need to wake up now."

Callie's voice and the soft touch of her hand pulled him out of the nightmare. He breathed deeply before opening his eyes. Mountain air. Pine. Bliss. He tentatively opened his eyes, and Callie smiled down at him.

"You were having a bad dream," she explained needlessly.

He shook slightly, trying to rid his head of the images. Zane on that fucking slab, pieces of his body still sizzling from where those assholes branded him. He'd been so still. Nate had thought he was dead.

"Asshole, your pansy-ass bad dream sent my butt to the floor."

Nate sat up. Sure enough, Zane was sprawled on the floor on the other side of the bed. Callie sat beside Nate, knees pulled to her chest. She was all soft skin and a hint of a smile. Zane, on the other hand, was one hundred percent pissed-off man. And he was alive. Nate could even look at the scars this morning without feeling so guilty he had to turn away.

"Sorry." Nate managed not to laugh. Zane was tangled in a very feminine quilt. It had come with the cabin. Maybe it was time to think about replacing some of the items that didn't go with their personalities, like the rose and bunny covered quilt.

Zane stood up, tossing the quilt at Nate's face. He scratched his belly and stretched. "I'm taking a shower, and then I'll start breakfast. Then I'm going to find a bigger bed. My legs hang off this one, and Callie elbowed me all night long."

She grinned. "Well, you two took up all the space. I had to sleep on top of Nate."

A bigger bed was definitely in order. Zane brushed his lips across Callie's and walked out toward the bathroom. The single bathroom. This cabin wasn't big enough for the two of them, much less for three. And pretty much everything was falling apart. Zane would be lucky if his shower wasn't icy cold because the water heater was wonky. All the appliances looked like they'd come from antique stores.

Damn it. He couldn't afford more. He couldn't even afford a separate living room. It was squeezed in with the kitchen and dining room.

At one point in time, he could have offered Callie a mansion.

"What is that look about?" Callie regarded him with a worried expression on her face.

What was he supposed to say? *Well, baby, I was thinking about the fact that I can't support you. I was thinking how sad it was that you slept with a man who can't buy you a Valentine's Day present, much less the ring you deserve.*

Her hand came out to cup his face. "It's okay, Nate. I promise I won't give you hell at work." There was a sad smile on her lips and a dullness to her eyes that hit Nate straight in the heart.

"What do you mean?"

She pulled her hand back and scooted to the edge of the bed. Her head darted around as though looking for her clothes. "I mean I'm not going to be some clinging vine, Sheriff. I'm a big girl. This was a fun fling."

Nate pulled her back down, pinning her to the bed. He needed to make a few things clear. He could handle it if she wanted to walk away because he had nothing to offer her, but this wasn't a fling. Not even close. He covered her with his body, spreading her legs wide with his knees. His cock immediately responded. He was hard as hell and seeking relief. There was no place for Callie to go, and she looked up at him with a sheen of tears in her eyes.

Nate stared down at her. She was so lovely. "How do you think this is supposed to work, baby?"

She tried to shrug, but he held her arms high over her head. His chest lay against her bare breasts. "I have breakfast and go home. I see you at work, and we behave professionally."

"Not going to happen." He couldn't help himself. She was close, and she was wet. God, she was so wet. What had she been dreaming about? Nate let go of her hands. He got on his knees and grabbed a condom, rolling it on with precision. "This isn't a fling. This is your future. Get used to us."

He fitted himself to that warm pussy and thrust home. Even after all the sex of the night before, she was still tight around him. He had to strain to get his cock in. He pushed in balls deep and held himself there.

Callie's brown eyes weren't dead anymore. They were alive with heat. "Nate, I don't know about this."

"I do. Trust me. You aren't going home. You're staying with us for the foreseeable future. And I have no intention of behaving professionally."

He pulled out and flexed back in. Her pussy clung to his cock, sucking at him. Last night had been fast and furious. This morning was different. This morning he wanted to take his time and make it last. He wanted to fuck her for hours. He could spend the morning exactly like this, pumping in and out of her pussy. He sighed at the connection humming through his blood. This was where he wanted to be.

"What did you expect?" Nate asked as he twisted his hips on the downstroke. "That I would pretend we aren't lovers?"

Her legs wound around his waist. She pressed back against him. He knew she had to be sore, but she accepted him anyway. "I guess I didn't think we would be. You won't stay here for too long. You only promised Stef you would work out Rye's term. That's up in less than a year. You don't like it here."

He wasn't sure what his feeling about the town had to do with anything. "I like you. That's what matters. I'm crazy about you." He twisted his hips slowly, grinding against her pelvis. He loved the way her eyes closed, and she groaned. He could see the pulse in her throat leap. "I am so crazy about you."

He kissed her and stopped talking. He showed her how he felt, worshipping her body with his. He thrust in and out, in and out. He lost himself in the scent, sight, and feel of her. Callie clutched at his shoulders. Her legs tightened, and she sighed as she came. The sweetest smile lit her face. He'd enjoyed the hot sex of the night before, but he loved this, too. After she came twice, he thrust as deep as he could go and let himself go.

He collapsed on top of her and cuddled against her. Zane could bring them breakfast. He wasn't leaving the bed. Maybe never again.

There was the sound of glass breaking, and Zane shouted. Nate was on his feet in an instant. His heart was racing, but he had trained long enough that he knew it wouldn't show on his face. His face would be stone cold, and every movement would be precise.

"What did he break?" Callie asked, wincing at the sound.

It hadn't been Zane. Nate knew it instinctively. His entire being had gone into protective cop mode. Two windows. Small, but of the proper height for a headshot. He stood clear. Callie was in a good place. The cabin walls were actual logs, built in the thirties. As a barrier to bullets went, they were about as good as it got.

The bedroom door burst open, and Zane plowed through. He had on a pair of jeans, and his hair was wet. "We have to go."

Zane tossed a T-shirt toward Callie along with her purse and pulled his Sig Sauer out of the nightstand.

Callie's eyes were wide as Nate found his Glock and quickly checked it for bullets and flicked off the safety. He pulled on a pair of sweatpants and reached for Callie's hand. He was proud of the calm way she was handling the whole thing.

"Barbarians?" Nate asked.

Zane's entire body was a study in concentration—his breathing steady, his hands curled around the gun. "Probably. Someone tossed a Moltov cocktail in the window. It caught the curtains on fire. I couldn't get it out. The living room is going slowly, but it's going."

Callie was reaching for her cell.

"No, baby. We have to go." They would have to leave everything behind. The cabin was solidly built, but the carpet was old and the curtains thin. They would catch quickly and burn hard.

She hit a single button. "You have your weapons, and I have

mine. Hello, Marie. I'm out at Marnie's old place. Someone's attacking us. Yeah. Okay." She let the phone fall into her purse. "Marie'll take care of it."

Nate wasn't sure what the fifty-plus-year-old owner of the Trading Post was going to do against an outlaw biker gang. He'd met Marie and her "life partner" Teeny. While Marie was solidly built, Teeny was a little bird of a woman. Nate peeked behind the curtain, making damn sure Callie was behind him. He couldn't see anyone waiting, but he knew they were out there. The fire was a way of getting them to flee. They would be walking right into a trap. God, he should have killed Ellis when he had the chance. The leader of the Barbarians was still a thorn in his side from his cushy prison cell.

"I'm going out first. I'm the one they want." Zane shoved back the curtains, and Nate pulled Callie out of the way.

She tried to get to Zane. "You can't go out there!"

Zane gave her a sad smile and pushed her hair back. She'd managed to get her glasses on, and he kissed the bridge of her nose. "I have to. They'll be looking for me. If I can distract them, Nate can get you to the car and get you out of here. Don't even think about disobeying me right now."

"I'll get her to the car and then come back for you." He had no intention of leaving Zane to the wolves. Callie could drive to the station house, lock herself in, and call for help.

"What the hell?" Zane breathed the question. His eyes widened as he looked out the window.

Nate joined him and shocked jarred through him. There were fifteen small cabins in this part of the valley. Every door was open, and their neighbors were coming out. Each man and a couple of women had a shotgun in their hands. In the distance, Nate could hear a siren wailing. Logan was on his way, somehow. He sighed. Logan was Marie's…sort of son. Apparently Marie hadn't made her boy quit after his foray into biker bars.

He heard the sound of shouting and then the unmistakable roar of a bike coming to life and driving away.

The citizens of Bliss–1. Barbarians–0.

Yeah, he might have to rethink his attitude about this town.

* * * *

Callie's hands were shaking as Zane helped her off the back of his bike. It was funny because while they'd been driving through the valley, her arms wrapped around his waist, she'd felt perfectly safe. He'd insisted she wear the helmet and it had been too big on her head, but something about being with him, feeling the sunshine on her skin as she rode, had calmed her immensely.

She knew that road like the back of her hand, but with Zane driving, it felt new. She'd never been on the back of a bike before. Now she understood why so many people drove through the mountains on them. There was a freedom she'd never felt in a car.

But now she was back to reality, and the reality was someone wanted to kill them.

Zane stood back while she opened the door.

"I won't be too long and then we can head into town. I'm pretty hungry. I think you'll like Stella's," she said. She wasn't sure she had enough in the place to feed him. Now that their cabin was no longer safe, she had to wonder if they would move in here. She would definitely need to buy some groceries.

"Why is your door unlocked?" He stared at her, his hands on his hips.

"Uhm, because I didn't lock it." She stepped inside. "And honestly I don't know where I put the key. It's okay, though. I totally know how use a credit card to get it open."

"That is not making me feel better," he said, examining the door. She could tell he was not impressed. "You don't even have a deadbolt."

"I don't even like the sound of that. And if I had one of those things and I used it, how would Stef get in when I'm in the shower? How would my neighbors get in when they need to borrow something?"

"They wouldn't and he shouldn't," Zane replied.

As though speaking had conjured the man, the door opened and Stef strode in.

"Callie?" He put a hand over his heart, breathing in deeply. "Thank god. I heard from Stella, who heard from Laura at the Stop 'n'

Shop, who talked to Mel who told her the invasion had started and Nate's place was ground zero."

"What?" Zane asked.

Stef looked at him. "Sorry. The Bliss gossip mill is powerful. At some point it goes through Mel and aliens get injected. Is everyone okay? I called Nate. He said there was a fire. He also said the Barbarians are back. What does that mean?"

Actually, she wouldn't hate having an answer to that question. She understood part of it. "This is some kind of motorcycle gang? Is that why Nate was so upset about the campsite we found?"

"They're camping here?" Stef turned to Zane. "You brought them into my town?"

Stef could be possessive. Of pretty much everything. And overbearing.

Zane stared a hole through her best friend. "I didn't exactly send out an invite, Talbot. And I've offered to leave."

"You're not leaving." She had to get that thought out of his head. Zane reminded her of an anxious predator. His shoulders were bunched up, fists tight at his sides. If she didn't bring the tension level down, Stef was going to get put on his backside. It was time to see if she had any influence over the man she'd spent all night making love with. She moved in, putting a hand on his chest and looking up at him. "I need you here with me. It's like Nate said. They wouldn't stop coming after me."

He seemed to forget that Stef was even in the room. His eyes softened, and she found herself wrapped up in his arms. "Babe, I'm not going to let them even get close to you. I promise."

Even Stef lost his hard edge. "I don't know a lot about what happened. Nate wouldn't tell me more than you got hurt and the operation went south. Do you honestly think these people are after you? The fire wasn't an accident?"

Zane was much more calm when he answered. "No. Someone threw a Molotov cocktail through the kitchen window. It wasn't a mistake."

"But I thought you put the president of the club in jail," Stef said. "Along with most of his members."

"Most of his immediate members," Zane agreed. "But the

Barbarians have chapters all over the southwest. Think of them almost like franchises, in a way. We weren't able to connect them all so they're still up and in operation, and they still answer to their president. Ellis was the president of the home club. Just because we put him in prison doesn't mean he's down for the count."

"Where is Nate and what is he planning on doing about this?" Stef asked.

"He's gone into the station house. He's going to make some calls," Zane explained.

"I'm going to send Callie out of town for a while. She'll go to Dallas and stay at The Club. The owner is a friend of mine and he's got connections to a security firm. She can stay there until this is all over," Stef said.

Oh, that was not happening. She turned, moving out of Zane's arms. "No. You put me in this position, Stef. You don't get to decide to pull me out of it now. I'm involved with Nate and Zane for better or worse. No one is going to protect me the way they can."

"And the first thing I'm going to do is get you a damn deadbolt," Zane groused. He took a deep breath, shaking his head as though attempting to shake off some unnamed emotion. "Look, Stef, this happened not an hour ago. Can we have some time to adjust? We need to figure out who's here and why. I'm going to stick to Callie like glue, and you have to know I would give my life for her. I think what happened this morning shook those bikers up, too. They weren't expecting an armed mob."

It had been such a relief to see her neighbors pouring out of their cabins. This was what she would never get in a city. Bliss was a family. They might bicker from time to time, but when the chips were down every man and woman in this town would be there for her. A whole lot of the kids, too. "I called Marie when it happened."

Stef's lips curled up. "That had to have scared the shit out of them."

Zane's hands found her shoulders, connecting them. "I know these guys. I spent years riding with them. They work in the shadows. They'll think twice about attacking us like that. And obviously we won't be going back to our cabin. We'll find someplace safe and hunker down. I know I haven't shown it, but I was good at my job, and part of that was protecting my partner. Callie is safe with me."

Stef seemed to consider that, and she prayed he came down on the side of reason. Stef was perfectly capable of kidnapping her and shoving her someplace he decided was safe if he was scared enough. He could be relentless about protecting the people he considered to be his family. And he definitely was serious about protecting his town. Jen sometimes jokingly called Stef the King of Bliss. It was a fitting nickname.

Stef held out a hand. "All right then. Callie's made her choice and I'll honor it, but you have to know that if this gets worse, my offer is still open."

Zane shook his hand. "I'll keep that in mind."

She thought she could trust them to not kill each other. "I'm going to take a quick shower and change. I'll be right back out."

"I'll be here," Zane promised her.

She started for her room, Stef following behind.

"I want to know you're okay," he said quietly.

She glanced back. Zane was facing away, his gaze apparently on the rows of framed pictures she kept on the wall. Her mother had put most of them there, lovingly cataloguing her childhood and their life together. God she missed her mom. She wished her mom was still in this room so she could walk in and ask her advice about Nate and Zane. What she wouldn't give for another few moments with her.

"I'm as okay as I can be." She loved Stef, but she wasn't sure she could confide in him about this. If she got a chance she would talk to Jen or Rachel or Nell. They wouldn't potentially punch anyone. Well, Rachel might, but she would blame pregnancy hormones.

"Are you sure? I know Nate's having trouble fitting in around here," Stef said. "I'll be honest I've started to wonder if I made a mistake by bringing him here. This particular plan of mine isn't going the way I thought it would."

"How did you think it would go?"

He leaned against the doorjamb, his voice low. "I was certain Nate would walk in here, take one look at you and realize how stupid he'd been."

She sighed because now she truly got it. Yes, he'd been trying to help Nate, but he'd also been trying to give her what she needed.

"Sweetie, I love that you love me so much and I'm thrilled to have this time with the two of them again, but I don't know that this is anything more than another fling. I don't think Nate stays here a long time. I think he'll want to move back to Dallas, or maybe New York or DC. He doesn't want to be a small-town sheriff the rest of his life. And Zane will go where Nate goes."

Despite how beautiful the night before had been, she knew it wouldn't last forever. She would get a few months, perhaps a year, and then they would move on and she would be left behind again. She didn't fit into their world. Though she'd thought about moving to Denver, she wouldn't live the way Nate would want to. She would find a group of outcasts and make a family. It was what she knew, what she genuinely loved.

"I don't understand. Why would anyone ever leave here?" Stef looked genuinely confused. "I thought if he came here, he would get it."

She reached up and touched his face. "Not everyone loves this place."

"Then they're crazy and they're not worthy of you," he insisted.

Her heart hurt as she realized what he was really doing. "When did you find out I was thinking about moving?"

He was quiet for a moment. "When you talked to Marie about putting your cabin up for sale. I won't let that happen, you know. I'll buy it and it will be waiting here for you when you come to your senses. You don't know what it's like out there. You belong here."

"Well, now I'm not going anywhere at all," she replied, trying to put a smile on his face again. He would do exactly that. He would buy her place anonymously and keep it as a shrine. "At least not until the threat passes, and who knows, maybe this whole episode will show Nate how nice it is to be in Bliss. I know he was impressed with how quickly we form an armed militia."

She should be more optimistic. Yes, they'd walked away once before, but that didn't mean they would do it again. And the truth was Nate was stuck here for a while. He might come around. Bliss had a way of working its magic on people. Zane hadn't even given it a shot yet.

She hadn't been fair to Stef. He had issues with being left behind.

Issues she knew all too well. "How about if I get serious about moving, I'll come and talk to you. I won't make that decision without talking to you. You know you're my family, Stef. You and Max and Rye. Even if I did move, I wouldn't ever stay away for too long."

He nodded. "Okay. I can live with that, but I think you should give the big idiot a chance. He might like it here now that you've got him to come out of the shadows."

"I heard that," Zane said from the next room.

Stef laughed. "You were starting to scare the tourists, man. There are stories of a wild man running through the woods half dressed. We already have enough Sasquatch enthusiasts. We don't need more."

"What the fuck is a Sasquatch?" Zane asked.

"Bigfoot, asshole. They think you're Bigfoot," Stef said with obvious relish.

"What?"

"It must be the fact that you could use a haircut," Stef said.

She sighed. Maybe she'd been hasty thinking they could get along. "I'm taking a shower now. Don't kill each other."

"My hair is fine," Zane was saying. "And I've got like zero body hair. This smoothness is all natural."

"All I can tell you is what I hear," Stef replied.

She left as they started to argue, but it was obvious the crisis had passed.

Men were weird that way.

* * * *

Three hours later, Zane watched Callie thank Stella as she placed a cup of coffee in front of her. He nodded from across the booth but kept his eyes down until the café owner left to wait on another table. Callie reached her hand out to cover his. He gave her a half-hearted smile that she seemed satisfied with.

She was dressed in a flowing skirt and blouse that she'd changed into when he'd taken her by her place. He'd walked around the small cabin while she'd showered and gotten ready. Callie's cabin was as small as his and Nate's, but there was a homey quality to it that called to him. He'd stared at the framed pictures spread out around the cabin, a map of her life. Pictures of her with her mother, of her as a child with her hair up in pigtails. There had been one of her and Nell when they were younger, the women smiling with flowers in their hair. He'd stared for the longest time at the one of four children sitting on a bale of hay. The twins, who had to be Max and Rye Harper, had been making silly faces for the camera while a young Stef had stared at it solemnly. Callie sat close to Stef, leaning into the boy as though letting him know everything would be all right.

It didn't make him want to punch the fucker less though. Bigfoot his ass.

He focused on Callie. Everything about her was calm, but Zane couldn't forget that not too long ago, her life had been in danger. Again.

"What's good here?" He picked up the menu and started to study it. He had no appetite whatsoever, but it would worry Callie if he didn't eat. His brain worked overtime. He could still smell the carpet burning, feel the heat and the panic when he realized what was happening. Because of the neighbors' quick thinking, the cabin had been mostly saved, though it would take a lot of money to make it livable again. A lot of money neither he nor Nate had. It was something he should think about. Callie would need someone who could provide for her. He wasn't sure exactly how he fit into that scenario.

"I would stick to standard diner fare. Pancakes, bacon, burgers, and such. Hal is a fantastic fry cook. Unfortunately, he considers himself something of an artist. Stella gives him complete control over the daily specials." She turned a little green as she spoke.

He looked up at the chalkboard over the counter. It proudly claimed that Ceviche de Hongos with black beans and lemon was the special of the day. "What is that?"

She shrugged. "I have no idea. It doesn't sell well in small-town Colorado. Although the people around here are free-spirited, their spirits still tend to like burgers and fries and ice box pie. Except for Henry and Nell. They're vegans. They protest here regularly."

Despite feeling sorry for himself, he felt his lips curl at the thought of the weird chick from the meadow protesting at a hole-in-the-wall diner. He tried to imagine the kind of man who married a woman like her. This Henry guy had to be a gentle soul who'd never once harmed another.

At one point in his life, he would have said people like that were naïve and deserved what the world gave them. But he was starting to think maybe those people needed to be protected. Maybe the strong of arm should protect the strong of heart.

Because scars could heal, and those naïve assholes out there still thought the scarred could be beautiful.

Because Callie, after all these years, still had that air of innocence about her.

The brunette from last night walked up to the table. She was dressed in jeans and a shirt with the diner's name across the chest. Her eyes were red and puffy. The night before had not been kind to her. Or rather, Stef hadn't. He couldn't forget how those two had gone at each other. Zane looked out the window as she talked to Callie, sensing she wouldn't want his pity.

He knew that feeling. He watched as people strolled down Main Street. Right down the road was the sheriff's office where he'd left Nate to deal with the reports required from last night and this morning. His stomach churned at the thought of what Nate intended to do. This afternoon Nate was going to call their old boss at the DEA. He was hoping to get some sort of backup. Zane was on Callie duty, and he couldn't think of anything he'd rather do.

Well, he'd be happier if they were back at her cabin. He didn't like to go out much anymore. Again, not a trait that led to gainful employment. She was really entrenched in this town. If he stayed here with her, where would he work?

"He's an asshole." The brunette, Jen—yeah, that was her name—had tears seeping from her eyes.

"Oh, sweetie, he's confused," Callie said, her hand reaching out to pat Jen's.

It had been like that all day. Wherever Callie went, hard luck stories found her. When the smoke had finally cleared and they salvaged what they could, he'd found Callie rocking a baby so one of the neighbors could grab a cup of coffee. A teen had begged her for a ride into Bliss, and Callie had obliged. Before they had even set foot in the station house, the crazy dude with the tin foil hat had run up to her and hugged her, telling her he was glad she hadn't been abducted. Apparently tragedies like fires or earthquakes were ripe opportunities for alien abductions. In the end, she'd ended up comforting the older man and promising him that some sort of detector thing would be here by the end of the week.

Callie had been a pretty butterfly, flitting around offering advice and comfort and an ear to bend to anyone she saw. Zane had been the big, hulking beast who followed her around.

No one was going to flatten his butterfly, damn it.

Jen sniffled. She looked Zane right in the eyes. "Well, I hope you're not an asshole."

Not sure what to say. "I'll have to work on that."

"You better. You take care of my friend or I swear I will…I don't know what I'll do, but it'll be bad."

The slender woman seemed perfectly serious. Zane had been intimidating all of his life because of his height and build. The scars had only added to his badass factor. People turned away from him in Dallas or stared in horrified fascination. Not this one, though. She'd said he was stunning. A fallen angel. She was a little crazy, but she seemed awful nice.

"Who's the asshole? You're Callie's friend. I'm Callie's man. I'll beat him up for you." He would get in good with Callie's friends. That seemed like a good thing to do. He might not be here for too long. Callie deserved far better than him, but he could certainly help her and her friends out in the short term.

"Stefan Talbot." Jen gave up the guy who hurt her really easily.

"Consider him broken." Zane sighed. Life was looking up. He'd wanted to kick that pompous rich boy's ass for years. Even more after the Bigfoot incident.

Callie poked her index finger at him like an enraged schoolteacher. "You most certainly will not, Zane Derek Hollister. You are going to behave yourself." She turned that judgmental finger on her friend. "And you are not going to put a hit on the man you love. He needs time. Give it to him. Pushing him will only make things worse. Now, we'll take the bacon cheeseburger loaded with fries and the special."

Jen nodded, and with a sigh of resignation, flounced off.

"I thought you said to avoid the special."

"Everyone avoids the special. It hurts Hal's feelings," she explained.

He reached for her hand. He loved how small it was in his. Small but solid. That was his girl. "You need a keeper."

Just like that, he was wondering if he wasn't exactly what she needed. Some douchebag rich boy would let everyone take advantage of her. Maybe she needed a guy who didn't care what people thought.

She grinned. "I kind of thought I had one."

Before Zane could reply, a sarcastic voice interrupted. "Well, damn, Cal. I thought I had to come rescue you, but it looks like you hired some muscle."

Zane glared up at the man who had walked into the diner and made a beeline for his woman. He looked like he'd ridden in off the range. A Stetson sat on his head. He wore jeans and boots and a shirt with pearl snaps. He stared at Zane for a moment and finally whistled.

"Damn, man, what does the other guy look like?"

"Max!" Callie turned to the newcomer, a startled look on her face.

He actually didn't mind. The cowboy was the first person he'd met in a long time to simply ask him about the scars. It should have made him self-conscious, but he found forthrightness put him at ease. "The other guy was actually ten guys, and they look pretty bad themselves. They drugged me and tied me down. They're mostly in prison."

The cowboy's eyebrows climbed into his Stetson. "Mostly?"

"I wasn't happy when I came to. Unfortunately for them, the only people in a position to help them were DEA agents. They were indisposed, and I managed a good ten minutes with a couple of them."

"Damn." The cowboy named Max slid into the booth beside Callie. His hand ran across the back of the booth. "That is impressive."

His arm went around Callie's shoulders, and Zane's blood pressure ticked up slightly, but Reasonable Guy was there, coming through for him with some sweet logic.

Everyone in the town is friends with Callie. Keep it cool. Keep the caveman buried.

Zane shook his head. "Nah, it was really just painful."

"So you with the DEA? What's drugs got to do with my girl Callie here?" Max squeezed her shoulders in a familiar way that had the caveman in Zane clawing to get out. Inner Asshole made an appearance.

If you break his arm, he won't be able to touch your woman with it.

When he thought about it, Inner Asshole was pretty logical, too.

He took a deep breath. His fingers tightened on the tabletop. He saw the way Callie playfully elbowed the cowboy. It did nothing to make him comfortable. It was past obvious that this Max fellow knew Callie really well. Max. That name triggered something in him. "It doesn't have anything to do with her. I'm not an agent anymore. And she isn't your girl."

"Really? You left a job like that?" Max completely ignored the important part. "Is that how you ended up as a bodyguard?" The cowboy reached over and grabbed Callie's coffee like he had a right to steal a sip.

He's being playful. They've been friends for a while and they're comfortable with each other. Explain who you are and he might back off. Reasonable Guy was still giving it a go.

"I'm not a bodyguard. I'm her boyfriend." That damn Max was riding an awfully thin line, but he had to think about more than his own possessive nature. Reasonable Guy was right. He should put the truth out there. "I'm one of her boyfriends, anyway."

Let that sink in. Maybe if he shocked backwoods Max, he would go away.

A big grin spread across the cowboy's face. He turned to Callie. "I hope the other one is a little smaller, darlin'." He took a long drink from Callie's mug. "This one looks like he could do some damage."

She flushed prettily and didn't seem to care that the jerk was drinking her coffee. "Max, you hush, and don't you say a word to Rye."

Just like that, it clicked. Max and Rye Harper were the twins she'd been in love with. They'd been the reason she wanted a ménage in the first place. This jerk with the perfect face was Callie's ideal man. He wasn't ridiculously oversized, and he didn't have a face full of scars. He probably didn't come with enough baggage to strangle an elephant, either. Old pretty-boy Max didn't have a past filled with regret. Max leaned over to Callie. He invaded her space.

"You know I gotta tell Rye, sweet thing. He's going to think it's real damn funny that you've taken to the lifestyle."

Max put a hand on Callie's head.

Zane listened for Reasonable Guy.

I got nothing. You should kill him.

And Inner Asshole took the reins.

He didn't even think about what he was doing. It was like watching a movie. He felt a bit outside of himself. He moved quickly, exiting his side of the booth, reaching for the asshole cowboy who dared to put a hand on his woman. He neatly picked him up by the throat and slammed him onto a nearby table. It was mere chance that it was empty.

"Zane!"

He heard Callie's outraged shout, but it seemed a far-off thing. There was only him and Max in that moment, and Zane needed to clear up a few issues before they could proceed. As for Callie, well, she'd made her choice the night before when she'd accepted him into her body. When she'd offered up that sweet pussy of hers, he'd taken more. She fucking belonged to him, and no goddamn cowboy was going to drink her coffee and touch her hair.

"Now, maybe we should talk about this, big guy." Max stared up at him, a slightly rueful expression on his face as though this wasn't his first time in this position. "You know, I think of her as my sister."

"You touch your sister's hair as often as you touch Callie's?" Zane wasn't letting him get off with that excuse. At least Talbot had taken a step back when he understood Zane and Nate had made their intentions plain.

"Yeah, but I'll be honest, Brooke is more like my daughter than my sister. I had to raise her after my mom died and my dad left town. I'm an affectionate guy. I swear on my unborn child's life that I have zero interest in Callie on a sexual level."

"Gee, thanks, Max," Callie said, sarcasm dripping as she stood beside him. Zane's hand was still wrapped around Max's throat, but he wasn't squeezing. Callie rolled those gorgeous dark eyes and sighed. "Do you mind, Zane? You're causing a scene."

He looked around the diner. Sure enough, every eye in the place was on them. Some were horrified at the scene and had cell phones in hand. Most, though, had big grins on their faces, including Stella, who was walking toward their table. She seemed completely unfazed by the potential ass kicking that was taking place in her establishment.

"Go rough on him," Stella said as she neatly placed their food on the table. "He deserves it." She looked at Callie. "I like your man, hon. He makes up for the other one. You gotta talk to the sheriff, girl. He keeps ticketing the tourists. I need the tourists in a good mood." She frowned as she looked down at Max. "You know, I've been around enough of these crazy threesomes to know that there's a hardass and a sweet one." She patted Zane's scarred face. "You're the sweet one, hon. You get free fries."

She walked off, her boots ringing across the floor.

"Damn," Max said, turning his head to watch Stella. "I don't get free fries. Cal, I think Stella thinks I'm the hardass. She doesn't know Rye at all, damn it. I am completely misunderstood."

A few things fell into place, and Zane let his hand drift to his side. "You're in a threesome?"

Max sat up and felt his neck for damage. "I don't consider it a threesome. It's a marriage. My brother and I are married to a lovely woman named Rachel. We have a baby on the way." A sly grin crossed his face. "Did you think you were shocking me, city boy?"

He wasn't sure how to answer that. He had thought it would shock him.

Max gave him a good-natured punch in the arm. "Nothing shocks a Bliss boy." His face suddenly went cold and dark, and Zane decided he'd completely underestimated the cowboy. "But we take our relationships serious, you understand? I wasn't joking. Callie's like my sister. You play around with her, and you deal with me and Rye."

"I'm not playing," Zane said automatically.

Max seemed to take his measure. Callie's arm wound around Zane's waist, and he pulled her close, waiting for the judgment of her childhood friend.

"All right then," Max said, scooting back into the booth. "As long as we understand each other."

This time Zane pulled Callie along and pushed her gently toward his side of the booth. Her sardonic look let him know she didn't miss his reasons for changing the seating arrangement. He slung an arm around her possessively but decided to play the white knight as well. She needed someone who looked out for her. He passed the amazing-looking cheeseburger over to her.

Callie looked up at him. "But I ordered the burger for you."

He winked at her and picked up the fork that went with the ceviche. "I'd like to try the special, babe. You take the burger."

He was surprised to find he really liked ceviche de hongos with black beans and lemon, and he was starting to like Bliss.

Chapter Nine

Nate hung up the phone and felt his stomach drop. It was worse than he could imagine. There really was a bounty on Zane's head, or rather on his chest, and there was next to nothing the authorities could do about it. It was all rumors. No one undercover was willing to risk his or her assignment for an agent who had gone down in a blaze of questionable behavior. He knew Zane hadn't done anything wrong, but his cover had been blown and no one had an explanation for how Ellis had come to find out Zane was a cop. Zane had left the agency without trying to fight for his job, but then he'd never really tried to fit in there in the first place. He wasn't a "climb the ladder" kind of guy.

Luckily, Nate was. Nate understood how important contacts were. Special Agents Ben Leander and Marcus Worthington were on their way to Bliss. He'd had to call in a couple of favors, but now they had some backup. Ben and Marcus were two of the best-connected men the agency had.

Nate sat back in his chair. His head was starting to pound. He'd had to promise his old boss that he would give serious consideration to coming back in three months. It meant breaking the deal he had with Stefan. Stef might understand, but he had to consider Callie and Zane. He always meant to return to the DEA once Zane was back on his feet. He'd been on the fast track there, and he'd been told what happened with Zane hadn't touched him. He would move up in the DEA and then look for a job in Washington. He might never get back the money his father had lost, but he could support Callie in the way she should be supported. He could give her a good life. He would find something for Zane. They would work it out.

He would buy a place with a guest house, and Zane could "live" there. Nate would marry Callie, and no one needed to know what their arrangement was.

That could work, right?

Of course, before they could figure out their living arrangements, he needed to deal with the problem at hand. Why were the Barbarians coming after Zane and not him? The question nagged at Nate. They had both testified in the trial that sent Ellis to jail. They had him locked up good and tight. The arrests and the trials were all solid. Years and years of information gathering had led to numerous arrests and the end of the largest drug operation in the southwest. Some of the group had gotten away, but given how large the operation had been, that wasn't so surprising. The fact that any of them would risk getting caught meant Ellis was damn serious about hurting Zane. They hadn't found all the money, but otherwise it had been a highly successful operation.

Those years with the Barbarians played in his mind. Zane had fit in there better than he had at the DEA. There was no bureaucratic bullshit to deal with or cocktail parties to attend. There was beer to drink. There were women to fuck and drugs to move. Zane had been damn good with the women and not at all bad with being the muscle Ellis needed to keep his business working. Nate had taken on the "guy who would do anything" role. It didn't get him close to Ellis, but it kept him and Zane safe. No one wanted to mess with Nate Rush.

If only his reputation could keep them safe now.

He needed to find a place to stash Zane and Callie until he'd figured out how to get the Barbarians off their backs. Their place was a no-go. The front room was a wreck. He didn't want to risk going to Callie's. It would be too easy to figure out who the woman from the bar was and where she lived.

He heard the door to the station open. Zane and Callie were

talking as they walked in, joking about something that had happened at the diner. Nate's cock responded almost immediately as she laughed. He hardened painfully at the sound of her voice. The night before played through his head. She'd been so sweet. She'd opened herself to them and never made a complaint when they took her over and over, trading places, giving her not a second to catch her breath before one of them was on top of her again.

Callie smiled as she opened the door to his office and held out a white bag emblazoned with red lettering stating proudly it came from Stella's Diner, established 1970. "Brought you some lunch."

Zane crowded behind her, his hands skimming her hips. "I tried to get you the special, but Callie insisted on a boring old cheeseburger."

Her face lit up as she passed Nate the bag. "Zane made a friend. Hal, the cook at Stella's, now thinks he hung the moon. Seriously, he's half in love with Zane because he ate the special."

Zane shrugged and threw his big body into the chair across from Nate's desk. It was the first time Nate had seen his best friend look comfortable in months, maybe in years. Zane's face was open for once. Callie had done that. One more thing to be grateful to her for. He reached out and ignored the burger, preferring to pull her into his lap. It might make him a bastard, but he had to have her. Right here. Right now.

"Oh!" Callie gasped. Nate circled her waist and planted his face in the nape of her neck. It had only been a couple of hours, but he'd missed her. Callie wiggled, and her ass was right across Nate's erection.

"Should I lock the door?" Zane had one eyebrow elevated. He looked ready to join in on the fun Nate had planned.

"No," Callie protested.

"Yes." Nate moved a hand up to her thigh. He thought about the stuff he'd saved from the cabin. It was sitting in his bag at Zane's feet. It contained everything they needed. They'd used Zane's stash the night before, but Nate had always been better prepared than his friend.

Zane moved quickly, locking the door to his office with a click.

"Sheriff, this is incredibly unprofessional." Callie sounded breathless, but she attempted to sit up.

He wasn't about to let that happen. "No, Ms. Sheppard. You will mind me. I'm your boss. You're my secretary."

She went still in his arms. He worried for a moment, but then he felt a little shaking in her chest. She was giggling.

"Seriously? You want to play right here, right now?"

He didn't want to play. He *needed* to play. He had a few hours before those DEA agents would show up and he would be confronted with his old life. He needed to be here with her, in the moment.

"I think we need to go over a few of your new duties, Ms. Sheppard."

She turned her head and grinned at him. "New duties, huh? I take it you're talking about something other than filing and sorting."

"You better believe it." He gave her a tiny shove, and she was on her feet. The small office suddenly seemed overly full with all three of them inside, but it felt perfectly intimate to him. "Slide your skirt off and hand it to Zane. He knows what to do with it."

Her mouth crooked up, but she seemed to be game. Sweet Callie was a dirty girl underneath all that sugar. His heart skipped as he thought about it. She was a dirty girl for them and only them. She'd never been down and filthy with anyone else because she'd never really wanted anyone else. It made Nate feel ten feet tall.

Her hands went to the back of her skirt. She fumbled with it, the gracelessness of the act endearing to his mind. He looked at Zane, expecting hot anticipation on his face, but there was a smile there instead. It was the goofy smile of a man insanely into a girl who was hot for him, too. It was probably a lot like the smile on his own face.

She managed to undo the button on her skirt. He heard the sweet sound of the zipper sliding down and then she pushed the skirt off, revealing inch after inch of skin. She was lightly tan without a single tan line. He got hard as hell thinking about how Callie had managed that. He could see her sitting by the river in nothing but her own perfect skin. He would love to lie next to her, feeling the warmth of the sun caressing him.

Of course, professional men with a mind toward a big-time career didn't sunbathe naked.

He shoved the thought aside as she handed Zane her skirt.

"I do know exactly what to do with this, babe." Zane tossed the skirt in the trash can next to Nate's desk.

Nate gave him a thumbs-up. Callie didn't need clothes. "On the desk, baby. Spread your legs."

"I'm going to need that skirt back," she said as she dutifully hoisted herself onto the desk. It was neat, but she had to move a few files. She spread her legs and couldn't seem to stop giggling. "This is starting to feel an awful lot like a gynecological exam. I'm not sure how sexy that is."

He sighed as he looked at that gorgeous, plump pussy. She kept it perfectly shaved. He looked forward to performing that task for her. It would be a sweet intimacy.

"I bet your gynecologist doesn't spend a lot of time thinking about how pretty your pussy is." Zane stood beside him staring down like he was appreciating a great work of art.

Her head came up. "I would hope not. She's almost seventy and has seven grandkids."

"I also bet she doesn't do this." Nate got on his knees. He leaned over and pressed a kiss on her pussy.

Callie's head fell back. "Definitely not, Sheriff."

He pressed kisses all over her pussy. Light butterfly caresses that had her quivering. Her clit started to peek out of its hood. "I like the way you call me *Sheriff*, darlin'. It makes me think of putting you in handcuffs and giving you a full body search. As a matter of fact, maybe we should do a little probing. What do you say, Deputy?"

Zane rolled his eyes. "No way. I am not your deputy, but I will most definitely help probe her. I have the perfect instrument we should use."

He had something else in mind. "That'll have to wait. If you grab that bag and look inside you might find what we need. It's clean and ready to be lubed up."

"It?" Callie asked with wide, curious eyes.

"Yep," he replied. He took hold of her thighs and neatly flipped her over. "Put that pretty ass in the air, Miss Sheppard."

"Nice. When did you have time to buy a butt plug?" Zane held the small pink plug in his hand as he poured lube across the plastic and readied it.

"Maybe we should talk about this." Callie sounded uncertain, but she didn't move from her place on the desk. She got on her hands and knees. Her heart-shaped ass was right there. He'd never be able to sit at this desk again without thinking about her gorgeous ass ripe and ready for use.

"No talking, Cal. You want to fuck us both, right?" Zane handed Nate the plug and his hand reached out to trace the curves of her ass. "We have to get you ready. We have to play with this hot ass of yours before we can fuck it."

Zane had hit the nail on the head. Nate wanted to get his cock in that tight ass. He wanted to screw her ass while Zane fucked her pussy. He wanted her between them.

He took the plug and nodded at Zane, who still held the lube in his hand. He knew what to do. He poured a line of slick lubricant in between her cheeks.

"Let me spread those for you," Zane said, his voice even deeper than usual. His eyes were caught on the globes of her ass. Zane's left hand came across the small of Callie's back. He gripped her and slowly pulled until Nate was able to see the puckered beauty of her backside. It was tight and closed. It would take work to get that gorgeous hole to admit him inside. His dick throbbed in anticipation.

Callie shuddered, her hips shaking slightly. Nate frowned.

"Baby, if you don't want to do this, all you have to do is say it." He didn't want to push her.

"Bullshit she doesn't want it. She wants it. I can smell how much she wants it." Zane breathed deeply and his sigh was all satisfaction.

"Maybe so, but it's rude to talk about it." Callie sounded prim and proper even with her asshole on display.

"Get used to it," Nate shot back. Now he could see that her pussy was dripping. She did want it. She wanted everything they could give her. "We won't be polite with you. There won't be anything staid about the way we fuck you. You're ours. We'll take you when we want, how we want. Be glad you don't wear panties, baby, because I'd simply rip them off when I wanted to fuck my pussy. And this pretty ass is ours, too."

Nate lined up the head of the plug and pushed in. The tight muscles refused him entry.

"Babe, you gotta relax. You gotta press back against the plug." Zane gave her soothing advice.

"Really, Zane? Done this much?" She didn't seem to be in the mood for advice. It was the most irritated he'd ever heard her.

Zane flushed. "No, but I've watched an awful lot of porn. You can learn the damnedest things on the Internet. Listen, babe, I am open-minded. If you do this and later on it leads to my dick sinking into this gorgeous asshole, I promise I'll let you play with mine."

"Me, too, baby." Nate wanted in so bad, he'd promise her the moon. He could take his sweet Callie playing around with his backdoor if it meant regularly getting inside hers.

She groaned and leaned forward, going down on her elbows. The plug slid in as her rosy ass opened up. It was a lovely site. Nate worked the plug in and out gently. He fucked her with the plug, pretending it was his cock taking the virgin hole.

Zane groaned beside him. He was watching, too. He was probably thinking the same thing. Nate slid the plug in and pulled back out, noting the way Callie began to sway with the rhythm.

"Not so bad, huh?" Nate asked, adoring the way she clenched around the plug.

"It's weird, but okay. I can handle it. I think it might feel good."

Zane leaned over and kissed the small of her back. "It will, babe. It's gonna feel so good. I promise, we'll go slow. We'll take care of you."

Nate pressed the plug in one last time before he decided it was time to take care of her. She'd done beautifully for her first time. Next time, he'd have her wear it for a while, but for now, he wanted her comfortable. He needed to pay her back for her openness. He pulled the plug out and dropped it discreetly in his desk drawer. Luckily, he was responsible for cleaning his own office.

"That was lovely. Now turn back over."

Callie flipped herself around, just a tad awkwardly. "Are you done?"

"Not by a long shot, babe. Now it's your turn," Zane said, proving he could read Nate's mind.

Her face was covered in a pretty blush. Her legs dangled off the desk. Nate reached down and rearranged them so her knees were up, her heels on the edge. It left her open and vulnerable.

"Let me taste this pussy." Nate let his fingers find her soft flesh, and she squirmed as he cupped her.

"Only if I can taste you and Zane after. I want you both in my mouth."

It took everything Nate had not to come in his jeans. He would fuck her mouth if that was what she wanted. He'd fill her up. But first, she was going to come and come hard under his tongue.

"That sounds perfect. Why don't you start on Zane, baby? I'll join in after I've taken care of you."

Zane moved from Nate's side. Nate looked over the expanse of Callie's beautifully bowed body. Zane was pushing his jeans down. Callie's head was at the edge of the desk. Zane cupped her chin and turned her head to the side. He pressed his cock against her lips. Her tongue came out, licking at the head. Zane put a knee on the desk so she didn't have to strain as he slid his cock into her mouth.

He knew how good that felt. He loved it when that hot tongue ran all across his cock. She gave the best head. It was only fair she got some back. Nate breathed in her scent. Cream coated her pink pussy with a sweet, musky smell. His cock twitched. He leaned down and licked, gathering her juice as he went. He licked her over and over. She tasted so good. He slid his tongue through her labia and up to her clit. That pink pearl was fully out of its hood and begging for attention. Nate sucked it into his mouth and tugged gently.

"Oh, Nate!" Callie's legs shook as she came. Her hands wound into his hair, tugging and pulling as she pushed her pussy against his face.

Nate got to his feet and his hand was on the fly of his pants when there was a knock on the door.

"Sheriff." Logan's voice cracked through the intimacy of the office.

Callie sat straight up and started fumbling for her skirt.

"Not right now, Logan," Nate barked. He wasn't going to interrupt this because Logan had trouble with a tourist.

"Sorry, Sheriff. I think it's important," Logan insisted.

Damn it. His cock would have to wait at least as long as it took to murder his deputy.

Zane cursed, too, but stuffed his cock back in his jeans. He helped Callie zip up her skirt. Nate nodded at Zane and sat back in his chair, pulling Callie into his lap. He needed her. He didn't want his deputy to see that he had a monster erection.

Rye Harper had the right idea. He'd been the one to put up that sign that announced he was fishing. Nate needed a new one.

Don't Commit Any Crimes – I'm Fucking My Secretary.

Zane unlocked the door and it swung open, revealing a red-faced Logan with a piece of paper in his hand.

Logan looked from Callie and Nate over to Zane and back again. His mouth came open and then closed. "Okay, well, I just wanted to tell you that some crazy-looking chick walked in a couple of minutes ago and handed me this note."

He held the folded piece of paper out toward Nate. Callie struggled to get off his lap, but he held her close. It was time for Callie to understand he had no intention of hiding the fact that they were lovers.

"Give it to Zane," he instructed. If he took his hands off Callie, he'd lose her. He fully intended to get back to his fun the minute he got rid of his deputy. Hell, he'd simply lift her up and bring her down on his dick.

Logan handed the paper to Zane, who immediately opened it and started to read.

Nate cuddled Callie close. She sighed and shook her head, as though trying to get him to understand how disappointed she was in his professionalism. He ignored her. He'd explained that he had no professionalism when it came to her. She would have to learn to live with it. "Thank you, Logan. Why don't you go and write the tourists some tickets? We could use a new microwave."

Callie slapped at him softly as Logan walked out. "He will be on the phone to his moms, his girlfriend, and everyone else he knows in just about…now. Do you know how the gossip mill works in a small town?"

Nate didn't care. Let 'em talk. "You don't think staying at our place last night escaped the town's attention? How about what happened this morning? Baby, I assure you they noticed you were in Zane's T-shirt and clinging to one of us most of the time."

He pulled her close. This was what he'd wanted since that first day when he walked in and realized how close he would be working with her. He cuddled her close and was satisfied when she softened against him, her head lying against his shoulder. He kissed her cheek and was about to tell Zane to lock that door again when he saw the look on his partner's face. Zane had gone white, his jaw tight. A slight tick in the muscle of his left cheek let him know his friend was deeply disturbed. After the events of the morning, he had a bad feeling who the note had come from.

Well, at least he didn't have an erection anymore.

Callie was watching Zane now, too.

Nate sat up. "What is it?"

"Bullshit, that's all." Zane folded the note again, and Nate could tell he was trying for a nonchalant look. "So, we checking into a motel or what? I don't think we should stay at Callie's. I wouldn't want someone chucking a fire bomb into her house."

"Let me see the note." Nate leaned forward. Callie hopped off his lap and went to sit in the chair beside Zane.

"Who was the note from?" Callie's voice cajoled, her hand rubbing a circle over Zane's denim-clad thigh.

Zane tossed the note on the desk. "He's someone Nate and I knew a long time back."

Nate unfolded the note, all that arousal he'd had a few moments before turning into anxiety. "Shit. How the fuck does this bastard run things from his prison cell?"

The note was from Ellis, though not in his handwriting. The "crazy-looking chick" must be one of the women from the gang.

"He probably dictated it to his lawyer." Zane's face was perfectly smooth. To an outsider, it would look like he didn't care, but he could see the wheels working in Zane's head. "You know some of those lawyers are as bad as the assholes they represent."

The note was simple.

Give up Zane or else.

It didn't list a place to drop him off or give them a time limit. Just a simple threat. That was Ellis's way. He would never tell you what he was going to do. He would rather his victim wondered. Nate let his gaze find Callie. She tried to get Zane to hold her hand, but he merely squeezed it and let it go again, shifting to get out of reach.

He knew in that moment that Zane was going to leave. Oh, he wouldn't tell them. He would wait until they weren't watching him and he would sneak off in a stupid attempt to sacrifice himself for the greater good. It would break Callie's heart. It wouldn't do much good for him, either.

"We need to think about moving Callie to someplace safe." He didn't want to get into it with Zane while she was around. It would worry her if they came to blows, and they just might. But when she was otherwise occupied, he was going to lay down the damn law with his partner.

Zane sat forward. He seemed perfectly happy to talk about something other than that note. "Absolutely. Maybe you should take her away for a while. You know, the two of you could go on vacation, maybe to the beach."

Or they could have this out here and now.

Callie sat back, her mouth open in shock. "I'm not leaving. This is my home. I already had this fight with Stef. Why would I leave?"

Zane's face hardened. "Because it isn't safe for you. I don't know if you noticed, but someone's tried to kill you twice in the last twenty-four hours."

"And I'm perfectly fine, thank you." She stood up and crossed her arms defensively over her chest. "I'm going to make some coffee and check the phones. I still have a job to do, you know."

The minute Callie was out of sight, Nate leaned forward. "Whatever you're thinking about doing, don't."

Zane's mouth was a flat, stubborn line. "You know it's for the best. I'll sit in that fucking bar until they come for me. I won't go in alone this time. I'll pack some serious heat."

He would go down in a blaze of glory. Nate got the message. Only he'd made a promise to himself that Zane wouldn't go down period. "Just sit tight. I've got this handled."

"Like you handled it last time?"

The words cut through Nate like a knife to his heart. He felt himself pale as though he'd gone bloodless, and his eyes weren't looking at Zane anymore, at least not the one in front of him. He saw Zane as he'd been that afternoon, laid out on a table, his skin smoking, blood leaking out onto the floor. When he'd uncuffed his partner, the big bull had managed to get up and beat the living shit out of a couple of his tormentors. It was only when he passed out from blood loss that he went down. He'd fallen and hit his head on a mounting block and slipped into a coma.

Nate hadn't been able to catch him in time. He could remember how hard he'd tried to get to him, how the whole world seemed to slow down, but no matter how hard he tried, he wasn't fast enough. He'd failed so terribly.

"Did you hear me?" Zane's rough voice brought him back to reality. "I won't let her get hurt."

Blood rushed back into Nate's body, pumping through his muscles with an angry vengeance. Damn it, how much did he have to do to make up for his mistake? Should he have rushed in to save Zane, guns blazing, when they were terribly outnumbered? He'd made the right call that day when he went for backup, and he was making the right one now.

"You think I intend to throw her to the wolves to save your ass?" Resentment bubbled up. He'd put his career on hold to take care of Zane, and had the bastard once said thank you? Now he wanted to accuse him of putting Callie in danger? "Let me tell you something, I will let them carve you up if it means sparing her a moment's pain, do you understand?"

Zane growled, baring his teeth. "Yeah, I got it, buddy. At least we're in agreement on something. So, I'll go and take care of this, once and for all. I would think you would be thrilled. You get the girl and ride off into the sunset, Sheriff."

Nate's fists came down on his desk, making the thing shudder. "Why do you insist on killing yourself? You know what? I'm tired to death of forcing you to live. You want to give Ellis the satisfaction of taking you apart, then go the fuck ahead. Who am I to stop you?"

Zane stood, shoving the chair back against the wall. He took up a lot of space in the small office. If only he had a big brain to go along with his bulk. Nate stood, too, facing down his oldest friend in the world.

"What are you waiting for, asshole?" Nate spat the question out. "The door is that way. I'll take care of Callie, don't you worry about it. I'll take her out of this two-bit town and show her a real life. We won't remember you at all."

He didn't mean a word of it. Even as the words spilled from his mouth, he knew that he would miss Zane. He would miss his friend forever, and there would be a hole no one else could fill. Why was he such a stubborn ass?

Zane hesitated. His face fell, but in the space of one breath to the next, he became hard as stone. "You don't know her at all. She's nothing but a freaking trophy to you, rich boy. You can't take her away from here. This is her home."

"Her home is with me and where I decide to make it." Even if Zane stayed, that held true. Nate was the only one of the three of them with a lick of ambition. Callie was a sweet thing, and Zane spent all of his time reading books and watching baseball. It was up to him. He would pull them along and make a brighter future for all of them. Zane and Callie had grown up without. They had no idea what real money could do for them. Callie lived in a run-down, two-bedroom cabin. Zane had grown up in a shitty apartment in a nasty section of town. When he found a proper job, Nate would make sure she had the best house they could afford, where any kids they had would have every advantage money could buy. He would use his old connections to make her comfortable in society. She would adjust.

Zane shook his head. "Man, she's not some high-society girl, and she never will be. She will never be some country-club woman. The girl likes to spend most of her time naked. How is that going to fit in at one of your charity balls? Face it, rich boy, your money's gone. You're down here in the mud with the rest of us, and you're going to stay here."

Nate's blood was boiling, bubbling right under his calm surface. Zane knew where to thrust that knife in. All of Nate's life he'd been groomed to take over his family's business. He'd rebelled when he joined the DEA, but the ambition that had been bred into him never went away. Now that the family business and money were all gone due to bad investments, a crooked accountant, and the condition of the economy, it was up to Nate to get his position back. It didn't matter that Callie had grown up here. Everyone had to leave the nest eventually.

It was a home with no future. He couldn't move up here. He couldn't get back what he'd lost in Bliss, Colorado. The most he could hope for here was another term as sheriff. No matter how nice the people were, Bliss was a dead-end town. "You won't have to worry about us, man. You'll have done your duty and sacrificed yourself. You've been trying to commit suicide for years. Well, I won't stop you anymore."

He would. Nate would lock his ass up if he had to, but he wanted to play this out to the end.

Zane was the very picture of half-contained rage. His muscles bunched and corded, his eyes flared. "I didn't have to commit suicide, asshole. I just had to follow you. You think I wanted to join the fucking DEA? I went to make sure you didn't get yourself killed."

The words rolled out of Nate's mouth before he could think to take them back. "Well, you could have saved yourself the trouble. I wasn't the one who fucked up and blew my cover."

When the punch came, it caught him across the face, and Nate's head snapped back with an audible crack. His eyes closed against the blinding pain of every nerve in his face firing off. He reached his hand up to wipe the blood away. Zane stared at him as though he wanted to apologize but couldn't force the words out of his stubborn mouth. It didn't matter. He wouldn't have accepted an apology. He needed something way more painful than an apology. This was a long time coming and something inside him thrilled at the thought of a fight.

Nate launched himself across the desk with no thought other than beating some sense into his oldest friend in the world.

The lamp on his desk fell to the floor with a crash. Zane shouted something, but Nate's focus had narrowed. He pulled back his arm and brought it down with every bit of force he could muster.

Zane fell back with a groan as Nate's fist met with his face. Zane was bigger, but Nate had always compensated by being more vicious. He didn't pull his punches, and he didn't pause to breathe. Zane was his punching bag, and he took all of his pent-up anger out on his big body. He got in a swift upper-cut to Zane's chin. He landed a fist on Zane's eye and noticed there was blood on his hands. His? Zane's? Didn't matter.

Zane finally managed to kick him off. Nate had the breath knocked out of him as Zane's knee got him in the stomach. His ribs ached, and his back hit the desk. He lay there for a moment, taking in the extent of his injuries. Then Zane grunted, and Nate knew they weren't done yet. Before Zane could get the drop on him, he brought up the heel of his boot and kicked him squarely in the nuts. Zane went down with a whimper, falling back into the chair he'd previously occupied.

"You motherfucker." Zane moaned, cupping himself.

Nate wiped the blood off his nose. He was pretty sure it wasn't broken. "Yeah, well, I'm not letting you sacrifice your ass to the Barbarians. We'll find a safe place to hole up and figure out what they want with you."

"Damn it, they want my head," Zane shot back. He shifted in the chair. "If they don't get mine, they'll take yours or Callie's." He let his head fall back, and his eyes closed. Zane seemed infinitely weary. "I'm tired of all of it. It isn't worth it, man."

"You are so selfish. You always have been." Nate managed to push his body up to a sitting position. He hissed slightly as he twisted. Damn, Zane knew where to kick a guy. He'd feel that impact for days. "Have you thought at all about how this affects Callie? The last time we left her, she was alone for six years. She's not some girl you pick up in a bar and leave behind the next morning. She deserves better than that."

Zane wiped blood from a cut under his right eye. "I never promised her anything."

"You promised you would take care of her."

"That's what I'm trying to do."

Nate's fists clenched. He was just about ready to start the fight again. The first beating hadn't gotten through Zane's thick skull. "You can't take care of her if you're dead. Who's to say that they won't come after me next? Should I go lie down and die, too?"

Zane kicked out. His boot caught the edge of the desk, making it shake.

"You think I want to die?" His hands shook, but he stopped and took a breath. He sat like that for a moment. "Fuck you, Nate. Maybe what I want is to be free of you. Maybe I want to start living my life without having to measure up to your standards. I am leaving, and there's nothing you can do about it."

The door slammed open, and Nate's head swung around. He noticed Zane was looking, too, his face as white as a sheet.

"Callie, baby," Zane started, but the words fell away.

There were tears shimmering in her eyes as she looked between the two of them. "You two through beating on each other?"

Nate noticed she was holding something in her hand. It dangled at the side, a nest of brightly colored vines flowing through her fingers.

Zane's face went mulish again. "We're done. Now, I gotta go. I have something to take care of. Nate can take care of you the rest of the day."

He pushed himself out of his chair, but Callie didn't move. Zane stared at his boots, obviously unwilling to force his way past her.

"Callie, it's just something we do from time to time," Nate tried to explain. It was true. At least once a year, he and Zane had it out. It was a guy thing. Callie paid him absolutely no attention.

"Tell me something, Zane," she began. Her lower lip trembled ever so slightly. "Was I going to get another note? At least last time no one knew about it. I didn't have to deal with the town pitying poor Callie, who can't keep a man to save her life. If you wanted to leave, if it didn't mean anything, why did you tell one of my oldest friends that I was your woman?"

Zane shrugged. He didn't look up. Callie might not know it, but it was a sure sign that whatever came out of Zane's mouth next was a complete lie. "I'm a good-time guy, darlin'. I like to fuck a pretty lady, and last night you were hot as hell. This morning, I want to move on. I don't mean to hurt you, babe. I'm not the kind of man who settles down."

"He's being a self-sacrificing idiot." Nate scrambled off the desk and forced his way in between them. He reached for her free hand. Despite the righteous ache in his bones, he felt the need to defend Zane, even against himself. "Don't believe a word he says."

Nate was surprised to discover his heart pounding. He knew why he was trying to save the big idiot's life, but he was also trying to save the relationship—between the three of them. It was important.

"You stay out of this. It's between me and Callie." Zane stared past him at Callie.

She turned to Nate. "I'm not stupid, Sheriff. I know he's lying, but in a way, he's not. I can't mean that much to him if he's willing to walk away without a fight."

Zane shrugged and gave her a grin that had Nate wincing. There was a wealth of arrogance on Zane's face. It was his "I'm an asshole" expression. "What can I say? I'm that kind of guy. I'd rather not fight, babe. It's easier to walk away."

She held up the nest of wires in her hand. "I'm glad you like to walk. This is a good portion of your motorcycle's electrical system. I trashed it. I grew up with three brothers. They might not have been blood, but they taught me things all the same. I also punched holes in your tires and took a club to the headlight. You might have heard that if you hadn't been beating on each other. You want to walk out on me, Zane? You *will* walk."

Zane took the wiring from her hands, his face a study in complete disbelief. "Goddamn it, Cal. How could you do that? It won't work. I'll get it fixed, and I'll be out of here by sunset."

"Where are you going to get it fixed?" She held her cell up, mocking him. It was pink with fake diamonds all over it. It was ridiculously feminine, like Callie, and just like its owner, it could do far more damage than one could imagine. "I already called all the mechanics in town who might be able to do the work. They won't have a place for you for weeks. They're already calling their buddies in Del Norte and Creede. You'll have to get that bike to Alamosa if you want it fixed, and no one will tow it for you. Good luck pushing it a hundred miles down the highway."

She turned. Zane's hand shot out, hauling her back. Nate watched warily. Zane wouldn't hurt her physically, but Nate was ready to beat the crap out of him if he pressed her further.

Zane had dropped the playboy act. His anguish bled through his eyes. "It won't work. Damn it, can't you see I'm doing this because I love you?"

A shadow crossed her face. "No, you don't."

"I am willing to die for you." Every word out of Zane's mouth sounded tortured.

"I know, but you're not willing to live for me. That's what I need. I'm nothing more than some fantasy to the two of you. I'm not real." Her shoulders slumped as she turned. "I found us a place to stay until you figure all of this out. It's well protected, and no one can sneak up on it. It's on high ground in an old fort, but the group has kept it up well. We have rooms there. One for each of us."

Nate crowded out Zane and reached for her now. Why was he getting punished? He wasn't the one walking away. "Callie, I told you I'm not hiding our relationship."

"No, but you're planning a life with a woman I don't know," she accused softly. "Zane is right. I'm never going to fit in where you need me. It's best if we call it all off now. I think the two of you should stay in Bliss until this group is caught. After that, Nate can head to wherever will give him the best salary, Zane can sit in a bar and drink himself to death, and I can move to Denver and go back to school."

A savage anger swept over him. If he thought he'd been pissed at Zane, that was nothing compared to what he felt now. He had to force his hands to relax or he would bruise her. "You'll go with me when I leave, darlin'. Make no mistake about it."

The wary look on Callie's face satisfied him. It didn't match her words. "I won't."

Zane pushed against him. "Babe, you have to let me go."

"I will. When you're safe, you can go wherever you like. You see, I love you, Zane. It doesn't matter that you don't love me. It doesn't matter that neither of you loves me. I'll keep you safe if it's the last thing I do, and then we can all move on."

"I have no intention of moving on without you." Nate growled the words. Damn it, he wasn't moving anywhere without either one of them. He needed them. He needed Zane for friendship and Callie as his lover. They were his soul mates. Somehow he'd gotten two, and he wouldn't lose either one.

Her eyes were clear now, though Nate could read the steady strength in them. "It's not your choice. We're playing by my rules now. We should get going. We need to meet with the director so he can go over the community guidelines. We'll stay there while we sort this out. I've called a town meeting for tonight at eight. If some biker gang is threatening us, then we need to get the town involved."

She pulled away from him. He checked the need to haul her into his arms. He wanted to show her that he wouldn't be dismissed. He wouldn't go down easy. There would be time for that when she'd calmed down. He had zero intention of sleeping alone tonight, but arguing wouldn't help. He'd have to get physical. She was responsive. She wouldn't be able to turn him down if he turned her on. "Where is this safe place?"

She paused at the doorway, her brown eyes slightly humorous. "The safest place I know—the nudist colony."

Nate groaned. He was never going to survive the day.

Chapter Ten

The big office was exactly as she remembered it. It had been almost a year since she'd been in this space. The pool, the grounds, that was a different story, but she'd seen little of the inside of Mountain and Valley Naturist Community.

"Hello, Callie. It is so good to see you again, sweetheart." Bill Hartman opened his arms, and Callie walked right in. He enfolded her in a hug. She heard Zane's gasp, or maybe it was Nate's. Probably Nate's. He was the one who could be the most easily offended. After all, Bill Hartman was completely naked as he hugged her.

Callie ignored him. It didn't matter what either of them thought. They were going to leave her, so she didn't have to care about what upset them.

"You, too, Bill. I'm grateful you could accommodate us." She broke off the embrace and stood back, taking in the man her mother had loved. He had never lived with them, but he'd funneled money their way. He'd been the reason her mother was comfortable in her final days.

He pulled away. Bill's clear blue eyes gazed down on hers, and Callie felt a bit strange. She was wearing clothes in a place where she had always felt comfortable being herself. Now she warred with the instinct to keep her armor tightly in place. She didn't want to be naked in front of Nate and Zane. Naked in front of them meant something different.

Bill nodded as though coming to a decision. Callie was pretty sure she knew what it was. He was going to let her choice to be clothed go unquestioned for now. Callie felt infinitely grateful. Bill took a step back and walked around to the chair behind his desk. He sat and indicated she should as well. There was only the heavy leather couch, and Nate and Zane were already there. They had left a spot for her in the center, but it would be tight. She sat down gingerly, trying to maintain her own space.

"I've informed our security team to keep a watch," Bill began. "We'll patrol the area on a regular basis to make sure no one sneaks up on us. And of course we'll have someone monitoring the security cameras at all times."

Zane's arm slid across the back of the sofa. She sat forward, avoiding his touch.

"We appreciate it," she said politely.

"You have patrols? And security cameras? What kind of security does a nudist colony need?" Nate asked with all the subtlety of a bull.

"Naturist, please, Sheriff," Bill corrected with not a drop of condescension in his voice. Of course, he was used to people belittling his lifestyle. They all were. "We're a small community, but we need the same things others need. We've beefed up our security recently. We now have cameras at every entrance, and we've made certain that our living quarters are safe. We're isolated. That has advantages and disadvantages. It gives us the freedom to live as we choose but leaves us open to those who would take from us. We're a wealthy community. We must protect ourselves."

Beside her, Nate was now sitting up straight as an arrow. "You said you recently upped your security. What's gone on that made you feel the need?"

Bill shook his head. "Times change. We recently reevaluated and chose to refresh our protocols. Rest assured, we can protect Callie and your friend. Our position on the mountain is unassailable. We know if someone sets foot anywhere close to the actual living area of our community. We own about two thousand acres of land on and down the mountain. Our closest neighbor is a horse ranch where the former sheriff lives. He has good security, as well, so we watch out for each other. My point is that as long as you stay on the grounds, we should be able to protect you."

"Exactly how will you protect us?" Nate's voice took on a harsh, suspicious air.

Zane's hand found the back of Callie's neck, and he cupped her nape in his big palm, the connection so sweet that it took her a second to remember that it wasn't real. She stood suddenly while Nate continued to interrogate the director.

"You better have a permit for every gun you keep in this place."

Bill's gaze went positively arctic. It was at times like this that Callie remembered the sixty-year-old had once been a Special Forces soldier. He'd also run a monumentally successful business. He'd retired at forty and spent his time running his true love, this peaceful community.

"Sheriff, I believe you will find there is no permit required to purchase either shotguns or handguns in the state of Colorado. And none of us needs a permit to carry concealed. We don't conceal anything here."

Callie stepped forward. Her heart ached a little. She hadn't meant to bring down Nate's condemnation on a place she loved so much. Tears pricked her eyes. How could he not see how much of her was here, in this place, in Bliss? He could take her out of Bliss, but she would always be the same girl. She could never be what he needed. "I'm sorry, Bill. I think I've made a mistake. We'll find somewhere more suitable."

Bill opened his mouth, but Nate stood up, hat in his hand. "No, Callie, we won't." He was quiet for a moment. "I apologize, Mr. Hartman. I know the gun laws. I'm a bit on edge, and it has me growling at everyone. You upped your security when I took over as sheriff."

She turned to Nate. "It had nothing to do with you, I'm sure."

Zane's eyes looked back and forth from the director to Nate. "You're wrong, babe. Nate made an ass of himself at some point in time. Your friend here was worried he wouldn't give a crap about the hippie nudists if something went wrong. I bet he didn't have trouble with the former sheriff."

Bill's shoulder came up negligently. "I've always found Rye Harper to be a tolerant man. He and Mr. Talbot helped install our new security. And, Callie, you and your friends are welcome. I begrudge no one. Please stay. I promise that the sheriff and I will find a way to get along."

"Damn straight," Nate said under his breath. "Let me make it easier. I apologize if I made you think I wouldn't help you. This community is a part of Bliss. I might be a bastard, but I do my job. If something happens here, I'll be right beside you, Mr. Hartman. Not only because it's my job, but because you're obviously important to Callie. I love Callie. I'll try to be less judgmental." He stood beside her, his hand on the small of her back.

A knowing smile crossed Bill's face. "As I said, you're welcome. I would love to have a better relationship with law enforcement." He stood and clapped his hands together. "Now, I believe our daily horseshoe contest is beginning. I shall leave the three of you to work out who gets the best room." His eyes narrowed.

"Uh, Callie does." Zane stood awkwardly.

Bill pointed at the big guy and gave him a wink. "That is the proper answer, son." He picked up the keys sitting on his desk and passed them around. "Callie is in a suite. The two of you have single rooms. Please remember, we are clothing optional except in the pool. No clothes allowed in the pool or the hot tub. Towels are available throughout the resort. Use one when sitting on the furniture. Have a nice stay."

Bill strode out of his office after handing Callie the keys. A silence descended, and she awkwardly stared at the small pieces of metal in her hand. There were three of them. She'd started the morning fairly sure they wouldn't need separate rooms.

God, she was going to be so lonely tonight.

Zane strode up, and his hand was on her nape again. "I'll stay with you tonight."

The very arrogance of the statement put her on edge. She thrust a key at him. "No, you won't. You have your own room."

He grinned down at her. She felt his satisfaction at her defiance. "Yeah, I will. You're the one who wouldn't let me leave, babe. I was ready to die to make sure you were safe. Look, I've thought about what you said. I can't stop thinking about it. You were right. I was looking for something easy because that's what I've done all my life.

But I love you. I won't leave you again, not until they carry me away in a body bag. I'm sorry for what I said before. This is the truth. I love you. You can't get rid of me. You want me to fight? I'll fight. Besides, you trashed my bike. You owe me."

Sweet words, but how could she believe him? The next time something threatened them, he would be right back to trying to leave. "I do not owe you a thing, Zane Hollister. I made myself clear back at the office. We're through."

He shrugged, and there was a light in his eyes that had been absent ever since he'd read that note back in Nate's office. "I don't accept your refusal. And I'm not taking this key. I'll sleep in your bed, or I'll sleep in your doorway. If you think I'll get a minute's rest with doors closed between us, you're wrong. Lock me out. Slam the door in my face. I won't leave you. You made your decision, Callie. You made it when you trashed my bike. You'll never get rid of me now."

She wanted so much to throw herself into his arms and sob out the tension of the day, but his previous words came back. Which Zane should she believe? The one who said he loved her, or the one who said she didn't matter? She took a step back. It was far past time to protect her own heart.

She thrust the key at him. "It's your room. Sleep in it or not. I don't care." She turned to Nate and handed a key to him as well. "Here's yours. Hopefully all of this will be over in a week or two and we can get on with our lives."

Nate's hand shot out, forming a manacle around her wrist. "You won't get rid of me so easily, either. I told you I loved you. I won't be dismissed."

Nate was an entirely different problem. "You don't love me. I'm convenient, and you think I'll be easily moldable. But I'll never fit into the niche you want to put me in. I'll be the hick you brought with you and I'll drag you down. You would resent me after a while."

He shook his head. "Don't tell me how I feel."

She was surrounded by them. Nate crowded her front, and Zane was at her back. They didn't respect her personal space. They were up against her, not attempting to hide the fact that they were aroused. She felt them. Nate against her stomach. Zane's erection pressed against the small of her back. It should have made her want to run. But she just wanted to drown in them, in their love, their care. It was false. It was a chimera waiting to rip her heart out.

She pushed them aside and made for the door. The keys dropped to the floor because neither would take them from her. She was left with one. The key to her room. "I'll see you when it's time to go back into town for the meeting."

She practically ran down the hall.

* * * *

Zane watched as Callie slammed the door behind her. Damn it. He'd screwed up on every level possible. He'd meant to keep her safe, and all he'd managed to do was break her heart. His every instinct told him to chase her down, get her under him. She wouldn't listen to a word he said, but maybe he could show her how he felt. Or maybe he should try to work everything out with Nate and present a united front. Maybe the problem was they were out of synch and Callie needed them both.

"I hope you're happy." Nate's frown covered most of his face. His nose was still a nice shade of red and pronouncedly swollen.

"Why would I be happy? You're the one who fucked up. You're the reason we'll sleep alone tonight." As much as he wanted peace between them, he wasn't about to take the blame for this debacle. He wasn't the one who had made Callie feel self-conscious. He'd just made her pissed. That he could deal with. Callie thinking she was less than she was made him mad, and that was Nate's fault.

He wasn't sleeping alone tonight. He'd meant every word he'd said. She'd made her choice. She hadn't let him walk. She would deal with the consequences, and one of those consequences was putting up with him in bed. He thought back to that moment when he realized how far Callie had gone to keep him here. He'd yelled at the time and moaned over the temporary loss of his bike, but damn she looked pretty when she got mad. What had it taken for gentle Callie to do that to his bike? She'd done a number on it, and to way more than the electrical system. He'd stood there and it had struck him for the first real time that she loved him. She loved him passionately and truly if she'd done that. Only the thought that he'd hurt her had kept him from tossing her over Nate's desk and having his way with her again. Her brown eyes had dulled, and he hadn't seen them flare back to life yet. He had some serious damage control to do, and he couldn't do it by sleeping in another room. He glanced down at the key on the floor but made no move to pick it up. "I was trying to save her, Nate. What's your excuse?"

Nate reached down and palmed both keys. "I have no idea what you mean. I'm not trying to hurt Callie. I told her I loved her and wanted to spend the rest of my life with her. How could that hurt her?"

Now who was being obtuse? Zane sank back into the couch. "You don't get her. You walk around insulting everything she loves and then wonder why she thinks you'll regret marrying her. And where exactly do I fit into this white-picket-fenced McMansion dream of yours? Am I supposed to slither off and let you keep the girl?"

Nate sat down beside him and a tired sigh escaped his lungs. "I wasn't trying to force you out. I think we can make this work, all three of us. I want that. But I want a career, too. You have to see that we can't stay here. There's no future in Bliss."

God, that was Nate's father talking. If only he could hear himself, he might see it. Nate's father had pounded ambition into him. He hadn't been happy when his son had gone into the DEA, but Nate had been ruthless in pursuing advancement. It had been as though he needed to prove to his father that he could rule the world, but in his own way.

Of course, now Nate's father was a shell of a man because ambition was all Peter Wright had. When his money dried up, so had his life. Nate hadn't learned the lesson. Zane had no intention of living that way. There was more to life than money, more than power. He'd started to learn that the day he'd come to this town.

There was love. There was friendship. There was bliss to be had if only he reached out to grab it.

"Maybe there's no future for you, but me? I don't know. I like it here." Maybe he shouldn't make such a big decision based on one day of following Callie around, but it was the way he operated. He made decisions based on his gut, and his gut told him that Bliss was a good place to be. His told him Bliss could be his home.

Nate's gaze pinned him. "Where are you planning on working? Or are you going to let Callie support you?"

That was something he'd been thinking about ever since last night. Bliss was rural. It relied on tourists, but there were enough people to support a few businesses year round. From what he could tell, there were tourists coming in and out all year. They came in the summer for the beauty of the high plains and the mountains. They came in the winter to ski. What did every tourist need? A drink.

"I'm going to open a bar, one where Callie doesn't get nearly murdered." He'd seen a place near the diner that might work. He'd tended bar in college. Surely he could figure the rest out. Now, money was another issue, but he'd cross that bridge if he lived long enough to actually get to it. "You didn't answer my question. Where do I fit into your perfect suburban paradise? You think I can pretend to be your roommate? Am I supposed to be some pathetic ass who lives at his friends' place when he's forty? Do I ever get to hold her hand in public or might that ruin your career path?"

Nate's face went white, and he had a sudden feeling that was exactly what Nate had planned. He meant to stroll off with the girl, and Zane could come and go, as long as he did it quietly. Maybe their fight wasn't over yet. His left fist tightened.

"What exactly would we do about kids?" He would poke all the holes he could in Nate's plan. "Callie wants a family. Are you the only one who gets to have babies with her? I get shut out? And what do we tell them? 'Uncle Zane is afraid of thunderstorms, that's why he's in bed with Mommy.'"

"Damn it, Zane. I don't know." Nate fell back against the sofa, and looked at him with weary eyes. "I haven't figured it out. I only know that I can't move up the ladder here. I haven't even started to think about kids."

He should because Callie would want them. "We have to think about them. You want her to give up her whole life and everything she's known for a place that will judge her, and probably harshly. I know you think I'm naïve. I know you think she is, too, but don't make this whole leaving-Bliss-because-there's-no-money-here about us. That's on you. You're the one who can't be happy without money and a job where someone kisses your ass."

"That's not what this is about," Nate insisted.

"If you can say that, then you're not being honest with yourself."

Nate sighed, the sound a weary thing. "Can we shelve this for now? As far as Callie's concerned, we can go jump in a lake. She's not wondering how our permanent threesome is going to work."

There was a short knock on the door before Bill Hartman entered, followed by two men he'd hoped to never see again. Special Agents Ben Leander and Marcus Worthington strode behind the director of the community. They were dressed in what he liked to think of as upwardly mobile asshole wear. Suits, ties, expensive shoes, and sunglasses they often wore whether or not they needed them. They were friends with Nate, or more importantly, they had been friends with Nate's father's contacts. Nate was one of them, an agent who could have a stellar career. Zane was not. Zane, as far as they were concerned, was just a fuck-up who'd blown his cover. It didn't matter that he'd done nothing wrong. It didn't matter that he'd simply walked in one day and Ellis knew. No one believed that he hadn't screwed up. Not even Nate.

Ben Leander slid the shades off, and there was no mistaking the contempt in his baby blues as he looked around. "Wright? I almost didn't recognize you in that costume. It looks like Halloween around here." He briefly inclined his perfectly coiffed head toward Zane. "Hollister. I should have known you would be hanging around."

Bill seemed strangely comfortable being the only man in the room with his dick hanging out. Zane respected that about him. "Please feel free to use the office as long as you need to, gentlemen. If I can be of any assistance, I'll be out on the lawn." He closed the door quietly behind him.

Worthington shook his head. The sunglasses came off, and he smoothly slid them into his pocket. His eyes narrowed on the closed door. "Why the hell was that guy naked? Is this some kind of a joke? I thought we were here for serious reasons. Wright, what kind of place is this?"

"Hell, as far as I can see," Leander replied, giving the office a once-over. It was obvious to Zane that Leander didn't care for the homey surroundings.

"Welcome to rural Colorado, city slickers," Zane said, throwing Max's earlier words out. It felt good. Finally a place where he fit in and these jerks stood out like sore thumbs. He couldn't believe Nate had called these guys in. Nate sure hadn't thought outside the box on this one. "Shouldn't the two of you be kissing someone's dress shoes in El Paso?"

Leander rolled his eyes and then pointedly ignored him. It wasn't the first time. Zane wasn't stupid. These two put up with him because they thought Nate was going places.

"The director wanted us on this as quickly as possible. So Ellis is causing trouble?" Leander asked.

Nate reached in his pocket and pulled out the note from earlier. He passed it to the tall, dark-haired agent. "He had some men jump Zane last night. Then earlier today, this note was delivered to the station house. Apparently there's a bounty on his head."

"I didn't think it was Hollister's head he was interested in," Worthington murmured. His lips curled slightly in distaste. Zane was pretty sure the agent was offended by the scars on his face.

Nate went a pale white. "Damn, you know that already? I didn't put that in the report."

Worthington raised a single aristocratic brow as he looked the note over. "You didn't have to put it in. I have my ear to the ground. Do we have the person who dropped the note off in custody?"

Nate paled, and it was easy to see he was embarrassed. "She dropped it off with my deputy. He didn't realize he should detain her."

"You should train him better," Leander said. "Well, I suppose we can check the CCTV cameras. We need an ID on her."

"They don't have cameras," Nate replied and there it was again.

Zane wasn't ashamed. "It's a small town. Not a lot of need, if you know what I mean. People are good to each other here."

Worthington snorted, an inelegant sound. "Sure they are. Well, at least someone was smart enough to call us in. I've already started the investigation. We have a whole network of informants and it didn't take long to get a snitch talking. Ellis still has men in Texas willing to work for him. I was surprised they managed to track you down, though. Hollister fell off the grid. He isn't even pulling a paycheck.

The Barbarians must be serious about him. The word on the street is that Ellis is offering a lot of cash for him."

"Where is he getting the money?" Zane asked the question with an exasperated sigh. "The man's in jail. We shut down his operations. I know he still has followers, but where is he getting the kind of cash he needs to put a hit out on me?"

Leander shrugged. "You didn't find all the cash. According to the forensic accountants, there's still millions missing. We can't figure out where he put it. It has to be in accounts somewhere, but there's no paper trail. We've taken apart every computer associated with the Barbarians and can't find the account numbers. He must have them memorized. We aren't allowed to torture him, so we'll probably never know. He kept everything hidden, even from his own lieutenants."

"Son of a bitch," Nate growled in obvious frustration. He seemed to shake it off and a professional expression took over his face. "Thank you for coming out. I've documented everything I know in the report I sent you. I want this guy taken down. I want to prove he's running his gang from prison and get him shut in solitary for the rest of his freaking life."

"That's not going to be easy." Worthington stared down at Nate. "We're going back to the motel to call the Denver office, and then we'll be at the meeting tonight. I hear there's some kind of town hall. That should be fun. We just wanted to check and make sure you found…suitable arrangements." A smirk lit the agent's face. Zane wondered if he'd still smirk if he broke his nose. "Obviously no one will look for you here."

Leander snickered. "Yeah, Wright, all you have to do is shoot anyone wearing pants, and you'll be fine. It should make the job easy."

Nate stood and sighed. "It's a good, defensible position, okay? I'm doing the best I can with a bad situation. Back off. I have enough to deal with."

"No shit," Leander replied pointedly, looking at Zane. "Everyone knows what you have to put up with, man."

Nate shook their hands. Zane stayed right where he was. No way was he kissing anyone's butt.

Callie was his focus now. If it wasn't the same for Nate, then they would part ways. Zane didn't like the thought of it. It left him unsettled. He'd watched Nate's back for years, depended on him for his very existence while they were undercover. They were closer than brothers.

And Zane would let him go if the choice was between Nate and Callie. A strange quiver hit his gut.

Callie was his future.

Nate was talking quietly to the agents while Zane had a sudden vision of building something here. He would have his bar, and he would have Callie. They could have a family. It wouldn't be some grand mansion and lush life, but it would be theirs. The only thing marring that vision was the thought of Nate being so far away.

The door closed as Leander and Worthington walked out.

"Well, that went as well as it could go. Damn it, Zane. Why can't you try to get along with them?" Nate stood over him, a disapproving frown on his face. "They have power in the agency. They can get things done. Why can't you play the game for once in your life?"

Because he'd tried, and he wasn't good at it. Zane got up. He was never going to be good at politics. Nate was a natural when he wanted to be. Nate could schmooze and cajole and get people to do what he wanted. He'd shown not an ounce of charm since the day they came to Bliss. Nate had saved it all up for those assholes from the agency.

Zane sighed. Nate's priorities were all screwed up. He compromised with people who didn't care and fought with ones who did. Well, he wasn't making the same mistake. He'd made his choice and that meant making nice with the people he would be neighbors with. It was a weird way to fit in, but he was doing it. He pulled his T-shirt over his head and let it fall to the ground.

Nate's eyes widened when Zane's hand hit the fly of his jeans and drew the zipper down. "What the hell are you doing?"

"You want me to play games and compromise?" He shoved his denims down with his boxers after kicking off his shoes. "I'll play, but only when it counts."

He walked out of the office as naked as the day he was born. This place meant something to Callie. He was going to prove he could fit in.

Chapter Eleven

Callie took a deep breath as she made it to the lawn. The air held a wonderfully crisp aspect, but she could feel her cheeks burning with heat. She forced a smile on her face as she walked by people she'd known since she was a child. They called out greetings and asked how she was doing. How was she doing? She was falling apart. The last twenty-four hours had been a hurricane of emotion, and she wasn't sure how to handle any of it.

She was in love, but naturally she couldn't be normal. She couldn't fall for a guy and settle in to something comfortable. No, she had to fall for two men, neither one of them easy. Zane had a death wish, and Nate wanted something she wasn't sure she could give him. If she looked deep down, she wasn't even sure she wanted to try. She turned at the edge of the lawn, preferring to walk for a bit before she headed to her room.

She strode down the narrow path that led to the front gates. The aspens were beginning to turn to browns and golds. It was almost fall, and soon it would be winter. Where would she be when the snow started falling? Would she be holed up here? Would she be packing to move to Denver? And where would they be? Nate would be waiting for his time to be up so he could move on to bigger and better things. Zane would be drinking in some bar, maybe.

She forced herself to slow down. She could hear the clang of horseshoes hitting the metal post and the jovial laughter of the men playing the game. A small group of women walked past. She recognized a few of them from her mother's old group of friends. She found a picnic bench and pondered the fact that she felt apart from everyone. She was surrounded, almost constantly, by people she knew and cared about, and she felt so alone. It was last night that had done it. Experiencing that kind of intimacy made everything clear to her. She never felt as connected as she did when she made love with Nate and Zane. She became a different person. When they were alone together, she felt loved and wanted and free.

How could she give that up? How could she keep it?

"Callie Sheppard?"

She turned with a gasp. She hadn't heard the man walk up behind her. Scratch that. Two men in some serious suits. Cops. She knew two cops when she saw them.

"Agents?" They had to be here about last night. Nothing else happened in Bliss. Certainly nothing that would bring out Feds. There was zero doubt in her mind that these boys were Feds.

"Agent Benjamin Leander. I'm with the Drug Enforcement Agency," the taller of the two said. His skin was bronze but with the slightest hint of orange that came from a salon rather than the sun. His dark brown hair was impeccable, and she bet he had a skin care regime. Definitely not a rough-and-ready cop. He was a bureaucrat. "This is my partner, Agent Marcus Worthington. We're investigating the threats against Zane Hollister. You were at the bar when Hollister was attacked last night?"

She glanced at the second man, who looked like a blond clone of the first. "Yes, I was there."

He studied her behind those mirrored aviators he wore. She couldn't see his eyes, and it was a bit unnerving. She felt like a bug under a microscope. His mouth was turned down as he took in her clothes. She was suddenly aware of how cheap everything she owned was.

"What were you doing at that bar? From what we understand, it's a rough and tumble place frequented by bikers. You don't look like a biker," Worthington commented.

She swallowed, trying to find a way to properly answer that question without being completely honest. She wasn't about to admit that she'd gone there to get laid. "I was getting a drink, as one does in a bar. Is there something illegal about that?"

Agent Worthington huffed and turned away. Leander leaned in. "There's nothing illegal about getting a drink, Miss Sheppard, but that is a known place where outlaw bikers hang out. You don't seem to keep good company."

"I didn't know anyone there except Zane."

"Like I said, you don't seem to keep good company, ma'am." Leander sat perfectly still, almost unnervingly so. "If you didn't know anyone, why did you go?"

He was starting to annoy her. Why exactly was he treating her like she was a criminal? "I've answered that question for you, Agent Leander. I was thirsty."

"Fine, we've established you were thirsty and can't pick your friends. Let's move on. What happened when you got to the establishment?"

She folded her hands in her lap and clenched them tightly. She was going to get through this interview for Zane's sake. "I ordered a drink and talked to Zane."

"How do you know Zane Hollister?" Worthington stood over her, one foot on the bench, arm negligently across his knee. "Or were you trying to pick up a date for the night?"

"Is this how you question a witness, Agent Worthington?" Nate's deep voice cut through the condescension. Callie turned, and Nate strode toward her. He sat down beside her, his hand entwining with hers. He didn't look at her but kept his eyes on the men across the table. "Ms. Sheppard is a witness, not a suspect. She's also my girlfriend. I expect you to treat her with some modicum of respect."

Leander sighed. "Sorry, Nate. I didn't realize you brought a girl with you."

"We thought she was some local piece Zane was doing." Worthington snorted dismissively.

Glancing at Nate, she saw his eyes narrow and knew he was about to explode. She needed to avoid that. He wanted to go back to the DEA, and beating the crap out of a couple of agents wouldn't help his case. It was time to start standing up for herself. A slow smile slid across her face. She wasn't about to let these jerks intimidate her or make her feel bad about herself. She could do that all on her own.

She pulled her hand out of Nate's. "I am local, gentlemen. And I'm definitely doing Zane."

Nate stiffened beside her, his shoulders straightening, jaw tight with obvious embarrassment. At least he wasn't thinking about punching the agents now. Her heart thudded dully in her chest when she realized his face had turned a bright red, and he wasn't trying to hold onto her anymore. This was what a relationship would be like with Nate. He would always be ashamed of what they were.

"I thought you said she was your girlfriend." Leander was talking to Nate but stared straight through Callie.

She shrugged. It didn't matter what they thought of her. She simply wanted Nate to get out of this with his pride intact. She loved him. She couldn't put him through this type of relationship. Zane could handle it, if he really wanted to. Nate would never be able to live the way a threesome required, and she couldn't handle the life he wanted. "I'm his friend, and I'm a girl. That's just the way we talk out here in the country. I'm not Zane's girlfriend, either. I've hooked up with him a couple of times. I'm the sheriff's admin. I run the station house."

"I bet you do." That came from Worthington. His sunglasses were off. He stared openly at her.

Then he was staring at Nate's enraged face. He pushed his big body away from the table and was in the other agent's space with the inherent grace of a predator. "You back the fuck off. She is my girlfriend, and she is Zane's girlfriend. It isn't a friendly relationship. Get it? And neither one of us is going to allow you to treat her with disrespect."

Worthington pulled back and held his hands up. "Sorry, man. Didn't realize you and Hollister were…like that."

Nate hauled her up. Callie stumbled and held on to his waist to stop from falling. Nate's arm slid under her shoulder and pulled her close. "Yeah, well we are, and it's really none of your business. I didn't call you in to judge my relationships. You find a way to get the bounty off Zane's head. That's your job."

Leander stood. He put a hand on his partner, neatly separating the men. His handsome face was all smooth and conciliatory. "Whoa, Nate, man, we didn't mean anything by it. It's just a surprise. Of course, we'll do our best for Hollister." He nodded Callie's way. "Ma'am, I apologize for the misunderstanding. We'll go now, but if you can think of anything that might help, give us a call."

Worthington backed off with a shake of his head, and the agents retreated through the community's heavy gates. Nate stared as they walked away.

"Why did you do that? I can handle them." She took a step back.

He turned, shaking his head. "Why should you have to handle them? They were being jerks. I knew they never liked Zane, but I didn't think they would be such pricks where a woman was concerned."

"I'm sure they wouldn't to a woman they considered a lady," Callie explained. "But I'm a country girl. We're good for a quick lay and not a lot else."

It wasn't the first time she'd come up against the type. She'd had more than her share of handsy tourists who thought she should be thrilled they were willing to give her a whirl.

Nate's jaw tightened. He forced her to look up into his face. "Is that what you think of me?"

She shook her head. Nate wasn't like that, but their problems were unworkable all the same. "I know I'm not an easy lay for you."

"Damn straight. You've actually been really difficult." His face softened, and he leaned over, brushing his lips sweetly against hers. The sensation made her heart clench. It took everything she had not to wind her arms around his neck and deepen the kiss. He pulled back, his face wary and a bit disappointed. "I love you, Callie. I won't let anyone put you down."

And they would in his world. Unless she was willing to change everything about herself, she would be an albatross around his neck. "It's okay, Nate. It didn't bother me. So those agents are going to figure out who's after Zane?"

It was time for a change of subject. She turned from the picnic table and began walking back toward the lawn.

Nate looked like he wanted to argue but fell into step beside her.

"We know who wants Zane. We don't know why, beyond revenge. If Ellis merely wanted him dead, he could hire a killer. I don't understand the game he's playing. I know Ellis. I worked with him for years. He's a bastard but a straightforward one. If he wanted Zane dead, someone would have shot him."

"Is it a tradition in that club of his to take a trophy?" She shuddered at the thought of someone carving up Zane's body to prove he was dead. It was a horrible thought, but these were criminals.

"Not that I've heard of. The only trophy these guys are interested in is money. This is a business, sweetheart. They can be brutal men, but I've never heard of taking someone's tat. If you leave the club you're supposed to get rid of the tattoo. If you left on decent terms, you get it lasered off or inked over."

"And if you get kicked out?" She wasn't sure she wanted to know.

"They burn it off you," he replied quietly, and she had to wonder if he'd been forced to witness an act like that. He seemed to shake it off. "But like I said, I've never known them to carve it off. I've tried to get Zane to start the process of getting rid of that tat, but he's a stubborn ass."

She thought of the elaborate tattoo on Zane's chest. It was a work of art covering his entire left pectoral muscle. There was a fierce snake at the center with flames weaving around it. The multi-colored design must have taken hours and hours to impress on his skin. Her gut twisted at the thought of Zane dying for that damn tattoo. "Are they any good? Those agents, I mean."

He stopped and took her right hand in both of his. "Baby, I know I haven't given you a reason to believe me, but I promise it's going to be okay. I'm not going to let them kill Zane, and I won't let them hurt you. Leander and Worthington are real movers in the agency. They can bring people together. They'll find out the information we need. This was a big case and there are still questions to be answered. We locked up the bad guy, but we didn't find all the money. The DEA still has people looking for Ellis's accounts. This is almost like a break for them. It's the first move he's made since going to prison. Besides, Zane used to be an agent. You have to understand that cops take care of their own."

She didn't think they had seemed particularly caring. They had been downright rude when talking about Zane. But she had to trust that Nate knew what he was doing. "All right. Let's go see if Zane's settling in."

"Zane's gone fucking insane, that's what he's done." Nate shook his head and suddenly his whole face flushed. "Oh, shit. They think I'm sleeping with Zane."

She smiled, with real amusement this time. She thought he'd misunderstood portions of the previous conversation, but she hadn't been about to point it out. "If it helps, I think they think you're sleeping with me, too."

"Damn it, I am sleeping with you. But this is a perfectly straight threesome. There is nothing weird about it at all. It's a normal threesome. Well, it's a normal twosome, and then there's Zane."

She stopped, catching her first glimpse of Zane. He stood on the lawn with a group of six other men. His arm came back and then pitched forward, a silver horseshoe flying through the air and perfectly circling the stake ten feet away. He nodded with satisfaction and shook Bill Hartman's hand before ceding his turn. He, like all the men around him jovially playing the game, was completely naked.

"He's trying to fit in." Nate's lips curled up, and he obviously was stifling a laugh.

Fit in? She looked at the men around Zane. Despite the fantasy of a nudist resort, the truth was it was mostly middle-aged men and women. Six-foot five-inch Zane had at least three inches on the next tallest man who, like many of his friends, sported a pot belly and a body gone mostly soft. There was absolutely nothing soft on Zane. He stretched unselfconsciously as he watched the other man pitch a horseshoe. He laughed at something that was said, his head thrown back, all that black hair shaking. He was broad shouldered and lean waisted. He had a six-pack that made her eyes widen, and his ass was one of the most perfect things she'd ever seen. Even completely relaxed, his cock swung in a…Callie had to take a deep breath. "He's never going to fit in. He's so obviously meant to stand out."

Nate frowned at her. "Like what you see, huh? Fine. He's not the only one who looks good. I work out."

Nate started to pull at the buttons on his shirt.

"What are you doing?" She grinned as she watched Nate take his clothes off. She wanted to laugh out loud, but she wouldn't do anything that might make him stop and think. Nate was running on emotion, and it was a lovely thing. He quickly unveiled his own hot body. It was different from Zane's, but just as gorgeous as the other man's. He was powerfully muscled with big arms, and every muscle looked like some artist had carefully sculpted it with beauty in mind. She longed to run her hands over the smooth skin covering his body.

"I can fit in, too, damn it." He made his declaration with the same look of determination she'd seen when he talked about his plans for the future.

He kicked his boots and pants off and strode arrogantly over to join the game. Callie noticed Bill's surprised expression when Nate walked up and asked if he could give it a try. Bill shook Nate's hand, and Zane said something that had Nate promising vengeance.

Gina Winters, a forty-something friend of Callie's, walked up to stand beside her. She was a pretty redhead. Her eyes flared as she looked at the sight in front of her. "Oh, my. When did the boy toys show up?"

An insane sense of satisfaction spread through Callie. "They're with me."

"Really?"

They were. At least for now. If she only had a few days with them, why shouldn't she enjoy it? Callie tugged her T-shirt over her head and toed out of her shoes. "Yes, really. Those are my boy toys, Gina. And I don't share."

She didn't. She didn't share. It was a freeing revelation. Callie Sheppard had two men, and she wasn't sharing them.

* * * *

He was naked. He was naked and holding a horseshoe. Nate took a deep breath. He eyed the stake and let his arm flow back. He could do this. It was the same game, despite the fact that his junk was hanging out for all to see.

Actually, now that he thought about it, it felt kind of nice. The air felt different on his skin, softer but strangely crisper. He was more aware of his body without the encumbrance of clothes.

His arm pitched forward, and he released the horseshoe. He'd never actually done this before, and he was horrible at it. He didn't even get close. The horseshoe landed in the grass with a thud. Nate frowned.

"Don't."

He turned to Zane. "Don't what?"

Zane put a hand on his hip. It was weird. Everyone was naked. There wasn't a place he could look that he didn't see skin. "Don't be an asshole. It's just a game. You can't be good at everything."

But he was supposed to be, a voice inside him said. Sometimes that voice wasn't so little. Sometimes that voice was a roar telling him that he wasn't good enough, and he had to do better. God, what would his father think of him now? He was standing in the middle of a nudists' colony with his dick hanging out, playing horseshoes. "It's all about practice. I need to practice and I'll be better at this."

Zane groaned. "That's your dad talking, man. You know, there was a time when I envied you. My mom couldn't have given a crap whether I made anything of myself. When I got the opportunity to get that scholarship to go to private school, I had to forge her name on the paperwork. She didn't even know I'd changed schools for six months."

"Your mom was a drunk." She still was, though he refrained from mentioning that. He didn't think Zane had spoken to her for years. When Zane had been in the hospital, he'd called her. She'd said she didn't have a son, but if she did, he owed her money. He'd hung up, and he'd been the only one sitting by Zane's bed when he'd finally woken up. "And you shouldn't be jealous. My parents wanted the perfect son. I never pleased them. I screwed everything up when I joined the DEA instead of taking over the family business."

Which his father had run into the ground. Could he have made a difference? Guilt burned through him.

Zane tugged at his elbow and led him away from the group. "Stop it. You aren't responsible for what happened to the business."

"How did you know what I was thinking?"

"I've lived and worked beside you for years. I know when you're letting the old man get to you. He pushed you so fucking hard you couldn't take a dump without wondering if you were the best at it."

Nate couldn't help it. He laughed, really laughed. It was true, and Zane knew just how to put it to him. His father had pushed him on his grades, pushed him at football, pushed him to date the prettiest girl. *Only the best for a Wright…* His father hated Zane.

His father wouldn't like Callie.

That thought sobered him really quickly.

Zane's brow was furrowed. "Now I don't know what you're thinking." It seemed to bother him.

"I was wondering how Callie and my parents would get along."

"They wouldn't, and you know it. He'll see her as a piece of fluff who could never help you socially. I know exactly what your father would say. He would tell you that if you simply had to have her, keep her as a mistress and find a proper wife. That's when I would go to jail for assaulting your dad."

Only if Nate didn't get to him first. Damn, Zane was right. Callie was far too sweet for his high-society world. They would question her on every level. They wouldn't like the way she dressed or how she did her hair. They would make fun of her for her lack of an education and the jobs she'd done in the past. They would tell her all the ways she wasn't good enough. "They would tear her up."

"I didn't say that," Zane corrected with a shake of his head. "She's no shrinking violet. She can be downright mean when she wants to. Did you see what she did to my bike? That was a custom-made bike. It took some strength to pry the seat off. And what she did to the tires… I'm kind of scared of her now. I don't think I'll piss her off again anytime soon."

Nate grinned at the thought. She had been one pissed-off sweetheart of a woman. Callie often allowed them to take the lead, but when she put her foot down, he had the feeling he and Zane would fall in line. She could handle herself, but that didn't mean she wouldn't get her heart broken. "You need to stick close to her. I don't trust Ben and Marcus with her."

Zane's eyes went positively arctic. "What did they do?"

"I didn't like the way they questioned her," Nate admitted.

"Why the hell did you call in those two? They're going to cause problems here. They're assholes."

He sighed. "I didn't ask for them specifically, though I do believe they'll get the job done. I actually asked them to send Tyler Williams out here."

Williams wasn't as senior, but he was a solid agent. He didn't mind getting his hands dirty and did undercover like he was born for it. He would have fit in here because he fit in anywhere. He was smart and quick. He didn't think Zane was a fuck-up.

"Yeah, he would be good here. So why send in the suits?"

Nate shrugged. "No idea. Maybe Williams is on a job. Maybe the director wanted to show he was taking this seriously. I guess they wanted their best agents on it."

"The director's blind. Those two are paper pushers. The only reason they move up is the fact that they went to Harvard and their dads are big in Washington." Zane laughed bitterly. "I know why they sent them. They want you back. They're really here to convince you to return to work."

"Well, I think they might reconsider now that I apparently outed us as a gay couple." He waited for Zane to roar.

A slow smile broke over Zane's face. "What?"

"Yeah, I was pissed about the way they treated Callie. They were acting like she didn't matter. Assholes. I might have outed us as a threesome, and they took it wrong," he explained.

"Nice. Now I'm not only the agent who blew his cover. I'm the gay agent who blew his cover."

He didn't seem upset. Zane was grinning from ear to ear. It surprised Nate. "This doesn't bother you?"

"Nah. I'm perfectly comfortable with my heterosexuality, man. I have no desire to jump your nasty ass, but our lady likes a little kink. I put up with you for her sake." His smile faded slightly. "It doesn't matter what they think of me. I'm never going back. But rumors like that could hurt you. Go and talk to them. Tell them you were only protecting your partner."

"Fuck that. It's the truth. I love Callie. I share her with you. I'm not hiding it." He wasn't going to hide it. He still wasn't sure about the future, but he didn't want to hide Callie and Zane. It didn't feel right. He looked at Zane and realized they had a problem. "Damn it, Zane. Try to be less comfortable with yourself." Zane's cock was lengthening by the second. “Seriously, you can’t walk around with that thing.”

Zane pointed to a spot behind him. Nate turned, and then his dick was hard, too. Callie stood next to a woman, a smile on her face and talking animatedly. She was gloriously naked, her skin glowing in the sun. Her smile was lit by a warm glow that came from deep within her. Even as his dick got hard, Nate felt his heart soften. She was so beautiful.

He heard a feminine squeal as two women ran to Callie. It was Callie’s friend Jen, who seemed to make Stef insane, and the twins’ wife, Rachel. The three women hugged enthusiastically, and he heard a bunch of questions about what had happened. Nate felt a definite affection for the women who seemed so concerned about his Callie.

“Damn, Sheriff, you gotta put on some pants,” a wry voice with a deep western drawl said. “The naked thing only works when you keep your dick calm, man.”

Nate cupped himself and reached for his pants as the Harper twins walked up.

The second twin laughed out loud and didn’t give him the courtesy of looking away. “Yeah, Rye, this is why we couldn’t live up here. I would be hiding too damn much of myself.”

Nate tried to quell his rising embarrassment. He carefully zipped up his pants and left the shirt off. He wasn’t going to show how uncomfortable he was. It was a natural damn reaction. She was his mate. She was naked. He would be worried if his cock didn’t react.

He glanced back at Zane, who was calmly grabbing a towel from the stack near the horseshoe pit. Zane wound it around his waist. There were piles of towels neatly stacked throughout the place. Like Nate, his chest was still on full display.

“Harper,” Zane acknowledged.

“Damn, Max, you were right about him.” Rye Harper wore a blue shirt while his brother was in a black T-shirt. Otherwise, they were perfectly identical. The former sheriff looked Zane up and down and finally whistled. “You are one big, scary dude. Callie has way more exotic tastes than I would have thought.”

Zane’s eyes were off in the distance, watching the women as they talked. A faint smile touched his lips. “Lucky for me, huh?”

Rye's eyes went hard as he stared at Zane. "It is lucky for you, you big son of a bitch, and it better stay that way. You need to understand that she has a family and we will watch over her. The way I look at it, you might have some nasty people after you, but you break her heart and I swear I'll make those bikers look like a toddler's playgroup."

Max sighed heavily as though they'd been over this a couple of hundred times. "Back off, Rye. I told you. The big guy and I have a deal. He takes care of Callie, and I don't kill him."

Zane's head was thrown back as his laughter boomed across the yard. "Yeah, believe that, Harper. We made that deal of yours with my hand wrapped around your throat." He looked at the twins seriously. "Don't worry about Callie. I'm staying close no matter what, even after the threat passes. I'm going to be here for her. She owes me. She trashed my bike, so I can't leave."

Nate didn't like the way any of this sounded. The way Zane was talking, he was taking responsibility for Callie on his own.

Rye Harper held out a hand and shook Zane's. "All right then. Just know that when you take on Callie, you take on her family. Rach will have you out to the house for dinner as soon as possible. She's completely obsessed with having a close family for our kid."

"You better be ready to play the doting uncle," Max tossed in.

Yup, Nate didn't like this feeling at all. "I think Zane and I can handle it."

Max turned to him with a frown on his face. "You're welcome, of course, Sheriff. For as long as you're here. The rumor is you're going to leave as soon as you can. I'm glad one of you has the sense to stay with Callie."

"Callie is going to have the good sense to stay with me." Nate heard himself grinding the words out of his mouth. Max Harper would have to find his close-knit family with someone else. Callie would leave with him. She would leave behind the Harper twins and Stef and Jen and all her friends at the diner. She would say good-bye to Logan and his moms, Marie and Teeny. There would be no more knitting sessions with Nell. She would wave a fond farewell to everything she knew to follow him to Washington and a cushy job where he never had to deal with alien invasions, naturists, or vegans declaring their rights at the stoplight on Friday afternoons. Zane could be a well-kept secret.

Yeah, the money he could make would be worth giving up all of this, right?

"Damn it, Rachel!" Rye Harper was yelling across the yard at his pretty wife. "You put your clothes back on."

The woman with the strawberry-blonde hair and a faint curve to her belly placed a hand on her hips and yelled right back. "No, I won't, Rye. I'm in Rome, damn it!"

Rye turned back to his brother. "She is pregnant. What the hell is she thinking? Pregnant ladies shouldn't be walking around like that."

Max's grin was broad. "I don't see why not, bro. That's how she got pregnant in the first place. I think she makes for some really nice scenery." He turned a black look back on Nate and Zane. "Not that anyone else should be enjoying it."

"You're safe, Harper. I only got eyes for one woman." Zane slapped Nate on the back.

Jen ran across the yard and practically threw herself in Zane's arms. Luckily, she still had her clothes on, but Zane seemed startled by it anyway. The slender brunette kissed his cheek enthusiastically. "Thank you so much. When I saw you earlier, I was so caught up in my own drama that I forgot to thank you for saving Callie this morning."

Zane gently disentangled himself. Nate looked over at the two naked females who were approaching now. Callie didn't seem bothered by her friend throwing herself at Zane. She was smiling.

"You know Nate helped, too," Callie pointed out.

Finally, someone acknowledged his contributions. He braced himself for Jen's impact. The brunette simply gave him a distant smile. "Thank you, too, Sheriff."

She went back to looking at Zane like he was a conquering hero.

The group crowded around Zane. In one morning, Zane had managed to make himself a part of this weird place. Nate had no doubt that Zane would be invited to the monthly poker game, behind Nate's back of course, since Nate had pointed out that gambling was illegal. Zane would spend family dinners at the Harper ranch. Zane would become a part of Bliss.

Zane would be happy here in a way he'd never been anywhere they had lived. This place was already ingrained on Callie's soul. Nate realized with a sudden ache that he was the one who didn't fit. After a lifetime of being on the inside, being outside the circle hurt like hell. Was this how Zane had always felt? Was this how Zane and Callie would feel if they followed him?

A warm hand slipped into his. Callie. Her brown eyes were luminous in the late afternoon light. The very air around her seemed soft. "You okay?"

He knew that she would go with him if he pushed hard enough. Despite her earlier protestations that she wouldn't have anything further to do with them, the minute she thought he was hurting, she was there at his side, trying to give him comfort. He could use that if he wanted to. She would go because she loved him. Zane would go, too. Zane would go because Zane loved him. They would leave behind the only place where they belonged because he wanted them to.

"Yeah," he lied. "I'm fine, baby." He wasn't anywhere close to fine, but the feel of her hand in his was helping.

Rachel slapped at Rye's hands. He was trying to wrap a towel around her. "Stop it."

Max was grinning like a loon watching them fight.

It was chaotic and surreal and somehow fun at the same time. He wouldn't get this kind of feeling in the outside world. He would always be thinking about how other people would judge him and his friends.

"Wow, I love this tattoo," Jen was saying as she stared at Zane's chest. She glanced back at Callie. "Have you really looked at this? It's so intricate. It must have taken forever."

"Days," Zane conceded. He nodded at Nate. "Nate got off easy. His only took a couple of hours."

Nate remembered the day they had first sat on the chair and gotten inked for the Barbarians. It was a statement of intent for the MC. It proved a man was in for life. Ellis took those tats seriously. Each one had the snake logo, but the art surrounding it was slightly different. Nate's had been relatively simple, Zane's insanely complex. There were at least four bikers with the same level of intricacy as

Zane. Two of them were dead.

"What do the numbers mean?" Jen asked.

Nate dropped Callie's hands as it all finally fell into place.

* * * *

Zane looked down at the artist. "What numbers?"

He turned his head down, trying to get a good look at his chest. He could see the tat that marked him as a Barbarian, but all he could discern was a mass of curly-cue-looking things around a big, mean-looking snake. He tended to not pay attention to the mass of ink on his chest. Of course, he tried not to look at the other side of his chest, too. It reminded him too much of that day when he was strapped down and tortured. Ellis had branded his right side with superheated metal, and he'd cut his face all to hell. The one part Ellis insisted on leaving alone was his Barbarian tat. That had been off limits when making the pig squeal.

Zane shook off the dark thoughts. He would never figure out how his cover had been blown. Someone had known and told, and then his life had gone to hell.

He would have to accept it because now things were looking up. He wasn't going to allow the past to stain the future he had here. His eyes moved around the small crowd of people on the lawn. They were smiling and teasing each other and he was a part of it. Max Harper elbowed him in a friendly way. Jen had hugged him and thanked him. Rachel Harper was apparently ready to accept him as an uncle to her baby. Callie made that possible. Callie couldn't know how much the gift of her home and family, of sharing it with him, meant.

Damn, he was getting misty-eyed just thinking about raising a family in this place. The last thing he wanted to do was think about his tat. He would get it lasered off as soon as he had the cash. Nate was right about that. He'd been stubborn and now he couldn't wait to start the process.

"These numbers," Jen was saying. She had called Callie over and ran her index finger over the ink. "See? They're kind of woven into the design. Did you do that? Are they meaningful?"

A cold knowledge rushed in, seeping into his bones. He might not have wanted a career in law enforcement, but he'd been a cop long enough to have instincts. "Ellis designed it."

He turned quickly to Nate, who was pale, his eyes locked on the tat.

"Damn it, that would explain everything," Nate muttered.

Zane swallowed as the full reality hit him. No wonder there was a bounty on his head. Hell, they didn't give a damn about his head—his chest was another story.

"What's wrong?" Callie's gaze moved back and forth between them.

Nate's face had already taken on that hard-as-granite look he got when he went into full-on lawman mode. Nate's eyes got cold, and his mouth became a flat line. Everything about him became still, like a rattler waiting to strike. Nate was a true cop—in a way Zane had never been—and that was a good thing because it looked like they would need one.

"Nothing's wrong, baby. At least nothing we can't handle." Nate stood beside Jen, who also seemed to understand that something was wrong. "Jen, I'm going to need you to write down the numbers you see. If you can discern a particular pattern off of them, I would greatly appreciate it."

"Oh, it's there." Jen's hand ran across the tat lightly, tracing the ink. "See how it flows. It starts here and winds around all the way back in a counterclockwise pattern. It's subtle and very distinct. This man was a true artist."

"Yeah, well, he's also a drug dealer and a sadist," he pointed out.

"Oh my god, the account number for the missing money is on Zane's chest!" Callie finally caught up. Her eyes filled with fear.

"We need to get you to El Paso first thing in the morning." Nate was already reaching into his pants, pulling out his cell phone. "At least we have something to talk about tonight. All the town needs to do is keep a watch out for a day or two. Once we get into that account and prove to Ellis we've found his cash, he'll leave Zane alone. This was never about revenge, thank god. It's always been about money." He turned away. "Yeah, Worthington, I think I have a solution to our problems…"

Nate's voice faded as he walked away.

Zane reached out and grabbed Callie's hand. The Harpers were now quiet and watching him with solemn eyes.

"You going to be okay, Zane?" Max asked.

Not Hollister. Zane. This group wouldn't use his last name. It wasn't intimate enough. His heart seized a little. Damn, if he played his cards right, this would be his family. He would even forgo beating the crap out of Talbot if it meant belonging in this close-knit group. He pulled Callie against his chest, needing to feel her close to him. "It's going to be fine. I'll give the agency the info they need, and then I'll be out of it. Once Ellis knows the game is up, he'll call off the dogs. He's ruthless but he also knows he won't have a chance of ever getting out of jail if he kills a former agent."

Callie wrapped her arms around his waist and held on like she would never let go. He kissed the top her head. If he had his way, she would never have to.

Chapter Twelve

Callie turned the shower to hot, as hot as she thought she could stand. It was only moments before steam started to fill the room. She watched in the mirror as her image faded in favor of a coating of moisture. She was an opaque ghost in the glass. Though she brushed the steam away, it came back immediately. In a way, she was glad she couldn't see her reflection. It would only show the truth—that she had aged more in the past couple of weeks than in the years before.

Tomorrow, Zane would leave, and there would be nothing here to bring him back. Sure he'd said a lot of stuff about wanting her, but he'd left her behind once. There was nothing to stop him this time. If Zane was safe and happy, then there would be no reason for Nate to return, either. He would, of course. Duty would bring him back until they could find someone to take his place, but he would be counting the hours until he could get back to his real life.

How had she run out of time so fast?

With shaking hands, she placed a towel within reach and stepped into the shower. They were going to El Paso in the morning. She had one last night with them and only two hours before they had to be at the town meeting she herself had called. She'd thought about canceling it so she would have more time with Nate and Zane, but these people were her friends and family. They had the right to know what was going on. The group coming after Zane was dangerous and would be until everything was sorted out. Bliss needed to be vigilant.

She felt sick at the thought of not being with them. For the first time, she really thought about going with Nate. He seemed to truly want her to go with him. Of course, he would probably regret it once she screwed up his career path by being a complete hick, hippy weirdo. Tears swelled in her eyes as she realized she couldn't risk him coming to hate her when she didn't fit into his world.

She was going to lose them both. This time it might break her.

"Babe?" Zane's deep voice cut through her misery. She turned away to hide her face as he pulled back the shower curtain. "Babe, are you crying?"

"How did you get in here? I locked the door." The cooler air from outside her shower stroked her skin, causing her to shiver. In an instant, the curtain closed, and she was warm again.

Unfortunately, Zane was on the wrong side of the curtain. She felt his hands cup her shoulders. "I spent years posing as a criminal. I can get through any door you put between us. If I can't pick the lock, I assure you I can kick the door down." He turned her around to face him. "Now tell me why you're crying."

She was too shocked to hide her face now. He was still in his jeans. "You're getting wet."

He groaned and lowered his forehead to hers. "Yeah, well, I wasn't thinking about my clothes. I was thinking about the fact that you're crying." His lips touched the tip of her nose. "Please don't cry, babe. It tears me up." His voice was rough, as though he was on the edge of tears himself.

He wasn't wearing a shirt, and Callie's hands smoothed over his skin, stopping at each puckered scar to run a loving touch over it. She loved his body, every inch of it. Every scar and imperfection made him the man he was. She wound her arms tightly around his lean waist.

"I love you," she whispered against his chest. It made no sense to hold it back. She would never say those words in this way to anyone but Zane and Nate. When they were gone, she would close off that part of herself. "I love you so much."

His hand tangled in her wet hair. "Then marry me."

Her heart lurched, threatening to pound straight out of her chest. Her head shot up to look into Zane's painfully serious face. His eyes were a dark green, and he seemed to be waiting for her to reject him. "Marry you? I thought you would leave."

Now a smile curled his lips up. His hands ran down her back, waking every nerve in her skin until he curved his fingers around her backside and gave the cheeks a sizzling squeeze. "Never again, Callie. I will never leave you again. I made a mistake leaving the first time. Nate made a mistake, too, but I can't force him to acknowledge it. We both love you so fucking much, but I think he's going to leave. He's my best friend. He's my brother, but I'm choosing you this time." He took a breath. "Do you think you would be okay if it was just you and me?"

The thought of Nate on his own made her eyes water, but there was no chance she would turn Zane down. She would love him and make a home for him and thank her lucky stars that she had a man like this. She managed to nod.

He kissed her, deep and long. His tongue reached out to caress hers. She felt his longing in that kiss. He would miss Nate, too. They would be incomplete, but at least they would have each other.

Zane urged her close, rubbing his jean-clad erection against her belly. "I love you, babe." He tangled his fingers in her hair and gently pulled her head back so she looked into his eyes, couldn't miss an inch of his scarred, gorgeous face. "I'll never let you down, Callie. I'll try so hard to be the best husband you could have." His throat worked up and down, choking on some unnamed emotion.

She easily read his face, knew what he was saying. She lifted her hands to cup his face. He would try to be everything to her. He would try to make up for the fact that Nate wasn't with them. She'd been so selfish. She'd thought only of how much she would miss Nate and not once of how much Zane would miss him. Nate and Zane might never have kissed or had any sexual feelings toward each other, but they were soul mates. Zane's life would be less for the lack of Nate in it. She went on her toes and kissed him, her tongue licking along his plump lower lip, causing him to shiver. She felt a thrill race through her. She had power over this big, glorious man. It was a good thing because he had so much power over her. "And I'll work hard to be the best wife for you. I promise. I love you more than you can know."

"Touch me," he demanded. His fingers tore open the fly of his jeans. He shoved them down over his hips, cursing the friction the wet denim caused. "Next time I'll take the damn things off before I get wet."

She grinned up at him, sliding her hands down over the hard plane of his chest to the well-defined abs. "No clothes allowed in the swimming pool. That should make it easier."

He groaned as her hand grasped his cock. He filled and overflowed her palm. "Oh, babe, this is a great place to visit, but we can't live here. I'm always hard around you. I can't walk around with a naked erection. I might get called a pervert."

He felt so good. Callie let her hand stroke him from the broad base of his cock to the engorged purple head. She was fascinated by the way he shook and moaned as her hand tracked across the silky skin. "That could be a problem. I don't think there's any way to hide this monster. It could scare the children."

His eyes widened in startled dismay. "There are kids here?"

She laughed at his horror. She also noticed that his cock was weeping. She swiped her thumb over the slit of his cock, and he gasped. "No kids. This is an adult community, but there are family resorts if you like the lifestyle. I was thinking about our kids. If you want them, that is. I'm not getting any younger."

She brought her thumb to her mouth and licked off the bead of arousal she'd found.

"Oh, god, that's sexy." Zane groaned. "Babies. You want babies."

"I do." She got to her knees. The water from the shower beat a nice rhythm along her spine. On this point, there would be no negotiations. She was going to have his babies. "You want something permanent with me, mister, then there better be some serious impregnation going on."

She licked the tip of his straining dick, and his head fell forward. "Way to play hardball, babe. Damn, all I can think of now is the fact that I can ride you bareback. I've never had sex without a condom."

She let her hand find his heavy sac. She rolled his balls gently in her palm. She was going to have to have him soon. Her pussy was throbbing, and her thighs were wet in a way that had nothing to do with the spray from the shower. "We can decide on the timing, but it better be soon."

Zane reached down, locked his hands under her shoulders, and lifted her up. With flawless accuracy, he hauled her up, shoved her back against the tiled wall of the shower, and slammed his cock home.

She gasped as he penetrated her, his cock forcing its way deep into her pussy.

"No time like the present." His face was strained as he held himself deep inside. "Fuck, you feel so good."

She felt so full. Callie forced her legs to move, to try to grasp his hips. She steadied herself by placing her hands on his broad shoulders. She could barely breathe he was so deep inside her. "You didn't even take off your pants."

"No time. Get used to it. Now that I don't have to use a rubber, I'll take you when and where I want to." His voice shook as he held her in place. She was grateful for the restraint. He was big. It took her a moment to get used to him, to relax. The startling intrusion was quickly morphing into pleasure. Her pussy was wet, and she felt herself soften around him. He slid in another inch, and she felt his balls against the cheeks of her ass. "God, I'll never stop wanting you."

She gripped his shoulders, sinking her nails into the flesh there, willing him to move. She was so ready, so eager to feel him. "Then you should fuck me."

"Your wish…" Zane grunted right before he started to thrust into her.

Every nerve in her body ignited. He held her so tight her nipples rubbed against his chest. His mouth covered hers. His tongue plunged and retreated in time to the rhythm of his cock. She could do nothing but hold on as he pounded into her. She was caught between the tile and him and the pulsing heat of the shower.

It happened suddenly. He hit that perfect spot, and she went flying. She moaned and buried her face in his shoulder as the sensation took her. A second later, he stiffened, every muscle tense. He pumped into her as though he wanted to fuse them together. As he slowed, he leaned over to kiss her again. This time he was gentle, nibbling at her lips as his hips pumped softly.

"Sorry for the quickie. You felt so good, so right. That was amazing. We're going to make a baby. Nate's going to freak out. He's always..." Zane's face fell.

She let her feet drop to the floor, though she held on to Zane. Her legs were wobbly, her body still pulsing. "He always wanted kids?"

Zane pulled her close. "Yeah. He wanted the whole white-picket-fence thing, though I suspect his fence would have been much more expensive than a plain picket fence. Maybe wrought iron. Don't take his moving on as a reflection of you. He loves you. But he needs more than this place can give him. He wants things he can't have here."

"Do we have to give up on him?" Callie asked, hearing the longing in her voice. "Maybe we should go with him. It's not like we have jobs we're married to."

"No. I don't want to live in that world. There's no place for me there. This is my home. I think I started to love it here when Nell welcomed me to her grocery store and I nearly got kissed by a moose." He kissed her forehead and reached for the soap.

Staying in Bliss was all she'd ever wanted, and she loved that he was getting used to the place. "The meadow. That's what we call it. It's technically on James Glen's ranch, but they don't fence it. Nell would protest. Besides, it's kind of Maurice's home."

"You named the moose?" He grinned as he soaped up her shoulders.

"Yep, though he actually got his name from Hiram," she explained. "You honestly want to stay? You don't think you'll regret it down the line?"

"I know I won't. Living here with you is the best decision I've ever made," he replied. "Besides, you like your job. I don't even have a job, but I know I'll like the one I'm planning to get. I'm going to take out a loan on the empty building beside Stella's."

Callie knew it well. "Oh, that's supposedly haunted."

Zane soaped his hands again and then started to clean her back. His fingers rubbed and massaged until she sighed and leaned against him. He was already stirring, his erection coming back to life. "Then the ghost better get used to me. I'm going to open a bar. I'll go to the bank on Monday. If I can't get a loan from there, I'll hit up Stefan."

His voice cheered measurably. "Yeah, maybe I'll do that. He's like your brother, right? A family loan. If you want, you can help me run it, or you can keep working with Nate until the new sheriff takes over. It's up to you. But I want you to know that I'll take care of us. I'll provide for you. When I get the bar running and making money, you won't have to work."

His hands skimmed along her breasts and down to her pussy, where he rubbed for an awfully long time. "I like to work, Zane. If we can't convince Nate to stay with us, I'll help you with the bar. I think I'll be a good waitress."

He cleaned her thoroughly. "As long as the patrons understand you're a taken woman, I'm fine with that. Maybe I should just beat Nate until he agrees to stay."

There was a loud snort, and Callie jumped.

Zane simply sighed and muttered, "Sneaky bastard. How long have you been out there?" He peeked through the shower curtain.

She stole a glance and saw Nate sitting against the wall of the bathroom. He had one knee up, and his eyes stared at some place below the shower curtain.

"Long enough to know I should leave."

Nate's words cut through her. She scrambled out of the shower. She dripped across the tile, but Nate's arms were open as she kneeled in front of him. He didn't seem to care that she was soaking him through. She felt his breath as his arms closed around her.

"Zane's right. I'm not very smart. But I need more than I can get here, Callie. Can you forgive me?"

She felt the hitch in his chest when he said the words and knew how much they cost him. She also knew she couldn't reject him. She loved him. Zane loved him. Wherever he went, he would be a part of them. "Know that you'll always have a home with us. You can always visit or come back to us. I love you, Nate."

His arms tightened around her. "I love you, too, baby."

She wanted him. For as long as he stayed, she wanted him. "Come to bed with us."

There was the saddest smile on his face. "You sure you want me there?"

Zane reached out a hand. He'd shoved his soaked jeans off his body and stood there in all his glory. "Come to bed with us. She misses you. I don't, but she does." There was a wicked grin on his lips and a twinkle in his emerald eyes. "Come on, Nate. Stay with us for as long as you can, man."

Nate kept one hand on her, but he reached the other out to Zane. For a blissful moment, they were connected, and Callie felt complete.

"Look at me, baby." Nate's voice was thick as he nudged her head up. He nodded at her, and she stood as he accepted a hand up from Zane. The minute Nate was on his feet he was pulling her into his chest, his arms capturing her. He lowered his mouth to hers, and she marveled in all the ways he was different from Zane.

Where Zane overpowered, Nate cajoled. His mouth moved gently against hers, an invitation to play. She flowered open beneath him, allowing his tongue full access. He glided into her mouth with velvety seduction. Though she'd recently come, she felt herself heating up all over again.

She pressed her body to Nate's. She loved the feel of him, even through his clothes. Unlike Zane, he'd gotten fully redressed, and now the fabric of his shirt rasped at her nipples. His belt buckle was cool against her belly. Her hands on the strong muscles of his back, she dragged the shirt out of his waistband. She pulled it up so she could get at his warm skin. Nate cursed and pulled himself out of her embrace.

His blue eyes were hot as he tugged the shirt up and over his head, not bothering with niceties like unbuttoning or folding. He simply tossed it away and went to work on his belt buckle. While Nate tore out of his clothes, Zane moved in behind her. His big hands ran up her torso and cupped her breasts. His mouth found the nape of her neck and kissed the supersensitive skin there. Zane's thumbs circled her nipples, making them ripe and hard.

She gave herself over to Zane's touch as she watched Nate. He kicked out of his boots and shoved his pants and boxers off, tossing them to the side. His dick was already at full attention. It jutted from his body, bobbing as though seeking something. Nate grabbed it with one hand and stroked up and down.

"She is the prettiest thing ever, isn't she, Nate?" Zane's deep voice was a grumble. He was pressed so close to her she could feel it on her skin when he talked.

Nate's eyes were firmly on her breasts as he stroked himself up and down. His hand smoothed his erection from balls to base. The head of his cock was already becoming coated with pearly liquid. "She'll be even prettier when I'm done."

There was a deep chuckle from behind. Zane pinched her nipples between his thumbs and forefingers. She moved restlessly under his hands. Her breasts were so sensitive.

"Are you going to use her for target practice?" Zane asked. His cock moved against her back.

"I want her covered in us, man." Nate's words came out as a harsh groan. His thumb brushed the head of his cock. She watched breathlessly as it seemed to swell and pulse.

"Bed, Callie." There was no doubt that Zane's words were a command. "Hurry. He won't last long."

She scurried out of the bathroom, unsure of what they were planning. It didn't matter. She trusted them. Whatever they wanted would end in her screaming in pleasure at some point. She was willing to do anything to make her time with Nate memorable.

She brushed back tears at the thought. Tonight wasn't about sadness. She was going to enjoy every moment she had left with him. She threw herself on the bed and watched as Zane and Nate placed themselves on either side.

"Lay back, darlin'." Nate's face was flushed as he pumped away at his cock. "Play with yourself."

She laid back and let her fingers drift down. If they wanted a show, she would give them one. She felt so free and powerful in that moment, she barely recognized herself. With these two men she wasn't Callie, the shoulder to cry on, the responsible one. With Nate and Zane, she was a lover, a sexy vixen who took two men at once and left both of them satisfied.

"I don't know what just went through your head, babe, but it was hot." Zane groaned, and his hand was stroking his cock, too.

She smiled as she plucked at her own nipples. One hand stayed caressing her breasts, but the other hand started to make its way lower. "I was thinking I can handle both of you. I was thinking I want both of you tonight. One in my pussy, and one in my ass."

"Fuck." Nate's cock strained, and she watched, fascinated by the way his heavy balls squeezed up tight. "Play with your pussy, baby. I want your fingers wet."

She slid her finger through her juicy pussy. Her clit was already pulsing as though the very air in the room was causing it to swell and beg for release. Callie's eyes darted between Zane and Nate, both watching her, both near to reaching a climax of their own. She pressed down hard on her pulsing clit and came forcefully. She closed her eyes and rode the wave.

Nate moaned and then something warm and sticky started to splash across her breasts. She opened her eyes to see Nate standing right over her, shooting across her skin. A second later, another stream landed as Zane groaned and came. Their cocks were so beautiful, pulsing and giving up their semen. Jets of pearly liquid splashed across her breasts, mingling their essences across her skin.

Heavy pants filled the room as the men came down. Zane got on his knees on the bed beside her, lining his softening cock up to her mouth. "Lick me clean."

She let her tongue come out to run along his cock, gathering the cream that had been left behind. Suddenly Nate was there, too, crowding her, holding his dick out for her ministrations. She turned her head from side to side, cleaning first one and then the other cock until both were clean but hardening again.

Zane pulled away and hopped off the bed. He placed a hand on her head and winked before walking away. She heard the bathroom door open. Nate seemed happy he was no longer competing for her attention. He pushed his cock at her.

"Get me hard again, baby." He groaned as he pushed his cockhead into her mouth. "God, I want to fuck you."

He loomed over. She relaxed back and let him use her mouth. She whirled her tongue around his rapidly reviving cock. He filled her mouth with a salty, manly flavor.

"Don't move, babe." Zane's voice cut through the quiet. "This should be warm." She felt Zane moving a cloth across her breasts, cleaning them. He chuckled as he worked, lingering on her nipples, getting her hot all over again. "This is so sexy right now, but it won't be when it cools off. I want you pretty and clean when we get you dirty again." He pulled away the cloth. "Nate, let her up on her knees."

Nate growled and continued to thrust softly at her mouth.

"Damn it, do you want me to get her ready or not?" Zane asked.

Nate pulled out of her mouth. He had her up and on her hands and knees before she could take a breath. "Take me. Your mouth feels so good."

She ran her tongue down to his balls, delighting in the way they squeezed up as she licked them. She closed her eyes and sucked one, and then the other, into her mouth. She could feel Zane get off the bed. She'd moved back to Nate's dick and was laving the head with little strokes when she felt the bed move under Zane's weight again. She had to concentrate on what she was doing because Zane's hands were suddenly caressing the cheeks of her ass.

"Stay still, Callie," Zane said behind her. "I'm going to play with you for a minute."

Nate groaned, and his cock seemed to swell in her mouth. Callie tried to hold her body still while she continued to work Nate over with her tongue. She shivered as Zane poured lube in between the cheeks of her ass. She took Nate deep. Her chin hit his balls as Zane spread her wide and pressed a finger in. Prickles of sensation sparked in her ass as Zane pressed deep, past the tight ring of muscles. It was almost pain but a bit like pleasure. She groaned around Nate's thick cock.

"How tight is she?" Nate said on a growl.

"So fucking tight. She's going to grip you like a vise."

Nate came out of her mouth with a pop. He put a hand on her head and stroked her gently. "Why me? I got her virginity. Why give up this?"

Zane pulled out and then pressed forward again. She let her head fall to the bed as she pushed back against him. Zane pulled his finger out.

"You were listening in, man," Zane said, getting off the bed. There was a wealth of arrogant pleasure in his voice as he spoke to them from the bathroom. "We can't make babies if I'm fucking her ass." There was the sound of water running and then turning off. In a moment, he was back and he pulled her up, twisting her around like a doll to bring her mouth to his. He pressed his lips against hers. "You okay with this, babe?"

Callie nodded and turned back to Nate. There was a stricken look in his eyes. "I want him. I think the question is does Nate want me?"

Nate's hands dropped for a moment, and he sat back on his heels. His voice was quiet, and he held her eyes with his. "I love you, Callie. I'll always love you."

There was a "but" in those words that she didn't need him to verbalize. He loved her, but he needed more. Tears pricked her eyes, but she wouldn't shed them. She leaned into him.

"I love you, too. Be my first, again." She whispered the words against his lips.

His head sagged, and when he looked back at her, he was haunted. "Always."

"Let me lay down, babe." Zane's hands were gentle on her back, urging her on.

Nate pulled her along, and Zane settled underneath her. She straddled his hips. His huge cock jutted up, naked and powerful. He took himself in hand as she lowered herself on top of him. Inch by inch he filled her. His cock stroked into her pussy. His green eyes watched as she sank onto him. She sighed as he slid home.

Almost immediately, she felt Nate's hand on her back, pressing her onto Zane's chest. Her nipples rasped against Zane's skin as Nate moved in behind her. She heard the crinkle of a condom wrapper and then the pressure of something way bigger than a finger pressing against her anus, seeking entry. She took a deep breath and tried to stay calm.

"This is the prettiest asshole I've ever seen. I can't wait to fuck it. Relax, Callie. I need you to push back against me. It's just like the plug. Flatten your back and press out."

Nate's hands gripped her hips as he pushed forward. Pressure made her shiver. She tried to follow his orders. She flattened her back, pressing her chest against Zane.

Zane kissed her. He whispered to her. He told her how beautiful she was, how much he loved her. Nate's cock pressed forward, fighting the tight ring of muscles that sought to keep him out. Tears welled. The pressure was almost too much, and then he slid in.

"Oh, god." She fought tears. It was like he'd shoved a hot poker up her ass. He was so much bigger than the plug they'd used before.

"Give it a minute." Zane soothed her, running his hands through her hair, kissing her forehead. "We'll try this once, and if you don't like it, we won't do it again."

Nate was holding himself still against her backside. He was covering her. It felt like there wasn't any part of her they weren't touching. Despite the discomfort, the intimacy of being completely enveloped by them was the best feeling she'd ever had. She'd never felt safer and more cherished than she did in that moment.

"I'm fine." She managed to talk though it felt like she couldn't breathe. She was so full. Her hands shook as she placed one on Zane's face and the other snaked around to touch Nate. "I want this."

She did. She wanted to be with them in every way possible, for as long as they had.

"Good, darlin', because I can't hold back any longer. I'll try to go slow." Nate's words sounded like they were ground between his teeth. He started to pull his cock back, and she felt her eyes go wide. She had nerves in her ass that she never knew she had, and now every one of them was screaming in pleasure at the slow, steady drag of Nate's dick.

Zane grinned up at her. "Not the last time then, babe?"

"Oh, no." She pressed back against Nate. She couldn't stand the thought of him pulling out.

He pressed back in with a groan. "Your ass feels so good. It's so tight. I can feel every inch of you."

"You done playing around back there?" Zane asked. "Because I really need to fuck this pussy."

Nate hissed and suddenly pressed forward. Callie could feel his abs against her backside. He was all the way in. "Damn straight, Zane. Let's fuck our woman."

She held on for dear life as they worked in tandem. When one pressed forward, the other pulled out. Zane's hands were on her waist, guiding her up and down his cock. Nate's pulled at her hips, forcing his big dick in and out of her ass. The sensations rushed along her skin. Her breath came out in rabid pants. Something was building inside her pussy, her ass. The twin pleasures were fighting for precedence. Then suddenly she couldn't breathe, couldn't see. She could only feel as she came apart. Her clit pulsed as she came and came. The nerves in her ass lit up and sparked a fire that raced through her.

She heard Nate shout as he frantically pounded into her ass. He stiffened behind her, and his hands tightened. Zane's face flushed, and she felt him pulse as he came, flooding her.

Nate fell forward, shoving her on to Zane's chest. She could feel him breathing heavily against her back. He pressed his lips to the nape of her neck.

"I love you, Callie," Nate whispered.

She wished that was enough.

Chapter Thirteen

The town hall was full to overflowing by the time Nate gently pushed his way through the crowd. He hadn't been sure what to expect when Callie had told him she'd called a town meeting, but it wasn't this crowd. He was used to citizens being fairly apathetic about what went on around them. He should have known this town would be different. It looked like everyone in Bliss had shown up. There was a loud hum of conversation going on around him as he settled Callie into a seat close to the front.

"Don't worry. I'll take care of her." Zane slid into the open seat next to Callie like he belonged there.

He did. Zane belonged next to her more than he himself did. Zane was staying with her. Zane was committing to her. Damn it. The thought made him ache inside. He nodded shortly and turned away from the sight of her scooting closer to Zane. If he was half as smart as he claimed to be, he would be sitting on the other side of Callie, vying for attention.

"Sheriff!"

The loud calls of the people around him reminded Nate that even if he was willing to commit his life to being the sheriff of Bliss, he wouldn't be sitting with Zane and Callie. Not tonight at least. There was a small raised stage at the front of the room with a long conference table and a place setting with his name on it. He had a meeting to run.

A frail figure stood in between the imposing bodies of Worthington and Leander. The agents looked ridiculously out of place among the locals. They were in perfectly pressed suits with hair that had been cut into the current style and wouldn't dare to look windblown. He snickered inwardly. They would shit their pants if they had his job. Just the other day he'd had to help the park rangers deal with a huge grizzly who decided to invite himself into the Farley family's cabin for supper. Then he had to talk to the boys, who had been luring the damn bear in for a science experiment. Yup, Worthington and Leander would have no idea how to handle a bear, much less the evil genius that was the Farley brothers.

When had he started thinking that way? Hell, he used to dress like the agents when he wasn't on the job. He had the best clothes, the latest haircut, thousand-dollar shoes. When did all of that become something he snickered at? *Clothes made the man*, his father would say. *Bullshit*, his increasingly loud inner voice chimed in. What a man did, what he loved and protected, that made a man.

And now that he thought about it, his uniform was pretty comfy. It didn't wrinkle so it was easy to take care of. He didn't hate putting it on. He'd hated what it represented, but he was kind of coming to terms with it. When he went back to the DEA, he would dress in suits when they had meetings, put on ties that threatened to strangle him, and he would have to give up his well-worn boots because they weren't snazzy enough.

He didn't like that thought.

"Sheriff Wright." The elderly man leaning on his walker looked relieved to see him walking up. Hiram Jones was the mayor of Bliss and had been for the last twenty years. He wore the town's version of formal, a clean western shirt, bolo tie with a shiny silver clasp, and pressed blue jeans. A Stetson sat on his head, and Nate realized that Hiram must have taken this meeting seriously. After all, he'd put in his teeth. Hiram usually didn't bother. Hiram scooted his walker with tennis balls covering the feet over closer to Nate. "I'm glad you're here. I don't think I like these two. Are you sure we need them around? Bliss can handle its own, if you know what I mean."

Nate nodded politely and gave the elderly man a hand. He started maneuvering Hiram toward a seat at the front of the audience. He saw a place open next to Stella who, for some reason, had decided to dress like Annie Oakley. All she was missing was a shotgun strapped to her back, though Nate had no illusions that she could have one in her hands before he could blink. For all her crazy dress, she was solid. Stella was dependable, and she would take care of the mayor.

They all took care of each other here. He wouldn't get that in DC.

"The special agents are merely here as backup, Mayor Jones," Nate explained. "I assure you, I'm still in charge."

Stella smiled up at the mayor and immediately began fussing over him. "You come on and sit down with me, Hi. Sheriff Wright will take care of those boys. Special agents? I don't see anything special about them."

Nate was satisfied the mayor was settled and walked back over to his former colleagues. He could hear them talking as they looked around the room. Now he wished this meeting was taking place in the town square in full daylight where their disdainful stares would be hidden behind their expensive sunglasses.

"This place is a complete joke," Leander said, not bothering to keep his voice down. "Not a one of these people know their head from their ass."

"Yeah, Wright, you gotta dump this place and come back to the real world." Worthington was shaking his head. "Seriously, how can you stand it here? No one in this piddly town has ever had to face anything. I can't stand all the syrupy sweetness. It's like fucking Mayberry in here."

"It's not so bad." Nate kept his tone moderate but had the sudden urge to wipe the snarky smile off Marcus Worthington's face. And what was actually wrong with Mayberry? It had always seemed like a nice place to him.

Leander sighed. "It's just a pity, a truly gifted agent like you getting stuck in this pathetic place because of misplaced loyalty. Look, Wright, I know he's your partner and you've been friends for a long time, but Hollister is dragging you down. Marc and I have a proposal for you. There's a lot of money to be made in our positions."

Doing what? The real money was at the top. Nate couldn't

imagine Worthington and Leander made that much more than he had. Of course, they made more than his Bliss salary, but they also spent more. He didn't need a ton of cash here in Bliss. No one judged him on the make of his car or how expensive his shoes were. They didn't care. He didn't want to hear the lecture on coming back to the agency right now. He had too much on his mind already. "We should get the meeting started."

Nate rushed on stage. He sank into his chair and touched the microphone to ensure it was on. "Settle down people. We're ready to start."

After a moment, Worthington and Leander took their seats at the podium, and Nate introduced them. He gave the town a brief rundown of what was happening and what to look for. The special agents interjected here and there, giving advice as though they were talking to two-year-olds rather than an entire town of people whose percentage of gun owners dwarfed the national average. They were patronizing. They were obnoxious. They were probably what Nate himself had sounded like just a few days ago. As Worthington went on and on, Nate sat, really thinking about his predicament.

What did he want? It was a question he thought he'd answered a long time ago. He wanted everything. He wanted to be a success. Success in his world was measured in money and power. So why hadn't he taken up his father on his offer when he finished college? His father had offered him a vice presidency in the family company. It was a straight shot to CEO. As CEO he would have had the world at his feet. Why had he joined the DEA? Because deep down he wanted to protect people. Because deep in his heart, he wanted to matter, and not because he had money.

His ambition had burned, certainly. He'd seen himself running a Bureau office in record time. He'd marry the right woman and be on a fast track. He would show his father that he could make his own way to the top.

Oh, god, Zane was right. He was thirty-one years old and still trying to prove to his father that he was worthy of his respect. And why? It wasn't like he respected his father. His father had gutted his trust fund in a vain attempt to keep up appearances as the ground was burning around him. Nate had trusted him to watch out for his interests while he was in deep cover, and his father's only explanation for why he'd burned through ten million dollars was that he'd needed it. Nate would be okay, he'd explained, but they couldn't be poor.

His whole world had been destroyed in one single afternoon. Zane had been close to death, and Nate had sat alone in a hospital room when he'd learned his future was gone. He'd spent every second trying to get back to that place where he had everything to look forward to.

Was he spending so much time mourning the past that he was missing out on his future? Sometimes things happened for a reason.

He was well aware that he was zoning out at the worst possible time. He tried not to stare at Zane and Callie sitting next to the Harpers and Stefan. No one gave Zane's scarred face a second glance as people leaned in to ask him questions. Zane looked cool and comfortable as he quietly replied to a woman leaning forward from the row behind him.

"Perhaps it would be better if you directed your questions to the agents in charge, ma'am," Leander stated in that gratingly pretentious tone of his.

The blonde stood up, and Nate noted Leander's interests rise. Laura Niles worked at the convenience store. She was also stacked and lovely. She had a small-town charm that belied what Nate knew were years of big-city living. She marched herself up to the microphone set up at the front of the audience. She was wearing jeans and an incongruous pair of red stilettos. Nate smiled a little. Laura would wear four-inch heels to shovel her driveway.

Leander placed a hand over his microphone and leaned toward his partner. "There's my date for the night. What do you bet I can get that naïve piece of ass in bed after this meeting is over?"

His blood pressure ticked up. Laura was a nice lady, not some piece of ass. She stood in front of the microphone, and he was aware of a certain protective feeling for her. Not because she was a lovely woman. She had nothing on his Callie. He felt protective because she belonged to Bliss.

"Please feel free to share your thoughts with the rest of us, sweetheart." There was an unmistakable leer on Leander's face. Worthington leaned forward, obviously sizing her up.

"Of course," Laura started with a deep breath. "My name is Laura Niles. I left the FBI five years ago when a serial killer nearly tortured me to death after my profile of him led me right to his doorstep. I'm not in Bliss because I'm some fruitcake, as you said to your partner. I'm in Bliss because I like it here. As for sharing my thoughts with the room, well, I was just telling Zane there that the two of you are assholes who probably don't know a Sig from a Ruger because you're too busy fixing your hair. I totally remember your type from the Bureau. You made us all look bad." She grinned brightly. "Thanks. I do feel better having shared that with the room."

There was a nice round of applause.

She sauntered off, leaving two frowning special agents in her wake. Before Worthington could speak, Marie had taken her place at the microphone. "My name is Marie Warner. I run the Trading Post with my wife, Teeny, who I rescued from her abusive ex-husband. I shot his balls off when he tried to kidnap our son and kill my woman."

Nate hid a smile behind his hand. Apparently word had gotten out that Leander and Worthington thought they were lightweights who had never faced danger in their pitiful, small-town lives. He frowned as he realized he'd said something close to that not too long ago.

Marie pointed a finger at the stage. "My boy is a deputy. I'll shoot your balls off if you get him killed."

"Damn it, Momma! You have got to stop that. I am an adult man and I can shoot balls off all on my own." Logan stood up at the back of the room where he'd been making out with some brunette he'd been seeing.

"Why don't we keep it to the topic at hand, which is how we're going to protect you until we can resolve these very important issues."

Nate had to hand it to Worthington. He sounded professional.

Rachel Harper stepped up to the microphone. She introduced herself and quickly got to the point. "I shot and killed my crazy stalker a couple of months back. I think you should post some pictures of the men we need to take care of. As Marie and I are the only ones here who've recently killed a son of a bitch, I think we should lead the hunt."

"And where the hell are you going to stash your gun, Rach?"

Max Harper didn't need a microphone. Rye was on his feet next to his brother, looking every bit as outraged. "Do your maternity pants even have pockets?"

"I would like to interject something." A light, frothy voice broke through the discussions that were rapidly multiplying. Nate looked up and saw that Nell had brought her own microphone. "I'm Nell Flanders, and while I am a pacifist, I am also a feminist. I believe that if Rachel wants to 'kill a son of a bitch,' she should be allowed to. Her state of gestation shouldn't come into it."

Her husband, Henry, leaned in. "Have we put any thought into passive resistance? It worked for Gandhi."

And then they were off. A delightful chaos reigned as Max and Rye argued with Rachel over whether or not she would lead an armed posse. Henry got into a heated argument with Stella over whether protests would, perhaps, change the hearts and minds of an outlaw biker club. Logan tried to explain to his moms that he was an adult and a man and shouldn't hide behind his momma.

"What the hell kind of town is this?" Leander asked, obviously disgusted with the whole event.

What kind of town was Bliss?

Nate looked at Zane and Callie. Callie was animatedly discussing something with Mel. Zane sat in the middle of it all with a huge grin on his face. His eyes lit up as he watched the clamor around him.

What kind of town was Bliss?

It was the kind of town where a person got a second chance. These people weren't naïve. They had all known pain. They knew what the real world was like and chose a different path. Nate was shocked at the way his eyes watered. What had these people done when their personal worlds had fallen apart? Had they spent their lives trying to get back something that was gone forever? Hell, no. When the world threw them out, they built a new one, a better one.

A new ambition started to burn through Nathan Wright. Why should he hold onto dreams that no longer meant anything? Callie mattered. Zane mattered. Bliss mattered.

What kind of town was Bliss?

It was *his* town.

Nate pulled his mike from its stand and got to his feet. His heart pounded with the weight of what he was about to do. "My name is Nathan Wright."

The crowd got quiet and turned to him. He noted vaguely that Leander and Worthington looked relieved that he was taking control. He figured they wouldn't be so relieved in a moment or two.

"I used to work for the Drug Enforcement Agency, but now I'm the sheriff of Bliss, and, damn it, I don't want to wear a condom, either."

There were a whole bunch of wide eyes looking up at him. Nell Flanders brought her microphone up. Nate cut her off. "Don't you talk to me about population control right now, Nell. Zane doesn't have to wear a condom, and I don't think it's fair that I have to."

Callie stood, her hands on her hips. "Zane doesn't have to wear a condom because he's willing to stay in Bliss and raise babies with me."

Zane had the widest grin on his face. It was a look of complete approval, and Nate felt it in his bones. His partner knew exactly what he was about to do. "Well, as to that, I'm staying, too. I'm staying in Bliss, and if this town decides to run a rubber duck against me in the next election, then you tell that damn duck to be prepared because I'm going to win. I am the sheriff of this town, and no damn inanimate object is going to do a better job than me. I promise to protect this town and all of her people. I promise to ruthlessly beat back the real world every time it encroaches. I promise to find the best alien-detecting technology that money can buy. I swear on my life that I'll do everything I can to keep my deputy alive and whole so his momma doesn't shoot my balls off." There was loud applause, hoots, and hollers as Nate made his first campaign speech. But there was more he had to promise than simply that he would do his job. He moved to the center of the stage and jumped off. He looked at Callie. "I promise to be the best husband and father I can be. I'll be the best friend and partner to you, Zane. And we'll be the best freaky threesome this town has ever seen."

"Hey," Max interrupted, only to have his wife's hand clasped over his mouth.

"I love you, Callie Sheppard. You agreed to marry Zane. Will you marry me, too?"

A smile curled her mouth up. "I never agreed to marry Zane. The truth is I don't necessarily believe in marriage as an institution."

"You do now!" Zane's outraged shout exactly matched Nate's own.

Callie looked between them. "Wow, way to double-team a girl."

"Have no doubt, you will marry us," he said with a light feeling invading his very cells. This was his future. These crazy, amazing people were his family.

"Hell, yes, she'll marry you," Stefan said with lazy menace. "I never thought I'd have to have a shotgun wedding in Bliss, but I will if you're stubborn, little sister."

"Fine, I guess I can compromise, but just this once." Then she was running toward him, her face open and filled with love. For him. Nate dropped the microphone and braced himself for impact. When his arms were filled with soft, sweet woman, he sighed and clutched her close, not giving a damn that the entire town had watched him proclaim his love. Zane was suddenly at Callie's back, the two of them crowding her the way they would for the next forty or fifty years.

"All of this is touching." Leander's sarcastic voice cut through Nate's joy, reminding him he had one thing left to do. "But none of it solves the problem that this town is woefully unprepared to handle the threat."

Nate turned and faced his former coworkers. It had been a mistake to bring them in, but one he could rectify. "Don't worry about us. We can take care of ourselves. You two should feel free to hightail it back to El Paso."

Worthington leaned forward. "I don't think that's a good idea."

Nate didn't want to hear it. "I said get the hell out of my town!"

The cheers erupted again, and Nate got lost in the crowd of people wishing him well.

* * * *

Callie felt like the whole world had a warm glow around it. All through the reception hall people she knew and had grown up with were talking about her, Nate, and Zane. She'd lost count of the people who had hugged her in congratulations.

Stella winked at her as she walked into the small kitchen. "You're the talk of the town, hon."

She felt her face flush. "I don't know about that. I think Nate and Zane are the ones people are talking about."

Stella shook her head. "We might be talking about them, but we love you. We're all happy that our favorite girl is going to be well taken care of. And don't you doubt that. Max, Rye, and Stef already had serious talks with both of those boys about how poorly things could go for them if they step out of line. I heard Hiram mention that he still knew how to use a shotgun to the sheriff. And me and Hal certainly can take care of business if either one of them hurts you."

Callie swung around quickly to try to see if Nate or Zane were running. They stood in the crowd, seemingly at ease, talking to the people around them. Zane laughed at something Jen said. Nate was surrounded by a small group of the county's ranchers, explaining something. Neither looked like they had been scared off by her friends and neighbors. Still. "Stella, you have to tell everyone to leave Nate and Zane alone. Couldn't we let them settle in before we show them how crazy we are?"

Stella held a tureen of coffee in her hands. Callie helped her pour it out into the sink. "Not a chance. And don't you worry. Those boys belong here. The big one knew it the minute he stuck his head outside of that cabin of theirs. And the sheriff is coming along nicely. It's going to be okay, hon. They love you. They aren't going to be run off so easily." She shook her head. "We're out of coffee in here. Can you go to the storeroom for me? It doesn't look like we're breaking up any time soon."

It was true. There was a vibrant energy in the room that couldn't be denied. The citizens of Bliss were talking and planning, enjoying each other's company. They needed coffee to fuel the discussions of how to protect the town. There was always something magical when they all came together like this.

And she didn't have to leave. She could stay in the place she loved, with the men she loved.

She walked out of the reception hall toward the small storage closet at the back of the building. The noise faded as she moved away from the crowd. She breathed a sigh of relief. It was great to be surrounded by friends, but she was looking forward to the time when she could climb into the Bronco with Nate and Zane and head back to "Fort Naked," as Zane had started calling the naturist community. Tomorrow morning they were all going to the airport. They were going to the field office in El Paso, and once all the reports were filed, Nate had assured her that Zane would be safe. She felt her heart clench and a smile cross her face. Nate would be coming home with them. Happy tears pricked her eyes. The three of them would come home to Bliss.

"Why wait? Why don't we do this thing now?"

Callie stopped in her tracks. She could hear voices down the hall. There was only one strip of lighting on in this hallway at night to conserve energy. It made the entire place seem gloomy. She'd been in this building a hundred times before, but a chill went through her. She went still, listening. There was nothing to be afraid of here. Her friends were close by. No one would hurt her here.

"You have to be patient," a deep voice said. "Wright is taking Hollister in tomorrow. That idiot will file a report with everything we need on it. The director has his head up his ass when it comes to stuff like this. The team might have the numbers, but they have no idea where the account is. It will take them weeks to figure out what bank Ellis used and to get a judge to sign off on taking the money into custody. We don't have the same problem. We simply get a copy of the report and disappear. No one will ever even know what happened."

Callie clasped a hand over her mouth to stop the gasp that almost came out. Worthington and Leander were dirty. She had to get to Nate and Zane. They needed to know. Had those two been the reason Zane's cover had been blown? How much had they cost her men? She started to back down the hall. Her sneakers screeched against the slick floor, the sound resonating through the quiet hall. She winced and held herself still, hoping the agents wouldn't notice. *Please, please don't let them come around the corner.*

But suddenly metal flashed as Worthington rounded the corner, gun in hand. "Scream and I'll shoot."

She turned to run anyway, but Leander was on her.

He turned to his partner as he shoved his gun in the small of her back. "Shit. What do we do now?"

"Change of plans," Worthington said as he pointed toward the door to the back parking lot.

Yep, it changed all of Callie's plans.

* * * *

Nate enjoyed a cup of coffee while he talked to a couple of the area ranchers. He looked up to see Zane in a discussion with Callie's friend, Jennifer. He was shaking his head no, and Jen didn't look like she was having it.

He nodded to James Glen and eased himself out of the conversation. He started to make his way across the room, intending to save Zane from Jen's pleas. She'd been begging him to sit for her. Apparently sitting meant allowing her to paint him. She'd explained it as capturing Zane's essence on canvas. Zane liked his essence just fine where it was. He was never going to be comfortable as an artist's model. Unfortunately, he was also not comfortable saying no to a woman. Even from across the room, Nate could see Zane's eyes darting around, looking for someone to come and save him.

Rachel Harper stepped in front of him. "Sheriff, have you seen Callie? I need to talk to her about the Winter Festival. It's coming up soon and we got volunteered by Marie to be on the committee. Considering her earlier speech, I'm not going to argue with her. Callie and I need to talk about setting up a meeting."

Nate looked around, his height providing him a view of the room. "I don't see her."

Rachel frowned. "I saw her walking out to the parking lot with those asshole agents you brought in. Has she not gotten back yet? I hope she was giving them directions on how to get out of town. Next time, Sheriff, trust us to handle our own business. The last thing we need is a bunch of outsiders coming in here and telling us how to live."

A chill went through him, heightening his senses. Leander and Worthington had left, and quickly, after the debacle of a town hall had happened. He hadn't thought they would come back. Why would

Callie be with them? The safety meeting had turned into a party, and Nate doubted that his former friends would have stayed for coffee and lemon pound cake. But then he also knew how they felt about Callie, and any interaction with her likely wouldn't be pleasant.

"Zane!" Nate yelled across the room. He didn't care that every head turned. "You seen Callie?"

Zane's face went a little white as he looked around.

"Has anyone seen Callie?" God, Nate hoped the answer to that question was yes. He was getting a sinking feeling in the pit of his stomach. A whole bunch of things were suddenly making sense. He thought back to Leander's earlier words. He'd said there was a lot of money to be made by men in their position. They were government employees, and at this level, there wasn't a big honking paycheck attached to the job. How did a law enforcement drone make real money? He sold out his fellow agents. He sold their covers for cold, hard cash.

He'd always wondered how Ellis had found out about Zane. It hadn't made sense. They'd been undercover for years, and never once had Zane said or done anything that could have exposed them. The only way Ellis could have found out was if someone on the inside was working with him.

His old "friends" had sold out Zane. Anger warred with fear in his gut. They had Callie and he was going to do anything he had to to get her back.

Chapter Fourteen

Callie pushed out against the bonds that held her hands together. Unfortunately, those suckers weren't moving. The SUV she'd been shoved into drove through the night. Every second took her farther away from Nate and Zane. The metal from the handcuffs was cold against her skin as she tried to twist her wrists. That jerk Leander had put the cuffs on tightly around them. They bit into her skin. He hadn't been willing to take any chances that she would be able to get away.

"You send the text?" Leander hands were tight on the steering wheel, his anger easy to see.

"Yeah." As Worthington said the words, there was a ping from his phone that let him know he had a text. "Well, that was fast. Looks like old Nathan is anxious about the girl. He says he'll meet us wherever we choose, and he'll bring Hollister with him. Maybe it wasn't all for nothing."

A low grumble came from Leander's throat. "I don't like it. I still think we should have taken Hollister out from a distance."

"We don't have that option now. That nosy bitch back there ruined everything. We can't be sure Wright won't go ahead and call the director. I'm sure he wrote the numbers down. He normally wouldn't give them to the boss over the phone, but he might if he thought someone would get there first. We have to have that money now because there's no way Wright hasn't told someone."

"Damn it. How did this get so fucked up? I'm not ready to run."

Worthington slapped his hand on the dashboard. "It's fucked up because you talk too loud, asshole. And because Wright's an idiot. I thought he would be easy to turn. He lost everything. He needs the fucking money."

"He needs Zane more," Callie said. They had thought they could turn Nathan Wright? They didn't know him at all.

There was an irritated huff from the front seat. Even in the gloom of the car, she could see Leander's hands tighten on the steering wheel. "Yeah, well, I never suspected those two were getting it on. I don't like to think about that. It's disgusting."

"They certainly are not, though there would be absolutely nothing wrong with it." The intolerance of some people constantly shocked her. "Both Zane and Nathan have a relationship with me. They are just very close friends."

"I'll say," Worthington snickered. "Look, sweetheart, I don't care about your perverted sex life."

Callie heard an offended squeak come out of her mouth. She wasn't sure why she was arguing the point with them. Maybe because it was easier than thinking about how they would kill her. There was no way they let her live. "It is not perverted. It is beautiful and loving. Maybe the reason you think everything is perverted is that you haven't dealt with your own sexuality. A good therapist could help with that."

Worthington leaned over. "Do you have anything we could use as a gag?"

She closed her mouth.

"Better," Worthington muttered.

He pulled out a gun and checked the chamber. She wished she'd paid more attention when Rye, Max, and Stef had taken her shooting. She knew her way around a rifle but not a handgun. If she'd paid them half a mind, she'd know what kind of gun they were going to kill her with.

She was surprised at how much she genuinely hated the two men sitting in front of her. Hate wasn't something she'd truly felt before, but it was a fire inside her now. They had ruined what could have been a perfect day. Nate loved her. Zane loved her. They were willing to give this crazy life a go. Her heart clenched. She could be pregnant even now. She could have the life she always wanted, but she'd been an idiot. She should never have been alone when she knew people were after her men. What had she been thinking? She'd thought the only danger came from the bikers, but now she could see that these men had been the real snakes all along.

Zane hadn't screwed up. Zane had been betrayed.

"You outed Zane." For some reason she needed to say the words out loud, needed them to know she understood how evil they were.

"And you're Nancy Drew," Leander replied. "Yeah, we gave up Zane. Nate was supposed to be gone that day. He'd told his handler he was working a deal out of Laredo, but he stayed in El Paso that day and fucked up everything. Ellis was going to pay us a million dollars for giving up the narc."

Worthington's laugh was like the cackle of a hyena. "Maybe we should thank Wright for screwing up that deal. Now we're getting twenty million instead of a measly one, and we don't have to worry about Ellis double-crossing us. What's he going to do from his prison cell?"

The car swerved suddenly, and she was tossed to the side. She narrowly avoided hitting her head on the side of the door. Twisting her body up, she tried to look out the window. Where were they? Her eyes adjusted to the low light, and she could see aspens and evergreens. The car was moving at an angle. They were going up the mountain. Given the amount of time they had been traveling, there was exactly one mountain they could be scaling. She knew it well. Max and Rye lived here. Mel lived on this mountain. She knew this place like the back of her hand. Was she going to die here?

Her chest hurt. She'd been so close to what she wanted. She'd almost had a life with both of them. When Nate had stood up in the middle of town hall tonight and declared himself, she thought her heart would burst. He'd stood up for her in front of everyone who mattered to her. Everyone in town knew that Callie Sheppard was loved and loved well. She'd sat by Zane in that meeting and watched Nate on the stage, and for the first time in her adult life, she hadn't felt alone. She'd been a part of something. She had a family of her own.

God, she couldn't die now.

"This better work." Leander's voice was slightly shaky. He twisted the steering wheel, trying to adjust to the winding road. "If he calls it in and we don't get that fucking cash, we're screwed. They'll be looking for us."

"Will you stop whining? I have the password." Worthington bit the words out of his mouth. The two were starting to snap at each other like irritated alligators. "All we need is the actual account number and we're golden. You might not be ready for this, but I am. It's going to be fine."

"If the Barbarians don't catch us. If the director doesn't set the dogs on us. I wish we'd done this before Ellis ordered the hit on Hollister." Leander's voice was tense and tight. He seemed more on the edge than his partner in crime.

"Yeah, well if he hadn't, we still wouldn't know where the damn account number was. We would still be working like idiots. I'm glad the bastard got anxious."

"Yeah, it's great that every asshole with a twelve gauge will be on the lookout for us. Once they find out Hollister is dead and the money is gone, they'll be gunning for us."

She'd known that these men intended to kill Zane if they got their hands on him, but her heart skipped a couple of beats at the verbal acknowledgment of their plan. She couldn't wrap her head around the idea that Zane might die. A vision of his big, beautiful body lying still on the ground swamped her senses, and she couldn't stop the small sob that choked out of her throat. The men in the front seat didn't seem to notice her distress.

"We'll be on a plane to Shanghai before anyone knows what happened. No one even knows Sonny is dead yet. The last I heard, Ellis thinks he's the turncoat. He put out a hit on him. Ellis thinks his own right-hand man turned on him and is planning this heist."

Leander's hand came out, and they shared an obnoxious high-five. "Damn straight he thinks that. It's what we told him. We didn't mention that we killed the asshole ourselves, but only after he gave up the password. It's too bad Ellis is such a paranoid bastard. If he'd given Sonny the account number, we'd be free and clear by now, but no, he has to hide the account number in a tat. Who thinks to do that?"

Worthington shrugged. "Hey, it worked for the dude. He hid twenty million dollars right under the nose of the DEA. Our own agent walked around with the evidence on his chest for years. I kind of admire the guy."

There was a long sigh. Leander's head shook. "Why fucking China? Couldn't we go to a country where they speak English?"

She knew the answer to that one. "China doesn't extradite jerks like you back to the U.S."

Worthington turned and winked at her. "The bitch is right. Even if Wright has already told the director what we've done, it won't matter. We'll get to China, buy a couple of new identities, and in a few years, no one will recognize us and we can enjoy our cash. Follow my lead, and we'll be fine." His hand moved down below the seat. He shifted as though he was shoving something into his pants. The gun. He nodded. "Turn here. The place Wright talked about in his report is right up the road."

The report? There was only one report he would have sent to these men. He would have documented everything that had happened in the last few days. There were only three places Nate might have mentioned in a report about the attempts on Zane's life. There was the biker bar, their cabin, and the campsite Mel had discovered. She'd typed up the report for him. He'd taken careful note of the longitude and latitude of the campsite. It had to be where they were going.

She closed her eyes as the car turned, visualizing the land around Mel's cabin. It was thick with aspens and firs, but there were several places that were clear. The campsite was one of the places with a bit of clear land. It was why Mel had designated it a potential landing zone. If it was a normal night, Mel would be on patrol. All she would have to do was find a way to let him know where she was, and Mel would take care of things. Despite his status as the town kook, Mel had spent time in the military, and he was beyond competent with a gun in his hands. She would pit Mel against these two any day of the week.

Unfortunately, Mel had been at the town hall. That plan was a no-go. He was likely still there, talking to Stella or discussing the coming invasion with Nell. She was on her own until Nate and Zane showed up and walked straight into an ambush. She was sure the treasonous agents had promised to exchange her for Zane, but she was also sure they didn't intend to leave any witnesses. Worthington and Leander would kill them all. It was up to her to keep that from happening.

She had to find a way to save her men.

The car stopped. The full moon lit the night. In the distance, she could see a set of caves Mel used to store some stuff she hoped Nate never found out about. Mel liked to be prepared, and some of those preparations involved a lot of firearms. He'd prepped for the aliens, but she would use those weapons against her captors. She had to find a way to get to those caves.

She breathed deeply, willing herself to be calm. Her hands shook behind her back as the agents got out of the car and slammed the front doors shut. She turned quickly when she realized the door to her left was opening.

"All right, sweetheart. Let's get this over with," Worthington said.

As hard as she could, she kicked the door open. It hit Worthington squarely in the gut, and he went down with a shout. She only had seconds before they would be on her. Callie scrambled out of the car and ran for the tree line. There was a shout behind her and a loud pop. She stumbled as something hit her shoulder. It felt like her skin was on fire. Through her tears, she got to her feet, unwilling to stay down. No matter what pain she felt, she had to keep moving. She had to survive or her men wouldn't either.

"Damn it, we need her alive for now."

Callie made it to the trees and was enveloped by the forest.

* * * *

Zane watched as Nate opened the locker containing the Bliss County Sheriff's Department's armory. He already had a Sig Sauer in a holster at the small of his back. Nate handed him a rifle and another handgun, this one a Glock. Zane checked each weapon carefully and forced himself to go slow, to be precise. What he wanted to do was grab whatever was handy and run as fast as he could to bash in two fuckers' brains and save his wife.

God, those assholes had Callie. What had they already done to her? Was she scared? Of course, she was scared. She was probably terrified. Did she understand they would do anything to save her? Panic threatened to swamp him, threatening to overcome every possible good decision he could make.

"Calm down, Zane. It's going to be all right." Nate's voice was even and sure as he passed Stefan Talbot a rifle.

Nate's eyes were as steady as his hands. His presence calmed Zane considerably. He'd never known anyone as calm under pressure as Nathan Wright. Despite Nate's former ambitions to move up at the DEA, Zane had always known Nate's true calling. He had been born to protect, to stand as a bulwark against violence. It was in Nate's blood, and nothing could change that.

The small sheriff's department was full of concerned townsfolk. The gleeful chaos that seemed to follow the citizens of Bliss had been replaced with a somber force of will. Zane looked around the room. The Harper twins were busy checking the rifles they had selected. Teeny was dividing her attention between Marie and Logan, both of whom seemed to be preparing for some form of all-out warfare.

Rachel Harper walked up to Nate with Jen Waters in tow.

"I can use a shotgun or a rifle." Rachel had pulled her strawberry-blonde hair into a tight ponytail.

"I've never actually shot anything, but I can learn really fast." Mascara tracked down Jen's face. She'd been crying from the moment she realized her friend was missing.

He saw Stef's eyes widen at the statement. Zane quickly stepped between them. The last thing he needed was Stef to start yelling at Callie's friend. Zane wasn't sure what was going on between those two, but it was intense. It also had no place here. "Jen, why don't you stay here and monitor the phone? We need someone to coordinate from here."

She shook her head. "No, she's my closest friend. Stella can answer the phone."

"Not a chance, pet." Stefan's voice was a silky threat. "If you think for one minute that I will allow you to walk into an ambush, you don't know me at all."

She turned to face him, her hands on her hips and stubborn will stamped on her face. "You don't own me, Stef. Hell, you don't even like me. I don't have to listen to a word you say. You want me to leave you alone? Well, I promise I won't make a fool of myself over Stefan Talbot ever again. And you can't tell me what to do."

"No, but I can." Nate stepped up. He nodded at the Harper twins. Max moved behind his wife while Rye strode to the single holding cell. He opened it and held the door wide. "Stef, if you would like to join Max and Rye, I believe there is plenty of room."

Rachel Harper gasped as her husband picked her up and started carrying her across the room toward the cell. She also proved she knew a whole lot of curse words.

"No way you're going with us, baby. You can yell all you like and call me every kind of name, but I'm keeping you safe. And I won't even try to blame the baby. I wouldn't let you do this whether or not you were pregnant," Max said as Rachel squirmed in his arms.

"Damn you, Max." She turned her head to take in Rye. "And you, too. Fine. I'll stay here. You don't have to lock me up."

"Yeah, I believe that one, Rach." Rye's voice was dripping with sarcasm. "You would form your own group and cause all kinds of trouble. In you go."

Stef moved quickly. Jen was in a fireman's hold over his shoulder before she could protest. She kicked and tried to scratch at his back, but she was in the cell when Rye Harper closed the door.

"I won't ever forgive you, Stef. You have no right to make this choice for me," she said through her tears. Rachel had her hands on the younger woman's shoulders.

"Yes, well, at least you'll be alive to hate me." Stef's eyes were hollow as he turned on Zane. "Is it you they want?"

Why hadn't they just taken him? Why had they taken Callie? God, if he'd known that was the choice, he would have turned himself over. "Yes."

Stef's mouth tightened, and he nodded sharply. "You're the bait then."

"I'm not the fucking bait," Zane said with savage intent. They needed to understand that he wasn't playing games. He wasn't taking the chance that something could go wrong. There was only one way to play this. "Once we find these assholes, I'm giving myself up, and you guys are getting Callie the hell out of there."

"I thought we knew where they were." Rye Harper was pointedly ignoring his wife's killer stare. "Didn't Nate get a text or something?"

Zane's attention swiftly focused on Nate. "He didn't get anything or he would have told me."

The words came out as a threat, and Zane meant them that way.

He knew in an instant that Nate was hiding something. His face had gone flat. Nate was an excellent poker player, but Zane had known him long enough to call his bluff. "You better spit it out now, man. If you know something and you're holding out on me, we're going to have trouble."

Nate's eyes narrowed. "I'd watch my tone, Zane, or you might find yourself in the cell with the women."

That was not happening. "I'd like to see you try. You want to explain why you're holding out on me?"

"What would you have done if I had given you the coordinates of the place where we're supposed to meet with Worthington and Leander?" Nate asked.

Frustration made his fists clench. "I sure as fuck wouldn't be sitting here. I would have gone there, and Callie would be out and safe by now."

"No, you would have gone charging in, and both you and Callie would be dead." Nate took the hat off his head and pulled out a Kevlar vest. He tossed it to Zane. "Put it on."

Zane let the damn thing hit the floor with a thud. "Tell me where she is."

Nate picked up the vest, his eyes steely as he held it out. "Put the fucking thing on or I'll Taser you and handle this myself. If you want to have anything to do with this mission, you will put the vest on and you will follow my every order. I'm in charge here. If you deviate from the plan, Logan is going to take you out."

"Umm, boss?" Logan's voice sounded reedy and thin. "I don't think that's such a good idea."

"Don't worry, Nate. If he steps out of line, Max, Rye, and I will take care of it." Stefan held the rifle like a man who knew what he was doing. "I'll make sure I don't actually kill him."

Zane's chest felt heavy. He stared at the man who had been his partner for most of his life. How could he not understand what was at stake here? "You can't do this, Nate. You have to give me up."

Nate reached out, putting a hand on his shoulder. "So they can kill you and Callie? Not going to happen. Leave this to me. I know I let you down before, but I won't this time. I promise. I won't lose you, and I certainly won't lose our wife."

The words made his heart seize. Their wife. They didn't need a piece of paper to make her theirs. He didn't need some marriage certificate to know that Callie was his. She'd given herself to him when she said "I love you." She couldn't take herself back, and there was no way in hell he was going to allow some assholes to take her away from them.

His eyes held Nate's, and Zane suddenly realized the real intimacy of this threesome he found himself in. It wasn't about the sex. It wasn't about getting her in between them. It was so much more. It was about sharing this life with Callie and Nate. It was about having another person who knew what it was like to love Callie. He could rely on Nate. Nate loved Callie, and in a completely nonsexual tough-guy way, Nate loved him, too.

Damn, Nathan Wright was his hero. Why hadn't he seen that before?

He picked up the vest and fitted it over his head. He tried to close the straps around the waist. They locked together, but just barely.

"Damn big bastard. Who thought we should get such a fucking small vest?" Nate asked no one in particular. He walked around Zane, shaking his head at the fit.

"It's a large." Rye Harper shrugged as though apologizing. "And I had to fight for that one. This is Bliss, not the DEA. We don't have a ton of money set aside for law enforcement. I managed to get exactly one Kevlar vest out of the chamber of commerce, and I had to win at dominoes to get it. I was surprised because I think Hiram cheats. We've always known that if the shit hit the fan, Logan was going down."

Logan snorted. "I ain't going down. The shit hits the fan, and I'm hiding behind Momma number two." He shrugged. "I might be a man, but I'm not stupid."

Marie smacked her child upside the head and told him to watch his language. Nate shook his head and started giving orders. Stella would man the phones and wait for the backup Nate had already called for. Marie and Laura Niles would guard the station house in case some of the jerks Ellis had set on him showed up again. Logan, the Harper twins, and Stef would head out with him and Nate.

They took their small armory and split into two vehicles—Nate, Zane, and Stef in the Bronco and the rest in Max Harper's truck. They were splitting up in order to try to come at Leander and Worthington from two different sides. They would attempt to give the men nowhere to run. Of course it also meant Callie would be stuck in the middle if the bullets started flying.

Zane's stomach roiled. He'd never gotten used to the adrenaline rush of a dangerous situation. Though he'd been good at his job, he'd never enjoyed it. He'd never liked the danger, the anticipation of a fight. He knew he looked like a bruiser to the outside world, but deep down he wanted some fucking peace.

Nate, on the hand, was born for this. His hands were steady on the wheel as he turned out of town and toward the mountain that dominated the landscape.

"You want to tell me where we're going now?"

"Are you going to behave?" Only the tightness of the words gave away the fact that Nate was tense.

"Yeah. I'll follow orders. I promise." This was Nate's op. He was going to trust his partner and not make trouble for him. Nate loved Callie. He wouldn't put her in more danger than he needed to.

Nate turned his head slightly, as though studying him for deception. "You better. Worthington sent me a text with coordinates about a half an hour ago. It's a place up the mountain on Mel's land. I tried to find him, but he'd disappeared. It would be nice if the man would carry a damn cell phone."

"He's never going to do that. Mel isn't a great believer in technology. I'm sure he's off somewhere patrolling. It's what he does at night. Be careful about who you shoot at. I wouldn't want Mel to get caught in this. There's a clearing about a quarter of a mile from Mel's cabin. It's isolated, but those city boys didn't think about the fact that there are several great sniper perches. Laura was right about those two. They are dumbasses." Stefan Talbot wasn't hiding his tension. He was like a well-dressed, highly coiled rattlesnake waiting to pounce. "We need time though. Max, Rye, and Logan are going to have to ditch the truck at the base of the mountain, or Leander and Worthington will know they're coming. It's not an easy climb."

"Do they need gear?" Nate asked.

"Max and Rye? Hell, no," Stef replied. "They were born in these mountains. They'll be there. They just need a couple of minutes."

"I don't know if we'll have that," Zane muttered under his breath. His knee bounced nervously, an unconscious show of anxiety.

Stef leaned forward. "She's alive, Zane. She'll be alive at the end of this. She's no delicate flower. She was born in these mountains, too. If she had any chance to run, I promise she's hiding right now. She knows the woods. She's tough."

"God, I hope she's not running around in the woods." Nate said.

They were thinking the same thing. They wanted her waiting patiently to be rescued. They wanted her to play it safe and let them take the chances.

There was absolutely no way in hell she would do that. She would take the first chance she got, and he had to hope she was lucky enough not to get hurt.

His hand tightened on the gun in his lap. The weight and feel was comforting. There was a real chance one of them wouldn't come out of it. If it had to be that way, then Zane hoped to hell it was him. Nate thought he was being self-sacrificing. Hell, he was being selfish. He didn't want to live without them. He couldn't even stand the thought of a world that didn't include Nate and Callie. He would rather die than live with the hole in his soul. But before anything happened, he needed to do something.

"Nate, I want us to be okay about what happened to me. It wasn't your fault. I know that. I've always known that."

Nate's jaw clenched. He swallowed before he replied. "I should have known something was wrong. I should have done something then and there."

"You did. You went for help. You saved me. I'm alive because you got the team and came back for me. If you'd tried to save me on your own, we would both be dead."

Nate didn't look at him. His eyes were focused on the road. "You were only there because you followed me."

"Yeah, I followed you," he replied. "You didn't make me sign up. I wanted to go. I was there because I believed in you, and you didn't let me down. You did your job and got Ellis off the street. Now it's time to finish it, and then we can move on to the good part of our lives."

Nate nodded shortly and turned the car up the long dirt road. "We finish this tonight."

The car got quiet. Zane firmly intended to finish it. Nate might be honor bound to try to take Worthington and Leander in, but Zane was under no such oaths.

He was going to kill them.

Chapter Fifteen

The stinging pain in her shoulder was reaching epic proportions. Callie tried to blink away her tears. Her left shoulder felt like it was on fire. She'd hit the tree line at a sprint, but now she moved slowly, carefully studying the ground so she didn't trip and fall and make things worse. The instinct was there to run as fast and far as she could, but that would be a mistake. Patience was required in this case. Panic would get her killed.

She forced herself to stop, to hide behind a huge tree and take stock.

She needed to be quiet. The moon was blocked by the forest here, and it was very dark. She could hear one of her attackers moving through the woods like an elephant clomping around. He gave away his position with every move. He'd been behind a desk for too long. He'd forgotten how to stalk his prey, if he'd ever known how.

She hoped he couldn't hear the thundering beat of her heart. It was galloping. *Breathe slowly, let yourself focus.* Nell had taught her meditation. She'd done it in an attempt to balance Callie's soul with the energy of the earth, but she could use the lesson to find her inner calm, to keep the panic at bay.

She took a long, cleansing breath. It was cool and getting cold.

"You better come out now, bitch!" Leander's voice bounced around the forest.

Callie listened carefully. She was pretty sure he was behind her and to her left. It was like when she was a kid and playing games. She, Max, Rye, and Stef would play hide and seek in these woods. A much younger Mel had warned her even then that she might get abducted by aliens. He'd taken them all out here and shown them good places to hide. He'd taught them how to survive.

The caves. She had to get to the caves. How was she going to climb with her hands behind her back?

She would deal with that problem when she got to it. Mel had a stash in that cave. The moonshine still he kept there might not help her, but the guns he hid would. If she had to, she would shoot those men with her hands behind her back. She would start firing and hope she hit something.

"Come on, sweetheart. You don't want to be out here. The woods are scary." A more soothing voice was trying to coax her out. Worthington sounded a bit closer. "You have no idea what's out here. There are probably animals out here that would love to get a bite of you. Just come out, and we'll take care of you. Nate should be here any minute, and he'll take you home."

Not likely. She rolled her eyes. Did they think she was a complete idiot? Probably. She hadn't used a whole lot of common sense around them, but that was about to change. There was no way she would willingly go back to them. And she knew what was in these woods a hell of a lot better than they did. Where was a bear when she needed one?

She eased from her hiding place when she heard them move away. She kept her step light, moving slowly, from one tree to the next, inching toward the clearing. She would have to run once she got there, but if they were still in the woods, she should be all right if she was careful.

She broke from the woods and made a beeline for the caves. The entrance was hidden, but she had no doubt where it was located. She'd snuck into it far too often. When she was a kid, she had played there with the boys. Only a year ago, she'd snuck in and sat and cried after her mother's funeral.

The trouble was the entrance to the cave was about ten feet up a pretty steep incline, and she had to climb without the aid of her hands. She stumbled and fell, her knees hitting the hard ground. Pain flashed through her and she bit back a cry. She had to get up, but she struggled. It was so hard to balance.

"Callie, this can go easy or it can go hard." Worthington's voice sounded closer now.

She swung her head around, praying he wasn't actually walking toward her. Her breath came out in a harsh pant. She saw a flash of something moving and forced herself to get off her knees. Her entire body trembled violently. Fear threatened to take over her every cell. She decided to give the cave one last shot. She backed up slightly and took the hill at a run. She fell forward, her face hitting a rock. She groaned and tried to turn over.

Get up. Move. Don't just lay there.

She felt something tug at her shirt. She opened her mouth to scream, but a hand came down across it. She bucked and tried to get her teeth to sink into that hand because if they were going to kill her, she was going to make them feel it. She was going to fight.

"Callie, calm down."

She knew that voice. She stilled and opened her eyes. Mel's face loomed over hers in the gloom. She breathed a huge sigh of relief.

"Come on." He hooked his hands under her armpits and hauled her up.

"There!"

Callie heard the masculine shout as Mel was pulling her up. Her shoulder screamed in protest.

"Someone's up there with her!"

Mel whirled her around and was setting her on her feet at the mouth of the cave when Callie heard the loud crack of gunfire. Mel's body jerked, and he pushed her roughly away from him. She hit the hard rock of the cave on her ass and immediately scrambled to get up.

"Mel!" Her voice echoed through the cave. She got to her knees and started to make her way toward him.

Mel crawled through the entrance. She could barely see the outline of his body as he struggled to get through. He turned, and Callie could see he'd managed to hold on to his rifle. He turned and fired, the report shockingly loud.

"Sorry, Callie." Mel practically shouted the words. He scooted backward slightly. "That should make them think twice about coming up here. You in cuffs?"

"Yeah," she replied breathlessly. "Where are you hit?"

She could hear the pain in Mel's voice, but it remained steady and even. If the aliens ever did come to Bliss, Callie was going to run straight to Mel. For all his paranoia, he was damn cool in a crisis. "They hit my left thigh. It's bleeding pretty bad, but I'll live. I won't be running anytime soon." He fired off another shot. "Come over here and I'll get those cuffs off you. I can pick that lock in no time at all."

She scooted to him on her knees, wincing at the pain lancing through her. Everything hurt, it seemed.

"How did you find me?" She turned to give Mel access to her hands. She heard the click of metal against metal and suddenly her hands were free. She stretched to get her circulation going again.

"I saw them take you from the town hall. I was getting into my truck to come home and start my patrol, and I saw them put you in their car. You're a good girl, Callie. I knew you wouldn't leave with two strange men, not when you already have two strange men." Mel's eyes were already facing front again, watching for the agents.

She winced as she started to get circulation back in her hands. Her shoulder hurt, but she breathed through it. Her pain was nothing compared to what these men had done to Zane, what they would do to Nate and Zane if she gave them a chance. She kneeled beside Mel. "Can you take them out?"

"If they're stupid enough to come close," Mel replied quietly. He sent out another warning shot. "They're playing it smart for now. Don't worry. Your men will be here."

That was what she was afraid of. "They're walking into an ambush."

Mel shook his head and chuckled a little. "No, Cal, they're walking into what we used to call a clusterfuck in the Marines. Excuse my language. You see, these boys didn't think this out at all. There are far too many places here to come up on a man. Why do you think I chose this spot for my stash? You have to know this place intimately to find all of its hidey holes. Otherwise, you're a sitting duck. Those boys are sitting ducks. I don't know what they're thinking."

"I screwed up their plans," she admitted. "They didn't mean to end up here. They intended to steal twenty million dollars, and I overheard them talking. Hence this crazy plan. Do you see them?"

Mel was still for a moment. "No. They're quiet, too." His voice went down a notch. "I heard someone coming up the road though. They stopped a little way back. I think your men are here."

She let her eyes close and sent a silent prayer to anyone who would listen. She'd done her part. They wouldn't be able to use her to pull Zane and Nate in. Now it was up to them to save themselves. A sudden thought occurred to her. "Mel, I need a shotgun."

"There's a flashlight about ten feet to your right. When you find it, move back another ten feet, and you'll find a stash of guns."

She started crawling, feeling her way along the stone floor. If it came to it, she would do whatever it took. She wasn't going to lose them.

* * * *

Nate cut off the engine about a half a mile from where he needed to be. He had no intention of walking into an ambush. What Zane didn't seem to understand was that he had no intention of losing either of the most important people in his life. He needed Callie, and he needed Zane, and he wasn't willing to let either of them die.

His hand curled around the gun he carried. "Stef, you take the long way around. I want you coming up on their backs. If they're where they say they are, Zane and I are going to come out of the forest in front of them."

Nate was watching Stef through the rearview mirror. His jaw tightened. "I won't let them hurt Callie. If it looks like they're going to make a move, I'll take them out."

Zane turned quickly. "They won't get the chance."

"They won't." Nate wouldn't let it happen. He wouldn't even allow himself to think about it happening. "We're going to have them surrounded once Max and Rye get there. If I can't take them out, the Harpers will. If you get a decent shot, you take it."

Stef slid out of the car and into the woods like a wraith. Zane held his rifle to his chest.

"Let's go," he said. "You stay close to me."

Nate got out of the car. He let his mind roam and remembered everything about the day he and Callie had come here. The place where he was supposed to go was right inside the clearing. If he and Zane were quiet, they should be able to sneak up on Worthington and Leander.

There was the loud report of a rifle. The sound made his heart speed up and his gut clench. That sound meant something had gone wrong. Zane took off, and Nate ran to keep up. He pumped his legs, adrenaline flowing through his body. There was another shot. This one sounded like a handgun. Had Max and Rye already made it into position? Why would they have started shooting without the signal?

There was only one answer to that. Callie. They would have started shooting to save Callie.

He forced himself to go cold, to push the panic and terror that threatened to engulf him down. A fleeting image of Callie's body on the ground flashed across his mind, but he pushed that down, too. He couldn't afford to panic, and he couldn't let Zane panic, either. He pushed himself, trying to keep up with Zane, but the big bastard was fast and had longer legs.

"Damn it, Zane, stop." He tried to keep his voice down, but Zane either didn't hear him or ignored him. Desperate, Nate launched himself at Zane and tackled him, pulling him to the ground. "Calm down."

"She could be dead right now." Zane's low whisper sounded tortured.

"You think I don't know that?" God, he was right back where he'd been that day when the Barbarians had Zane. His heart hurt, but he was going to do the same thing he'd done that day. He would have done anything to spare Zane the pain, but he would rather have Zane hurt than dead. Whatever they had done to Callie, he and Zane would heal her. And if those bastards had killed her, then it didn't matter. His badge would mean nothing. He would kill them, and slowly. "We follow the plan. Any deviation could mean her life. We have no idea what we're going into. Please trust me."

Zane got to his knees. In the gloom of the forest, Nate could see Zane's nod. "All right. This is your show."

He got to his feet, leaned down, and helped Zane up. "You go left and stay in the trees. I'm going out to the right. When we get sight of them, we're going to surround them. Once we're all in place, they won't have anywhere to go. We'll take 'em out from the high positions if they won't give up Callie."

Zane's eyes suddenly went wide, and his gun came up.

Something cold and hard pressed into the back of Nate's skull.

"Or we could just have it out here and now, Wright. Drop the weapon." There was a nasty lilt to Worthington's voice as he put a hand on Nate's shirt.

He ran through a hundred possibilities, every single way they might get out of this. None of them worked. They all ended in his head getting blown off his body. He let the rifle fall out of his hands.

"If you want to live, I would let him go." Zane was much calmer now, to Nate's everlasting gratitude. His training seemed to have come back online. Zane had been a damn fine agent, despite the fact it didn't come naturally to him.

Nate searched the woods in front of him, hoping for any sign that Stef or the Harpers were out there. He glanced behind Zane's back, praying he didn't see Leander walking out from the trees. So far the woods were quiet, with the exception of the tense standoff they were in. Where had those shots come from? Rifles weren't standard issue DEA weapons. He doubted either of the agents was using a rifle. That meant someone else was out there, or had been.

"Where's Callie?" Nate asked.

"Leander has her." There was the slightest tremble in Worthington's voice that scared the shit out of him. If Leander didn't actually have her, what had happened? "If you want her to live, you'll put down that fucking gun, Hollister."

Zane shook his head. "I need proof of life, asshole. You'll forgive me if I don't take your word for it. You produce her, and I'll think about not taking your head off."

Nate kept his voice calm, even as his heart raced. "You better listen to him. He'll let you kill me, you know. He's still mad because I left him in El Paso. Now that he knows you're the one who gave him up, I think he might rather have his revenge on you. Producing Callie is the only thing that will keep you alive."

Nate's heart nearly stopped as Leander came out of the forest behind Zane. Then he got a look at the agent's face. It was stark white, and his hands were empty and in the air. And thank god, Stefan

Talbot was behind him.

"I caught your friend," Stef said. "You're about to be surrounded. Let Nate go and lay down your weapon or I'll blow his head off."

Calmly, Worthington pulled Nate close, lifted his gun, and fired. The report nearly took Nate's ear off. His head rang as Leander's body slumped forward. He looked down at the hole in his chest, and then the light in his eyes died. Leander slumped forward, hitting the ground.

Worthington's hold on his shirt became vicious. "I never meant to leave that idiot alive. He's served his purpose. And I don't buy the crap you're selling, Sheriff. Hollister would never hurt his fuck buddy. He 'loves' you. Bunch of freaks. Now here's how it's going to go down. Hollister, you'll put the rifle down, and so will that other asshole. You'll let your friend there cuff you and put you in the trunk of my car, then you and me and Wright will take a ride. Otherwise, I can simply kill Wright here and now."

"You kill him, and I kill you." Zane held his position.

Worthington's laughter was an ugly sound. "You won't do anything to put him in danger. I saw the way the two of you were looking at each other in that pathetic excuse for a meeting. You would never hurt your partner. Now, put the gun down, Hollister, or I start taking your boy's body parts off. I'll start with his dick and see how you like that."

Nate saw the instant Zane made up his mind. Zane's hand tightened slightly on the trigger, and his eyes flared. He'd worked with him long enough to know what was going to come next. Fuck, this was going to hurt. His body tensed.

"You don't scare me at all, Worthington, and you never did." Zane pulled the trigger. Nate felt his shoulder fly back as he and Worthington were sent off balance. The bullet went straight through his left shoulder like a freaking arrow on fire. Nate hit the ground. It wasn't more than a second or two before Zane was hauling him up. He turned to see that the bullet had struck Worthington in his shoulder. Nate groaned as his body started to shake. His left arm wouldn't move.

Zane stood over Worthington. The agent panted and held his shoulder. Blood was squeezing out from between his fingers, but the asshole would live. Zane had his rifle pointed straight at Worthington's head.

"Nate can handle a little pain." Zane looked fierce in the dim light. Stef came to stand beside him. "Tell me where Callie is, or Stef and I will start filling you full of bullets. I am inclined to let you live now that I really think about it. I think Ellis might have a few things to say to you when you hit the prison system, and I am really looking forward to your execution for killing a federal agent, but if you don't tell me where my wife is, I'll make sure you go out real slow."

"She's alive," Worthington replied quickly. "She got away."

Zane's sigh of relief mirrored his own. He nodded shortly and turned to Stef. "Call it in. We need at least one ambulance. Tell Stella to call Del Norte for backup. Nate, you got some cuffs on you?"

Nate leaned back against a tree and then thought better of it when every nerve on his left side sparked to painful life. "On the right-hand side of my belt."

He gingerly moved aside his jacket to give Zane a chance to get the cuffs. He really hoped that ambulance got here soon and brought large amounts of painkillers with it. Getting shot fucking hurt.

"There they are."

Nate turned and saw the Harper twins coming up from behind them and Callie, *thank God*, was with them. She had a shotgun in her hand and was the most beautiful sight he'd ever seen.

"What happened? Is everyone all right?" Callie rushed toward them.

"Looks like we missed all the fun, Rye." Max Harper slung his rifle over his shoulder. "Sheriff, we found Callie holed up with Mel in a sniper position. Nell's not going to let Callie into her pacifist club anymore. Logan is helping Mel down. He took a bullet to the thigh. We'll have to make sure the doc who works on him is fully human. Looks like you could use a doc, too, Sheriff."

"Oh, Nate." Callie stared at his shoulder.

"Yeah, maybe it's time I found this town a doctor," Stefan mused.

Nate turned in time to see Worthington reach behind his back with his good hand. He started to shout a warning, but Zane was turning to cuff the agent. Nate tried to get between Zane and the bullet

Worthington was about to put into him. He wasn't thinking, merely running on pure instinct. He saw a flash of metal and then there was a horrible blast.

Worthington's gun fell uselessly to his side as he slumped down. Callie stood over the body. Her hands started to shake and the shotgun she'd used to blow half of the DEA agent's head to hell and back fell to the side. Zane managed to catch her before she hit the ground.

"She passed out." Zane cradled her gently against his chest. "She killed him."

Rye Harper looked at the mangled body of the man Callie had killed. "She did a damn fine job, too."

Stef joined him. "Nah, she still pulled to the left. I never could get her to shoot straight."

"Yeah, well, it was effective," Max interjected. "Hey, now Callie can join Marie and Rach in their 'I killed a son of a bitch' club."

He heard what they were saying, but he was staring down at Callie. He winced but used his good hand to smooth back her hair. "Baby, are you okay?"

Her eyes fluttered open. "Nate?"

Zane's arms tightened around her.

"I'm here, baby. I'm fine. Zane's fine, although he did shoot me." He was going to use that to get all the sweet affection from her he could.

Callie's eyes came wide open now. "What!"

Zane stood with her in his arms. "He'll forgive me, babe. Come on. Let's get her to a place where the EMTs can find us easily. I want them to take a look at her. She's got blood on her arm."

"It's okay. I got grazed when…oh, I killed him, and I'm not even sorry." Callie's eyes were wide with tears.

Nate kissed her gently. He would have to be careful with her because this would haunt her for a long time. "It's going to be okay, Callie. It was us or him. You made the right call."

Her hand came up and pulled him close. She kissed first him and then Zane. His eyes met Zane's. They held for a moment of perfect harmony, and then Zane turned and began to walk. Nate gritted his teeth and forced his legs to move. They were his family. He would follow them anywhere.

Chapter Sixteen

Callie stood by and watched as Zane flipped the light on. The whole front of the building was lit up in electric blue and red.

Trio was open for business.

Zane grinned as he turned, and she couldn't help but go a bit gooey at the sight. His dream was coming true, and way faster than they'd imagined. This ceremony was strictly for show. Most of Bliss was sitting in Trio's booths or at the bar when the place was officially opened. There was a great cheer as the beer started to flow.

"Congrats, little sister," Stefan said, sliding an arm around her shoulder.

"Thanks." She watched as Zane accepted the heartfelt congratulations of his friends. "And thank you for giving him the loan."

Stef nodded. "I figure if I'm trusting the big bastard with my little sister, I can trust him with some cash. And I was right. The place looks great. I think it's going to do well."

Stef looked around the bar. There was a blank look on his face that was replaced with a forced smile the minute he realized she was looking at him. Callie sighed. He'd been that way ever since the night Nate had been shot. The next morning, Jennifer Waters had taken a bus out of town, and Callie hadn't heard from her since. Stef refused to talk about Jen or what happened that night after he let her out of the cell.

She let it go. He would talk about it when he was ready. As for Jen, she'd left without even a good-bye. It worried her to no end, but she had to believe Jen had her reasons.

Even without her friend, the three months they had spent putting together Trio and rehabbing Nate's shoulder had been the best of her life. Even when Nate had been crabby, she'd felt like she was working toward something. She was building her future with her husbands. She glanced at Zane. On paper, he was her legal husband, but Nate had stood right beside them at the courthouse, and when the town had thrown them a reception, he'd taken the congratulations right along with Zane.

Now she wished her other hubby would get his sweet tushy home.

Zane pulled her away from Stef and into his arms. "Like it, babe?"

"You know I do." She went on her toes to place a kiss on those amazing lips of his. "I just wish Nate had been here."

"Where the hell is Nate anyway?" Stef asked. "Wasn't his plane due at four?"

Nate had been in El Paso for three days clearing up all the paperwork he needed to end the case. Once the DEA had control of the accounts, Ellis's money had dried up. The bounty was off Zane's chest. She had wanted to go with him, but Zane needed her more. Still, there was a knot in her stomach. They hadn't been apart in months, and there was still the smallest anxiety in the back of her mind that he would realize he'd made a mistake.

Zane smiled down at her. "You worry too much. He's coming home."

"She thinks he's staying in El Paso?" Stef suddenly looked concerned.

"I think they're going to offer him a job, probably with a promotion," she admitted. It was her fear. Nate would finally get the offer he wanted, the chance to move up, to be what he'd always wanted.

"I already have a job." Nate's voice rang out over the loud crowd.

She turned and ran into his arms. He looked super sexy in jeans and a T-shirt. His arms closed around her.

"Miss me?" The smirk on his face told her he knew the answer to that question.

"You know I did."

"Well, I missed you. I've been doing all the heavy lifting around here." Zane slapped Nate on the back. He looked down at Callie. "I told you he would come back. He's here now, babe, and let me tell you, once Nathan Wright decides he's committed, it's for life."

"Damn straight." Nate's eyes gleamed in the light of the bar they had all worked to build together. "I took the job in the DEA to get somewhere in life, but I also wanted to protect the things I loved. Everything I love is right here in Bliss. I'm never leaving, Callie. This is my home. You and Zane are my family."

"Yo! Can I get a beer here?" Max Harper yelled over the jukebox.

"Yeah, man, we might have way more family than we can handle." Zane groaned as he jogged back behind the bar.

"Get to work, gorgeous." Nate patted her behind. "I need a beer, and I want the hottest waitress in the state to get it for me." He looked toward the bar and frowned. "Damn it, Zane. Get rid of that duck."

She laughed. Nate had seen the rubber duck Zane had fixed to the bar. He'd managed to fit a tiny cowboy hat on the yellow duck and had glued on a gold badge. There was a donation box for the duck's eventual run for sheriff.

"I am not running against that duck."

Callie watched the two men she loved more than life argue about a rubber duck.

"Callie, baby, you got to get him to get rid of the duck."

"I am not getting in the middle of that." She shook her head, but Nate was already hauling her to his side.

"You say that now, but later…"

She gave him a wink that promised all the things she'd do later.

"Babe, order up." Zane passed her a tray filled with two beers for Max and Rye and a glass of tea for Rachel.

Callie picked up the tray and started her new life.

* * * *

Join me this summer for Stefan and Jennifer's story, *One to Keep*, the next book in the Bliss, CO series.

Author's Note

I'm often asked by generous readers how they can help get the word out about a book they enjoyed. There are so many ways to help an author you like. Leave a review. If your e-reader allows you to lend a book to a friend, please share it. Go to Goodreads and connect with others. Recommend the books you love because stories are meant to be shared. Thank you so much for reading this book and for supporting all the authors you love!

Sign up for Lexi Blake's newsletter
and be entered to win a $25 gift certificate
to the bookseller of your choice.

Join us for news, fun, and exclusive content
including free short stories.

Go to www.LexiBlake.net to subscribe.

There's a new contest every month!

Siren Beloved

Texas Sirens Book 4
By Lexi Blake writing as Sophie Oak
Coming Summer 2018

Aidan O'Malley left his fiancée, Lexi Moore, and their best friend, Lucas Cameron, after a night of passion left him shaken to his core. Years later, Aidan is back and he knows what he wants. He wants Lucas and Lexi forever.

Lucas has always been in love with Lexi, but he knows they need something more. They need the perfect Dom to complete their family. He never expected Aidan would be the Dom of their dreams.

Lexi is hiding a secret. She knows she's drowning and the time has come to heal, but her anger at Aidan holds her back from moving on with Lucas.

When Lexi's life is in danger, Aidan knows he'll do anything to win them back—and keep them alive.

* * * *

Lucas turned in his seat and faced the only woman he'd ever really loved. She'd been his friend, his heart and soul, his whole world since the day he'd met her, but he wasn't that for her. Her whole world had walked out the door when Aidan O'Malley left.

"I love you, Lucas Cameron."

His heart almost stopped. How long had he wanted those words? She'd never said I love you, not once. He'd waited to hear those words forever, but now he could hear the "but" somewhere in there like a little jolt of poison waiting to kill his happiness. "You know I love you, Lexi. I've said it every day for the past couple of years. I've asked you to move in with me. I've asked you to marry me."

"But you won't sleep with me."

It was the only thing he'd withheld. It had been easier when she was in Austin. He'd known her for years, been in love with her for that whole time, but they'd gone their separate ways while she finished school and he started a career. He'd thought he would never have her, thought she was out of his reach. She'd been ready to get married and have a happy life in Austin with her fiancé, Aidan. He'd been the one to screw that up. Yes, it had been much simpler when all he had were phone calls and texts and long instant messenger chats on the computer.

When Lexi moved to Dallas, his life had become a testament to the power of patience. She slept at his place more often than not. He took her to The Club. He'd introduced her to the lifestyle. He'd given her more orgasms than he could count but taken none for himself because he refused to be her rebound man. He wanted more. He wanted forever.

"Marry me and we'll talk about it." He wasn't going to let her use him for sex.

She laughed. "God, you are just like your brother. Except I think he's smarter than you."

Jack went home every night to two subs who loved him and each other more than life itself. Jack had two gorgeous kids. Jack had a job that meant the world to him. Damn straight Jack was smarter than he was. "He got all the brains."

She reached up to touch his hair. "Not all of them. Lucas, I did something really stupid last night, and I hurt some people I care about. I don't want to do that anymore. I need a solution, and it's not going to come with you compromising. You've done enough of that for me."

He felt like she'd just kicked him in the stomach. This was the moment he'd been dreading for the last three years. She didn't need him anymore. That was why she was willing to say I love you. It was a goodbye gift of sorts. She would steep it in all kinds of bullshit about how this was for him, but she was leaving. He didn't say anything. He couldn't. He kind of wished she would get it over with now that the moment was here.

"I love you, Lucas. I won't stop saying it. I've been selfish to hold it back. Selfish and afraid. I know if I had an ounce of sense, I would take what you're offering and run with it, but I think we would end up unhappy."

Bitterness welled. He'd done everything he could to prove how much he loved her. Why couldn't he be enough? "Yeah, unhappy. Really, I'm thrilled with the fact that you're breaking up with me.

That's going to make me really fucking happy."

"Babe, what are you talking about?" Lexi put her hands on the sides of his head and forced him to look at her. "I am not breaking up with you. I could never do that. Ever. I need you, but I think we both need something more. I think we need to find a Dom. Even if it's just for play, we need to admit that you're missing something you crave. Come on, let's see how things go with this Master A person. Maybe he has something he can teach us. I want what my mom has, and I can have that with you. But we need to move on. Aidan left us."

His heart ached, but he wasn't about to show it to her. He needed to be strong. "Aidan was never with me."

"Oh, my memory says differently. I remember a night when he was with you, and it was a beautiful thing."

Lucas couldn't remember it that way. "Damn it, he left you because of that night."

Her lips curled up in a sad smile. "Because he couldn't handle it. And he left *us*. That's the way I've come to think of it. It wasn't anything you did. He enjoyed what we did that night, and my only regret was that I didn't get to have you. Aidan was far too busy playing the Dom to let us be together. It was an amazing, beautiful night and I won't let Aidan's cowardice taint it anymore. I want to move past Aidan. I have to. It's killing me."

A kernel of hope lit inside Lucas. He pulled her into his arms, loving the feel of her against his chest. This was where he lived. "All right. We'll move past him. I love you, Lexi. I'll never love another human being the way I love you."

It was an easy thing to say since he'd only really loved once before, and Aidan was gone from him as surely as he'd walked out on Lexi. Aidan had left them alone and adrift. She was right. It was time to put the pieces back together.

"We'll meet this Master A, and then maybe we can decide what we want to do from there," he conceded. "But I still want to marry you."

She snuggled close to him. "And I still want to have wanton, disgusting, uncommitted sex with you."

He groaned. "You are so frustrating."

"I know." Her arms tightened around him. "You're right about the sex thing, Lucas. I want it to be special. I want it to be right."

He would make it right. And poor Master A had no idea what was coming for him.

One to Keep

Nights in Bliss, Colorado Book 3
By Lexi Blake writing as Sophie Oak
Coming Summer 2018

Stefan Talbot let Jennifer Waters run from him once. He knew she was far too young for him, but he kept a watchful eye on her, protecting her from afar. When she's arrested for a crime she didn't commit, Stef knows the time has come to get close again.

Jennifer ran from Bliss only to find herself in hot water in Dallas. She's longed to return to Bliss, but not in handcuffs. The only thing she longs for more than her mountain home is the man she ran from—Stef Talbot.

In the middle of the Winter Festival, Stef and Jen find themselves fighting for their love and their lives because danger has followed them back to Bliss.

About Lexi Blake

Lexi Blake lives in North Texas with her husband, three kids, and the laziest rescue dog in the world. She began writing at a young age, concentrating on plays and journalism. It wasn't until she started writing romance that she found success. She likes to find humor in the strangest places. Lexi believes in happy endings no matter how odd the couple, threesome or foursome may seem. She also writes contemporary Western ménage as Sophie Oak.

Connect with Lexi online:

Facebook: Lexi Blake
Twitter: authorlexiblake
Website: www.LexiBlake.net

Sign up for Lexi's free newsletter at www.LexiBlake.net.

Made in the USA
Middletown, DE
03 May 2018